Acclaim for Erin Dutton's Books

"*Sequestered Hearts* tells of two very private women dealing with the magnetic attraction between them. It is the story of the difficult dance between them, and how each is able to resolve h~~ ~ ~~ and find happiness. Cori and Bennett a ~~ ~~ ers and their story will keep the read ~~ ~~ all works out." – *Just About Write*

"*Sequestered Hearts* is packed wit ~~ ~~ .er moments too. The author writes ~~ ~~ ..on that one would expect from a veteran author. She builds anticipation and demonstrates Ben's and Cori's obvious attraction at the beginning of the novel, but we also see the antagonism and frustration these two characters experience with each other. Ben leaves Cori after she gets the interview with every intention of walking away from this enigmatic woman, and that is what Cori wants, too, or so we are led to believe....A romance is about more than just plot and character development. It's about passion, physical intimacy, and connection between the characters. The reader should have a visceral reaction to what is going on within the pages for the novel to succeed. Dutton's words match perfectly with the emotion she has created. Every encounter oozes with Ben's and Cori's hunger for each other. *Sequestered Hearts* is one book that cannot be overlooked. It is romance at its finest." – *L-word Literature.com*

"*Fully Involved* explores the emotional depths of these two very different women. Each woman struggles with loss, change, and the magnetic attraction they have for each other. Their relationship sizzles, flames, and ignites with a page turning intensity. This is an exciting read about two very intriguing women." – *Just About Write*

"Back when Isabel Grant was the tag-along little sister who annoyed them, tomboy Reid Webb and boyhood pal Jimmy Grant considered the girl an intrusion into their bucolic and—after Reid came out to Jimmy, blunting his amorous interest—platonic friendship. Years later, Isabel is a ravishing (and to all appearances) straight professional, and Jimmy and Reid are firefighters—and still best friends, living next door to each other, with Reid helping to raise Jimmy's son, Chase, after the death of his wife....[When]...Isabel comes back into Reid's life as young Chase's guardian, and childhood frictions—complicated by Reid's guilty attraction to Isabel—flare into emotional warfare....Dutton's studied evocation of the macho world of firefighting gives the formulaic story extra oomph—and happily ever after is what a good romance is all about, right?" – *Q-syndicate*

By the Author

Sequestered Hearts

Fully Involved

A Place to Rest

by
Erin Dutton

2008

A PLACE TO REST

ISBN 10: 1-60282-021-X
ISBN 13: 978-1-60282-021-0

THIS TRADE PAPERBACK ORIGINAL IS PUBLISHED BY
BOLD STROKES BOOKS, INC.
NEW YORK, USA

FIRST EDITION: JULY 2008

CREDITS
EDITORS:SHELLEY THRASHER AND STACIA SEAMAN
PRODUCTION DESIGN: STACIA SEAMAN
COVER DESIGN BY SHERI (GRAPHICARTIST2020@HOTMAIL.COM)

Acknowledgments

With every new project I'm reminded how lucky I am. Thanks to my editor, Shelley Thrasher, for your patience and expertise. Working with you has been both an education and an absolute joy. And thanks to copy editor Stacia Seaman. I'm amazed at how you see every detail.

As always, thanks to Radclyffe and Jennifer Knight for your continued support and guidance.

Connie Ward, thank you for all that you do for BSB and for each of us individually. You're a good friend and I've enjoyed getting to know you.

There are so many people behind the scenes adding to the amazing environment of Bold Strokes Books. I'm privileged to be connected to such a talented group.

Dedication

Family is a big part of this story. So it seems only right
that I dedicate it to mine.
For always giving me a place to belong.

Chapter One

Sawyer Drake rolled over and squinted at the bedside clock through eyes that weren't quite sharp enough without the correction of her black square-framed glasses. *Seven a.m.?* Who the hell was calling her at seven a.m.? She snatched up the receiver, pressed the button to end the offending noise, and growled into the phone.

"What?"

The voice that greeted her was far too cheery for the time of day. "Is that how you answer your phone? Really, Sawyer, I raised you to be more personable than that."

"Morning, Mom. I'm not usually personable until at least nine."

"I know, dear. That's why I called at seven. I was hoping to catch you off guard."

Sawyer laughed at her mother's candor. Tia Drake was nothing if not honest, and when she wanted something she made it clear. "What do you want, Mom?"

"I need a favor, Sawyer."

Sawyer pushed aside the covers and crawled out of bed, then padded down the short hallway of the two-bedroom apartment she shared with her best friend. In the kitchen, she moved from carpet to cool tile and grabbed a bottle of water from the fridge.

"Of course you do." Sawyer sipped from the bottle, letting the cold water soothe her dry throat. "Ever since you and Dad moved to Florida, you only call when you want something."

"Yes, I know," Tia said sarcastically. "Next you'll tell me I call your brother and sister more than I call you."

Sawyer cringed. Though she'd been teasing and knew her mother was doing the same, Tia had touched a nerve in talking about Sawyer's siblings. At thirty-two, Sawyer was four years older than her brother and sister, fraternal twins. She supposed it was normal for one child to think another got preferential treatment. And over the years she probably should have gotten used to her siblings getting more attention, especially when they were younger. People tended to coo over twin babies.

Tia interrupted her musings about her family dynamics. "Sawyer, I need you to do something for me. Have you found a new job yet?"

"Not yet." She'd been unemployed for two weeks since she left her job at the zoo. Although, in her defense, how long could they expect her to sit in a bamboo shack and sell tickets before she got bored?

"I want you to consider going to work with your sister." When a health scare had encouraged their father to consider early retirement, her parents had finally decided to leave Nashville and make that move south they had been talking about for years. Sawyer's sister, Erica, had reluctantly taken the reins of the family restaurant, Drake's.

"Mom—"

"Hear me out, Sawyer," Tia said in a tone she knew better than to interrupt. "I know you've never been interested in working at the restaurant. But Erica needs your help."

"She didn't say—"

"When was the last time you talked to her?"

Sawyer took a deep breath and mentally counted to ten. Her mother had a habit of not letting her finish a sentence. "I don't know. A few weeks ago, I guess."

"She says you haven't been by Drake's in months."

"I haven't had time." Sawyer regretted the white lie the moment it passed her lips. She wandered into the sparsely decorated living room and settled on one end of the sofa. Beige sofa, neutral carpet, and white walls. She kept promising herself that she would decorate the apartment, but it just never seemed to take priority. Her friend and roommate, Matthew, had added the few personal touches, such as the large burgundy vase and the colorful abstract painting.

"So then, daughter of mine, how have you been whiling away your hours of unemployment?"

"Ah—well—I—"

"Exactly as I thought. Erica's pregnant, Sawyer. You could at least go by there and check on her once in a while."

Her sister was nearly seven months along and planning to have the baby on her own. Every time Sawyer talked to her mother she had to listen to a monologue about how it must be so hard for Erica to be going through this all alone and how Sawyer should check on her more often. She would endure as long as she could before making an excuse to get off the phone.

"Mom, she works with Brady every day. It's not like she's by herself," she argued in vain, knowing her mother wouldn't see her brother's presence as a fitting substitute. From the time Sawyer was old enough, Tia had often left her in charge of her younger siblings while she and their father spent long hours at the restaurant.

"That's no excuse for you to not care about her."

"It's not that I don't care about her, you know that." It took some effort for her to keep from raising her voice. Her mother could be exasperating when she wanted to. It was how she wore a person down, and no doubt she knew Sawyer would give in. "Jesus, Mom. Okay. I'll go over there."

"And you'll work with her?"

"Now you're pushing your luck," she muttered, resting her feet on the oak coffee table in front of her.

"Try it for a few weeks. If you give it a fair shot, I won't bother you about it anymore."

Sawyer sighed. Well, what else was she going to do for the next few weeks? She hadn't found anything else yet, and a cushy job at her family's restaurant would be as good as any. She could just go in a few days a week and hang out with her brother and sister, and as an added bonus, her mother would think she was making an effort. This was a good opportunity to eliminate one of their arguing points. "If I do this and it doesn't work out, I'll never hear another word about working at the restaurant. Right?"

"Right," Tia agreed after a moment of silence.

"Okay, Mom. I'll try."

Minutes later she hung up and went back into the bathroom. She brushed her teeth and wondered, as she did every morning, if she should consider tinted contact lenses. Her brown eyes were very ordinary, so she thought about trying something in green or hazel. She'd considered contacts several times, mostly out of vanity, thinking her glasses made her look like a nerd. But as the years went by, she'd grown accustomed to them, even hiding behind them at times.

After a quick shower she ran a brush through her chin-length light brown hair and decided to let it air dry. She pulled a pair of khakis and a button-down blue striped shirt from the closet. *I should iron this shirt. But why bother?* Who did she need to impress? Erica? This would be the easiest job interview she'd ever had.

❖

"It's not too late to leave," Sawyer muttered to herself that afternoon as she shifted in a chair in her sister's office. "Erica hasn't even seen me yet."

She'd left word with the hostess on the way in that she would be waiting for Erica. So she tried to get comfortable in one of the expensive-looking chairs decorating the small office. Sawyer remembered many afternoons spent curled up in her father's old, comfortable furniture after school doing homework while he worked at the desk. Erica had redecorated earlier in the year after she had taken over and had obviously chosen the muted olive green-and-beige-patterned chairs for aesthetics rather than comfort. She seemingly hadn't wanted anything to compete with the bold artistic photos featuring some of their specialties that she'd had blown up and displayed on the walls. And she had replaced the scarred wooden desk that once held her father's old adding machine with a more modern-looking glass-and-chrome desk that now boasted a sleek desktop computer.

Sawyer was still considering her chances of escaping unnoticed when the office door opened and Erica hurried inside. She spared Sawyer only a quick glance as she moved behind the desk. Sawyer appraised her, thinking she looked tired. Her normally bright blue eyes had lost some of their sparkle, and her blond hair was pulled into a sloppy updo. Her stomach had rounded considerably since the last time Sawyer had seen her. Erica sighed as she lowered herself into her chair.

"How are you feeling?"

"I'm very busy today. What do you need, Sawyer?" she asked shortly.

"Well, I might be able to help you out." She leaned back and folded her arms over her chest. "I'm here for a job."

Erica stared at her. She'd been having a bad day already. Her vegetable delivery was late, one of her servers had quit, and her feet were swollen. Perhaps it wasn't fair, but right now she just wanted to slap that condescending smile right off Sawyer's face. She was quite used to that expression, having seen it when they were growing up every time Sawyer excelled where she faltered. School had been easy for Sawyer; she seemed to get good grades without putting in the hours of studying that Erica required. And she never seemed to tire of basking in their father's praise at report-card time.

Erica wondered what had motivated Sawyer to come in

today. She'd never had trouble finding a job before, but perhaps this time was different. It was just like Sawyer to sweep in and act like she was doing her a favor. She probably expected to be thanked effusively for bailing her out. She was tempted to refuse the offer, out of pride. Then she smiled as an idea began to form that would solve one problem and also put Sawyer in her place.

"Okay."

"Okay?" It was clear from Sawyer's expression that she'd been expecting an argument. "Great. When do you want me to start?"

"Tonight. Follow me." Without waiting to see if Sawyer was behind her, Erica stood and walked out of the office. She stopped at a linen closet in the hallway outside of the kitchen. "The entire dining room has been booked tonight for a fund-raiser for the mayor, and I'm down a server."

"Okay, cool. So—what? You want me to help out, hang around the dining room and make sure everyone's happy?" Though she wasn't really into politics, she thought she could handle an evening of socializing. She could throw on her best suit and glad-hand the guests, putting up a good front for Drake's.

"No." Erica held out a uniform. "I need another server."

"Are you forgetting I've been a waitress?" she said, remembering the summer she'd spent on the Cape waiting tables. "I didn't like it."

"If you want to come to work at Drake's, you have to start at the bottom. Learn the business from the ground up. Brady and I both did."

"You were sixteen when you were a server. I'm thirty-two years old and I have a business degree."

"Which you haven't used in ten years," Erica added, still holding out the black vest, tie, and apron.

Sawyer debated refusing but remembered her conversation with her mother. If she thought she'd gotten a guilt trip that morning, it would be nothing compared to their next phone conversation. She snatched the uniform from Erica. "I hope you're enjoying this little power trip."

"Wear black slacks and a white shirt with that, please," Erica responded, ignoring Sawyer's snide comment. "And be here at five," she called as Sawyer stalked away.

❖

"I should have figured she'd be late. She acted like she wanted to help, but that doesn't mean she's changed," Erica muttered as she walked through the kitchen.

"Erica, are you talking to yourself?" her twin brother, Brady, asked from across the room. She glanced at features so like her own and felt some of her irritation ease. Brady calmed her; she could rely on him in ways she'd never relied on Sawyer.

"Your sister came by this morning asking for a job, and she's twenty minutes late for her first shift."

Brady smiled. "She's always *my* sister when you're mad at her."

Erica crossed to the counter where her pastry chef was prepping. Jori Diamantina had been at Drake's for only six months, but she'd proved to be hardworking and creative. In just a few short weeks her dessert menu had begun to receive rave reviews. Erica had never regretted hiring her.

"Jori, have I ever told you about *Brady's* sister?" She heard Brady laugh as she turned her back on him.

"I think I've heard a thing or two." Jori regarded her with eyes that sometimes resonated with sadness, but today sparkled. Many times she had seen how Jori transformed when she stepped in the kitchen. Normally reserved in both public and private, she worked with sharp confidence.

"I'm sure you have. Don't get me wrong, I love Sawyer. But she's a bit flighty. She hops from job to job and never settles down. And don't get me started on her relationships. I mean, I don't think she's stayed with the same woman for more than a week since she was in the tenth grade."

"Maybe she simply hasn't found what she's looking for."

Erica appreciated Jori's attempt at diplomacy. "Well, that may be. But while she's out there searching, the rest of us are left to be the responsible ones and handle things around here."

"Geez, Erica, Sawyer has some good qualities, too. Don't just list her bad ones," Brady called.

"Oh, yeah," Erica continued. "Sawyer can be very charming when she wants to be. Believe me, Jori, within a few minutes she'll have you wondering why I'm complaining."

Jori nodded, uncertain how to respond to the obvious bitterness in Erica's voice. This was exactly the type of situation that made her uncomfortable. She enjoyed her job, and usually there was an easy dynamic between Erica and Brady. But tension surrounded any conversation about Sawyer. From what she'd heard, she didn't know why Erica wasted her time worrying about her sister when it seemed clear that the woman thought of no one but herself.

"I swear, if she doesn't get here soon she's going to make me regret hiring her."

"And that would ruin your perfect record, wouldn't it?" Brady grinned at Jori. "Erica takes all the credit for hiring you, even though I was the one who found you working at that dive on Fourth Avenue."

Jori laughed. "Granted, it was no Drake's, but that place wasn't a dive."

"Of course not." Erica lifted a freshly washed strawberry from the bowl in front of Jori. "But it was merely a stepping stone to this point in your career."

Erica remembered the day Brady had come to her raving about an assistant pastry chef he'd met. They'd just lost their own head pastry chef and invited Jori to interview. She won Erica over with the box of Key lime tarts she'd brought along. Erica went through with the interview mostly for show, already knowing she would offer Jori the job.

"You're a good fit for Drake's, Jori. And I hope we can convince you to stay with us for a very long time."

❖

Sawyer drove down West End Avenue in her white Toyota Solara convertible with the top down. A warm spring breeze feathered strands of hair across her face. She shoved them behind her ears and smothered a curse as the driver in front of her stopped quickly when the light turned yellow. She could already tell she wouldn't like working downtown. Traffic tested her notoriously short patience, and it would only get worse as summer progressed and country-music fans flocked to Nashville. Seeing a break in the lane to her left, she sped around the delivery van she'd nearly rear-ended twice already. During the summer Tia had taught her to drive, she'd also passed on her aggressive maneuvers and her irritation with traffic.

Since her meeting with Erica, she'd had time to think about the way Erica was flaunting her power, and it made her angry. As Sawyer's little sister, Erica had never been in a position of authority over her. Trying to please her mother was upsetting the balance of their relationship, and it wasn't in Sawyer's favor. She was convinced Erica's power play was unreasonable. After all, Sawyer was a Drake. How would it look for her to be toting trays?

West End turned into Broadway as she entered downtown. Crowds of people carrying cameras wandered along the sidewalks and paused at the open doors to several bars, no doubt hoping to glimpse the next big star. As she reached Fourth Avenue, the sounds of live music spilled out of a bar famous for its lavender exterior and for discovering new talent. Three blocks later, she took a left on First Avenue and slammed on her brakes, growling when a group of people decided to cross despite the Don't Walk signal. One of the men had the nerve to shoot her an offended look as he passed in front of her car. *Of course, that's nothing compared to the nerve he has wearing that shirt.* Sawyer didn't follow fashion too closely, but surely the old-fashioned cowboy-cut shirt with the pearl snaps and three-inch fringe running the length of the arms wasn't back in style.

When she was able to move again, she quickly covered the two blocks to the back of Drake's. She pulled up to the loading dock next to Erica's Land Rover and put the top up. Before getting out of the car, she grabbed the tie from the passenger seat and looped it around her neck.

As she walked through the back door into the kitchen, she paused. Brady, the executive chef, moved between the counters calling out instructions. The rest of the room's occupants, a sous chef and three line cooks, responded in kind. Erica had once told Sawyer that she loved the energy of a well-run kitchen, the sights and sounds mingling with quick, efficient movement. She said there was a choreography involved, each player gracefully playing their part. Sawyer knew she missed being the orchestrator in the kitchen now that she'd taken on a more administrative role.

Brady looked up from the lamb he was seasoning. A shock of blond hair just a shade darker than Erica's fell across his forehead. Though they were fraternal twins they shared the same soft features, and while they lent Erica a feminine beauty, they made Brady appear younger than his twenty-eight years. The baby face he had complained about as a teenager didn't offend him quite so much anymore. They were carbon copies of their mother, and Sawyer resembled their father with looks that she considered mousy.

"Erica's looking for you," Brady said.

Sawyer glanced at her watch. "No doubt. Is she mad?"

"She's always cranky these days," he joked.

"You wouldn't say that if she was standing here." Sawyer figured he knew as well as she did that Erica wouldn't like the reference to her pregnancy hormones.

Brady laughed. "Probably not. Paige said to invite you over this weekend. We're barbequing."

"Cool. Remind me later this week."

Brady's wife was quite possibly the sweetest woman Sawyer had ever met. Fortunately for them, both of their sons apparently took after her. During Paige's pregnancies Sawyer had tormented her with talk about them inheriting Brady's temper, another trait he'd inherited from their mother. "I guess I better get this over with. Where's Erica?"

"In the dining room," he answered, lifting his chin in that direction.

With a sigh, Sawyer headed that way. As she stepped into the dining room a feeling of warm familiarity engulfed her. The decor remained as it had been for many years. Subdued lighting cast pale circles of light on the tables peppered around the room. The far wall boasted a huge stone fireplace, and the large windows along the opposite side faced Second Avenue, bathing the room in natural light. The remaining wall space was covered with textured ivory wallpaper.

Erica intercepted her as she was passing the mahogany bar.

"It's five thirty." She flipped up Sawyer's collar, grabbed the ends of the tie slung around her neck, and deftly tied it. "I said five o'clock."

"Sorry."

"No, you're not. But you would be if I docked your paycheck."

"Slave driver," Sawyer muttered, pushing Erica's hands away and folding her collar back down. Between her mother and Erica, Sawyer was already thinking this was a bad idea. "I really don't need this aggravation. I can get a stress-free job tomorrow."

"Tonight is a big deal, Sawyer. A lot of important people will be here. Please don't let me down." Erica made the request softly as she drew the front of Sawyer's vest closed and buttoned it.

"I can dress myself." Sawyer stepped out of reach. "I'm already here, I may as well work. But after tonight I'm done."

Chapter Two

W hat's on the menu for tonight?" Sawyer asked as she entered the kitchen. The guests had started arriving, and many were sipping cocktails and milling about the dining room. Soon the hors d'oeuvres would be served, then everyone would be seated for dinner. After that Sawyer would be too busy to do more than pass through the kitchen. She touched her brother's arm affectionately as she peered over his shoulder.

"Chuck is working on an assortment of appetizers over there." He waved a hand toward his sous chef. The dark-haired man looked up at Brady and an indulgent grin drew the corners of his mustache upward. "For dinner, garlic roasted lamb with oregano pesto and steamed asparagus."

"Sounds good." Sawyer smiled at Chuck and smoothed her hand over the shoulder of Brady's pristine white jacket.

"It will be exquisite," Brady assured her, swiping the back of his hand across his forehead just below the band of his toque, the traditional pleated chef's hat. "But the real treat is dessert. Right, Jori?" He glanced over his shoulder.

Sawyer followed his gaze across the room to the woman standing behind a long stainless-steel table plating triangles of some sort of chocolate creation with pink stripes in the center. The woman's jacket appeared as clean and starched as Brady's. Instead of the toque she wore a navy blue bandana. Tendrils of shiny black hair curled out and clung to the edge of the fabric.

When she glanced up, Sawyer found herself staring into slightly almond-shaped eyes so dark that from across the room they appeared black. *Stunning.* This woman possessed a smoldering beauty that brought to mind sultry summer nights spent making love beneath a starry sky. *And she probably knows it, too.* In Sawyer's experience, women as attractive as this one were often very aware of what a pair of carefully batted eyelashes could garner.

"I guess you two haven't been introduced. Sawyer, Jori Diamantina is our pastry chef. Jori, this is my sister Sawyer."

"It's nice to meet you." Sawyer stepped forward and extended her hand.

"Yes, you, too," Jori said, taking Sawyer's hand.

The flush that spread up Jori's neck was unexpected, and her shy smile charmed Sawyer even more than the dimple that appeared in her right cheek. The hand within hers was soft and warm, and Sawyer's heart raced as she held it for a moment longer than was necessary. "Have you been working here long?"

"A few months."

"It's been a while since I've stopped by," Sawyer said. She couldn't even recall the previous pastry chef's face, but she was certain she would remember this one.

"I guess you need to come around more often," Brady said.

"I think I will." Sawyer's eyes didn't leave Jori's face. When Jori's blush deepened, Sawyer knew she'd sensed the innuendo behind her words.

"Really? Erica was just in here and said you'd only signed on for tonight."

"No. I'll be helping out for a bit," Sawyer told him. Despite her conversation with Erica, she thought she might have found something worth sticking around for, at least for a little while.

"Good." Brady opened the oven and pulled out a large pan bearing several lamb roasts.

"So what are you working on here?" Sawyer asked Jori,

stepping closer to study the dessert. The rich aroma of chocolate teased her senses, making her mouth water.

"Princess cake," Jori said. Sawyer raised an eyebrow and she continued. "Chocolate sponge cake with layers of triple-sec syrup and buttercream and a ganache icing." Jori's features lit up as she talked about her creation. Her eyes danced and her face was animated, and Sawyer glimpsed a passion that she envied.

"Sounds absolutely sinful," she purred, purposely lowering her voice.

"It is." The flirtation in Jori's tone surprised Sawyer. Already she thought of Jori as timid and hadn't expected this response to her teasing.

"My sisters both have a weakness for sweets," Brady said from behind her, effectively breaking the spell between them. Jori looked away and immediately her gaze was once again impersonal. "It's one of the few things they agree on."

"It's true," Sawyer said, missing the spark in Jori's eyes already. She kept her gaze on Jori's face, hoping she might see it again. "Chocolate in particular. I can't turn it down."

"There you are." Erica burst through the swinging door into the kitchen. "I need you out there with the other servers. Take these." She grabbed a tray of canapés and passed it to Sawyer.

"Yes, ma'am." Sawyer smiled once more in Jori's direction, then headed for the dining room.

After Sawyer was out of sight, Jori steadied herself with a few short breaths.

"Something wrong?" Brady asked without turning around.

"Um, no. No, everything's fine." Jori felt like her insides were shaking and wondered if her inner state was visible to her co-worker. Trying to distract herself, she went back to arranging slices of cake on gold-rimmed dessert plates.

Even after her earlier conversation with Erica, she hadn't given Sawyer much thought. Now she was certain she would be thinking about her for the rest of the night. Behind a pair of small rectangular glasses, the longest eyelashes Jori had ever seen framed rich brown eyes. Otherwise her features were unremarkable, pleasant and symmetrical, except when she was teasing her, one eyebrow arched more than the other. Her skin was smooth over prominent cheekbones and a strong jaw. Sawyer's smile as they had been introduced was wide and infectious and warmed her eyes. Jori couldn't help smiling back, albeit somewhat self-consciously. Sawyer's gaze had been focused when she looked at Jori, and it seemed as if Sawyer saw nothing but her—well, her and the chocolate cake between them.

This is ridiculous. You should be concentrating on work, not your boss's sister. You've been through this before. Do you want to lose the best job you've ever had? The admonishment worked, at least for a little while. Her concentration only flagged when Sawyer passed through the kitchen to pick up another tray of food.

Jori tracked the progress of dinner by the courses of food the servers came in for, and as they retrieved the main course she began to garnish the dessert. Each plate got a fan of strawberry slices and a drizzle of chocolate syrup, and then they were loaded onto trays for distribution. She was putting the finishing touches on a serving when she looked up and saw Sawyer standing there staring at the plate with an expression of absolute hunger on her face.

Sawyer watched Jori trail a curving line of chocolate across the china and felt her insides tighten unexpectedly. She was suddenly imagining herself dripping chocolate over Jori's skin. She swore her taste buds twitched at the thought of licking the sweet syrup from her bare stomach. *Man, do I need to get laid. I'm standing here fantasizing about a woman I've just met.* Sawyer had seen plenty of attractive women, some of whom had inspired lustful thoughts. But she couldn't remember the last time she'd reacted to someone this powerfully and quickly.

"Something wrong?" Jori asked.

"Nope," Sawyer answered. She scooped up the tray and dashed out of the kitchen, running from the warm concern in Jori's voice as well as the still-vivid visions of chocolate-covered sex.

❖

Sawyer's wrist cramped as she swung the tray up to hover over her right shoulder. The tightness in her arms and shoulders would no doubt manifest itself as a persistent ache in the morning. But she would not admit defeat. She had done much more physically demanding jobs before. She had spent the better part of one summer loading mulch at a landscape-supply company. So she carefully schooled her features into a pleasant smile as she drew close to the table nearest the kitchen and distributed desserts.

When her tray was empty, she hurried back to the kitchen, almost colliding with another server at the swinging door. She spun into the kitchen and slid her tray onto the counter in front of Jori, hoping she looked much smoother than she felt.

She leaned against the counter and waited while Jori garnished another half dozen plates and transferred them to the tray. Watching her brother and sister expertly wield a knife had always impressed her. Their motions were deft and quick. But somehow watching Jori's slender hands move quickly and confidently over the plates was different. As fingers tipped with nails kept short and neat manipulated the tender flesh of strawberry slices, she imagined them against her own skin.

When Jori reached for the melted chocolate, Sawyer turned away, unable to watch anymore. *Jesus, who knew food could be so dangerous?*

"All set," Jori said from behind her. Sawyer grabbed the tray without looking at her and headed back to the dining room. By the time she'd once again passed out the desserts, she had calmed her racing heart, but it had taken more than a few minutes out of Jori's presence to regain her senses.

"Ready for more?" Jori asked without looking up when Sawyer returned to the kitchen once more.

"Am I ever," she mumbled, her gaze once again drawn to Jori's hands. She wondered when she had developed an unnatural obsession with hands. Her imagination was working overtime and her libido was having no trouble keeping pace.

"What?" Jori glanced up.

"Um, yeah. I've got one table left." She averted her eyes, hoping the lust churning in her stomach wasn't evident there.

"Jesus, what a night. I forgot how much work waiting tables was." Sawyer perched on a stool at the bar, her elbows resting on the polished surface. The last guests had left over an hour ago, and she had helped Erica get the dining room back in order. She reached back and rubbed at a knot in the muscle where her neck and shoulders met. It had been several years and twice as many careers since she'd had a job that required so much physical strain.

"Are you still sure you want to come back tomorrow night?" Erica asked, moving behind the bar and getting a bottle of water from the cooler. She took a bit of pleasure in her sister's discomfort, knowing she had expected to breeze right through the evening and obviously failed to do so. She didn't want Sawyer to struggle, but she was tired of seeing her always land on her feet. She had been surprised when Sawyer sought her out during the salad course to tell her she had reconsidered and now wanted to continue working at Drake's.

Before Sawyer could answer, the door from the kitchen swung open and Brady walked through, leading Jori toward them. Erica watched as Sawyer's eyes immediately tracked to the pastry chef.

"Yeah, I'm sure," Sawyer murmured.

"How about a beer, sis?" Brady called as he slid onto the stool next to Sawyer. "And get the lady whatever she wants." He hooked a thumb in Jori's direction.

"I really should get going," Jori said.

"The fund-raiser was a big success. It should be good for business. Relax and celebrate with us," Erica suggested, sliding a local microbrew across the bar to her brother. "What can I get you?"

"Just water, please." Jori sat next to Brady.

Erica shifted her gaze between Jori and Sawyer, wondering what was going on in her sister's head. She certainly didn't want her pastry chef getting involved with Sawyer. Jori was sweet and a great addition to Drake's, and Erica didn't want to see her get hurt. Maybe she was being selfish, but she also didn't want to risk losing an employee when it ended. It *would* end, Erica was certain. Sawyer had a bad track record with women. It wasn't that she was a player. She apparently made honest attempts at relationships, but her short attention span prevented her from sticking around when the initial glow wore off. And Erica had watched one too many women, namely a good friend of hers, fall victim to Sawyer's fickleness.

Brady draped his arm over Sawyer's shoulders and beamed across the bar at her. "It's so great that we're all working together. It took you long enough to come around," he said, squeezing Sawyer.

"I don't think this is a permanent move, Brady," Erica interjected. Despite Sawyer's assertion that she planned to stick around, Erica still had her doubts. She would lose interest in Jori or the job, either of which would end her commitment to Drake's.

He looked expectantly at Sawyer, who just shrugged. "Oh, come on. This place is in your blood. I don't know why you keep trying to fight it," he said, dismissing her indecision.

"Are you kidding me? In my blood? This place has never meant to me what it means to you guys," Sawyer argued.

"Then why haven't you stayed at any other job?" Brady wasn't letting her off the hook.

"Jesus, Brady, get off my back. What is it with this family? Does everyone think they can just nag me until I give in?" Still sensitive from having her mother manipulate her so easily, Sawyer fought to keep her voice from rising. So what if she'd had a few jobs in the past several years. Why did they all think that gave them the right to dictate how she should live her life?

She glanced at Jori and bit back a retort. Her siblings sure knew how to make her seem irresponsible, and though she wanted to defend herself she decided that now wasn't the time. Jori was staring at her water as if she wished the floor would open up and swallow her. She hadn't spent any time around the three of them, so she couldn't know that the sniping was typical behavior for the Drake siblings.

"Well, I'm beat, and if you expect me to do this again tomorrow, I need some sleep." Sawyer stood.

"Be here by four."

"Okay."

"I should go, too." Jori rose.

Brady followed. "I'll walk you ladies out. Don't forget to lock up before you go upstairs, Erica."

The top floor of the building had been converted into a loft-style apartment that their parents had moved into after their children were all grown and had occupied until they retired. Tia had liked being close to the restaurant, and when Erica took over as manager, she'd moved in upstairs.

"Hey, Sawyer, how about a ride home? I was supposed to call Paige to pick me up when we got done. But she'd have to wake the boys and get them out," Brady said as they walked out the back door.

"Sure." Sawyer fished her keys from the pocket of her worn leather jacket and disengaged the automatic locks. "What's wrong with your truck?"

"I think it's the transmission. I dropped it off at the garage yesterday."

"When are you going to trade that thing in?" She didn't expect a response. Brady loved the old Ford, and she knew he'd keep patching it until his mechanic told him there was no hope. "What about you, Jori? Do you need a ride?"

"I'll grab a cab."

"Nonsense," Brady said, pulling open the passenger door. "Sawyer will drive you home. You're in Green Hills, right? You two are practically neighbors."

Sawyer slid behind the wheel and put the top down. "I hope you don't mind. It's a beautiful night and I thought we could enjoy it."

Jori nearly stumbled as she climbed into the low-slung car. Sawyer was watching her and the softly spoken comment felt intimate, as if they could forget Brady was trying to settle his long body into the small backseat. Sawyer slipped off her tie and tossed it on the center console between them.

"Brady, I'd probably fit back there better than you," she said. She estimated that Brady was six to eight inches taller than her own five foot five.

"He's fine." Sawyer waited until Jori closed the door, then put the car in gear and backed onto the street.

Brady leaned forward and rested his forearms along the top of their seats. "The boys are excited to see you this weekend," he said, clapping his hand on Sawyer's shoulder. "Daniel wants you to teach him to throw a football. I offered to show him but he won't hear of it."

"That's because he knows you throw like a girl." Sawyer

smiled. She loved spending time with her two nephews. At four and six years old they were at a great age. They were up for anything and still thought Aunt Sawyer was the coolest person on earth.

"Oh, yeah? Who taught you how to throw?"

"Mom did," Sawyer shot back with a wink in Jori's direction.

"Mom does have a pretty tight spiral," Brady conceded.

Sawyer laughed, but it wasn't far from the truth. Their mother had taken a very hands-on approach to parenting. Whenever she could, she was there cheering them on at baseball games and school plays. In fact, everything Tia did, she did it full throttle. After finishing her training as a chef, she started working at Drake's where she met and soon married their father, Tom Drake. Tom had grown up in the restaurant that his parents had founded, in much the same way Sawyer herself had. If he was the head of Drake's, Tia was the heart. The Drake family and the restaurant were hers from the moment they met.

"Jori, do you have any plans for this weekend? My wife and I are having some people over for a barbeque Sunday afternoon and you're welcome," Brady offered as Sawyer pulled up next to the curb at his house. He vaulted over the side of the car before Jori could open the door.

She hesitated.

"It's an open invitation, just let me know. See you ladies tomorrow." Brady didn't wait for a reply before he turned and strode up the walk.

"You should come," Sawyer said as she steered back into the street.

"I don't want to intrude." Jori studied Sawyer's profile and felt the same flutter she'd experienced throughout the night. She remembered how a wide grin had transformed Sawyer's face. Her brown eyes sparkled and the easy smile made Jori feel inexplicably warm. Something about Sawyer definitely brought butterflies to Jori's stomach, but Erica's warning about her charm lingered in her head.

"It's not an intrusion. There's always room for one more."

Realizing she'd been staring, Jori looked away as Sawyer glanced at her. She was certain this initial awareness would fade. Since they would be working together almost daily, Jori figured she would become accustomed to Sawyer's energy. *Charisma.* Jori had heard the word applied to others and it definitely fit Sawyer Drake. In just one evening, she had seen how people seemed to be drawn to Sawyer. They would stop midtask to talk to her, and when they turned away they did so with a smile on their face. Sawyer noticed things that others wouldn't. Jori had heard her compliment one of the cooks on his weight loss, and Jori, who worked with him every day, hadn't even known he was dieting.

When Sawyer looked at her, she felt as if Sawyer saw nothing else but her, even if just for that moment. And somehow the glow that spread inside her radiated from Sawyer, not from within.

"So you'll come, then." Sawyer had taken her silence as agreement.

"If I don't say yes, will the three of you be ganging up on me for the next three days?"

Sawyer laughed. "Most likely. We're definitely a force to be reckoned with when we have a shared goal. It's a good thing that doesn't happen very often."

"I'll keep that in mind," she said quietly. "Turn left on Woodmont."

"Nice neighborhood."

"Brady said you're around here, too, didn't he?" She pointed to a house on the left. "You can pull in the driveway. I'm around back in the garage apartment."

"I share an apartment in a complex farther down Hillsboro Road."

Sawyer steered carefully up the drive. The Bradford pears,

slim trees topped with shadowed puffs of foliage, guarded either side. About a hundred yards off the road, a Tudorbethan-style home was surrounded by immaculate landscaping. The white stucco and the gray half-timbers were accented with light stone. Sawyer guessed the house dated back to the early 1930s.

As they rounded the house, she saw a large three-stall garage painted to match the gray trim on the house. A wooden staircase with a moderately sized landing led to an exterior door on the second floor.

"Thanks for the ride. I've finally saved enough to buy a car, but I haven't had time to shop around."

"What are you looking for?" After putting the car in Park, Sawyer turned to her.

"Something inexpensive and reliable. I don't need much, just a good used sedan."

Sawyer smothered an offer to go shopping with her. Her roommate Matt was a salesman at Aces Toyota and had gotten her a great deal on the Solara. But she'd just met Jori and already had threatened to browbeat her into going to Brady's that weekend. She didn't want to scare Jori away. And though she barely knew her, something told her there was a good chance that could happen if she came on too strong.

CHAPTER THREE

Jori stepped out of the shower and rubbed a towel over her hair. It was almost time for a haircut. When she let her thick curls get too long they became frizzy and unruly, especially during the humid summer months. Since she wore a bandana while at work, she chose a short, low-maintenance style.

She pulled on a pair of black chalkstripe pants, tied the drawstring, and tugged a white T-shirt over her head, bumping her elbow against the wall in the process. She bit back a curse as the nerves in her arm tingled. The tiny bathroom was her least favorite part of her apartment. It was barely large enough to house the shower stall, a pedestal sink, and the small towel cabinet in the corner.

Her frustration with the size of the bathroom was worth the trade-off for the rest of the apartment. The remainder of her loft-style living area was open and boasted plenty of natural light. The apartment was tucked beneath the gable roof of the garage but had large windows at either end of the room. In the summer she opened them both and enjoyed a cross-breeze that nearly eliminated the need for air-conditioning.

Since she'd been saving every penny for a car, she had only furnished with the bare necessities. A futon and secondhand coffee table faced one of the windows, and an Asian-inspired screen she'd picked up at a yard sale divided the room from the platform bed on the far side. The corner opposite the bathroom housed what was really nothing more than a kitchenette. She didn't bemoan her lack of a full kitchen since she rarely put together anything more complicated than a salad at home.

Having been on her own since she was eighteen, she had sacrificed comfort at home to pay for her education. But after she'd graduated and got her first job as an assistant pastry chef, she began saving for the day she could find a new place. Then about a year and a half ago she happened to see the listing for this apartment in the newspaper and had quickly called the landlords, praying no one had already snapped it up.

It was much nicer than the last apartment she'd lived in, which was little more than a roof over her head in an undesirable neighborhood. The incredibly reasonable rent she paid made the apartment even more attractive. Her landlords were generous and had told her to do anything she liked to fix it up.

She descended the steps outside and crossed the aggregate drive toward the main house. She actually enjoyed the fifteen-minute walk to the bus stop on beautiful afternoons like this one, and as she strolled down the tree-lined drive she realized she was unusually excited about going to work. Since she'd started at Drake's, she'd always enjoyed her job, but today she buzzed with uncharacteristic anticipation. She recalled the flutter in her stomach while she had studied Sawyer's profile against the backdrop of the city speeding by. She still didn't know much about Sawyer, but somehow she knew if they worked together for any period of time she would.

"Good afternoon," Sawyer called as she strolled into the kitchen.

The kitchen was empty except for Erica, who carried a clipboard and was checking off items in the large stainless-steel refrigerators along the far wall.

"You're early," she said with a note of surprise in her voice. Sawyer shrugged. She knew she had arrived an hour before Erica expected her. She had awakened early, and even after showering, lingering over breakfast, and running some errands, she had plenty of time before dinner.

"Don't you have someone who can do that for you?" she asked, nodding at the clipboard in Erica's hand.

"Are you volunteering?" She turned toward Sawyer with a sigh and set the board down on the nearest counter. "Until you signed on, I was short a server. Brady and Chuck are handling dinner six days a week with their assistants filling the gaps. Jori has been a godsend because my assistant pastry chef was definitely not ready to step up. So to answer your question, no, I don't have anyone else to do this stuff. I'm the manager. It's my job."

"Well, maybe you should hire someone to help out, at least until after the baby's born." The fatigue in Erica's voice had immediately made Sawyer feel guilty, and she could practically hear her mother chastising her for baiting her sister. She knew Erica was a chef at heart, yet she'd stepped in when neither Sawyer nor Brady had volunteered to take over their father's managerial duties, making her a heck of a lot less selfish than them.

"I can't hire someone just because I don't want to do this stuff. I have to consider a little thing called profit."

"Geez, Erica, you don't have to talk to me like I'm a child."

"Well, stop acting like one," she snapped.

Sawyer bit back a sharp reply. A crack about hormones would only earn her a dose of Erica's temper.

"What the hell are you so mad about?" Sawyer asked.

"I didn't plan for any of this. I'm supposed to be cooking, not running the place. I never thought I would be pregnant and facing raising a child alone. I always thought the father would be in the picture. And he's not."

"He's an asshole. You're better off without him. And no one could've predicted Dad would get sick." Erica's outburst startled

Sawyer. She seemed to have everything together, so much so that she had time to critique Sawyer's life. It had never occurred to her that it might be a façade.

"But he did. And here I am, ignoring everything else for Drake's. Just like he did."

"That's not fair. You know he wasn't ignoring us."

Sawyer didn't have many childhood memories of her father that didn't involve being at the restaurant. When she was old enough, she had come to understand that he didn't spend so much time away from his family because he wanted to, but rather because he felt he should. Examining her grandparents' relationship, Sawyer had finally realized that Tom was raised to believe that working hard and making sure they didn't want for anything was his way of providing for his family. And he relied on Tia to fulfill their emotional needs.

Erica snapped up her clipboard from the counter and returned to the inventory. "Just forget it, Sawyer."

A strained silence still hung between them when Jori walked in.

Jori was several paces into the room before she noticed the tension that hung between its occupants. She hesitated, but it was too late to retreat so she continued silently to the pantry and pulled out the supplies she would need for that day's dinner. From the corner of her eye she saw Sawyer leave the room without a word.

Drake's was famous for varying their desserts. Instead of a printed menu they had several different daily selections. The servers were briefed before each shift and were responsible for letting the patrons know what the menu was. Usually Jori arrived in the early afternoon to begin preparing the evening's dishes.

She had picked up some fresh peaches from the farmers' market the day before, so one of tonight's desserts was a cobbler. She set a large pot of water on the stove, then measured ingredients.

"Everything okay?" she asked when Erica came over, picked

up one of the peaches, and smelled it, then absently passed it back and forth between her hands.

"Yeah, just family stuff," she said dismissively as she slid onto a nearby stool.

"How are you feeling?" Jori sensed that Erica wanted to change the subject. She loaded the peaches in a steamer basket and lowered it into the boiling water.

"Well, other than the fact that by the end of the night my shoe size goes up two sizes, I feel good."

"It's no wonder. I rarely see you sit down until well after the dinner rush." She leaned around Erica and grabbed another large pot, which she filled with ice and water.

"I don't have time to sit down. What are you doing with these peaches?"

"Peach cobbler." She pulled the basket from the hot water and submerged it in the cold water. "This will make the skin come off easily."

"Cobbler? You're going to make me gain a hundred pounds before the end of this pregnancy."

"It's quality control. You have to taste the dish before we serve it, don't you?" Jori joked.

"Of course."

In the weeks after she'd hired Jori, Erica had worried that her new pastry chef wasn't fitting in. After closing, when they would all gather around to talk, Jori busied herself cleaning up her area and rarely joined their conversation. But slowly she had begun to come out of her shell. And Erica soon figured out that she was just uncomfortable in a group.

She had soon seen Jori occasionally joke around with Brady and Chuck throughout the night and made an extra effort to converse with her when a lot of people weren't around. But Jori still seemed reluctant to talk about her personal life. She had responded to all of Erica's inquiries about her family with unspecific answers and a quick subject change.

Jori seemed uncomfortable talking about herself and

obviously struggled with the social ease that came so easily to Sawyer, which was one reason they seemed an odd match. But clearly there was a glimmer of interest, at least on Sawyer's part. Erica only hoped it didn't blossom into anything; maybe Jori's shyness would hinder Sawyer's efforts.

She felt a little guilty for rooting against Sawyer's success. But she was still irritated with her assumption that she could solve all of her problems by simply hiring someone. She didn't expect Sawyer to understand what it meant to sacrifice her desires for the good of the business. After all, she was free to flit from one job to the next and one relationship to the next, never caring about the state of the one she left behind.

Five years earlier one of Erica's closest friends had confided that she'd started seeing Sawyer. Erica had tried to stay neutral and wished them the best. But when Sawyer broke her heart, Erica lost a friend as well. Sawyer, however, went on about her life unaffected, as always.

Now that Erica had to make decisions for the good of Drake's instead of herself, her resentment of Sawyer was twisted up with jealousy of Sawyer's apparently carefree life.

❖

Sawyer shoved through the swinging kitchen door and yanked off her apron. She resisted the urge to sling it onto the nearest surface and instead draped it over her arm. The aromas of that night's menu mingled in the air, each competing for her attention. She drank them in and they separated inside her senses—something fried, roasting meat, and a dish with a touch of jalapeño. She'd grown up in this kitchen; sorting the flavors was automatic and something she'd done since she was a child.

Brady moved efficiently between two saucepans, a frying pan on the range, and the large oven nearby. Sawyer passed him up in favor of the counter where Jori worked. As she approached, Jori swiped her forearm across her temple, then picked up a lemon and rolled it between her palm and the metal surface. She pulled a knife from the magnetic bar attached to the wall. The sharp scent of citrus accompanied the smooth glide of the blade through the fruit.

"Hi." Sawyer leaned against the counter, one palm pressed to the cool surface.

"Hey," Jori said, barely glancing up.

"Sawyer." Erica crossed the kitchen, and when she got close enough to keep her voice down, she said, "I need you out front. Not back here hanging out."

"I've been running my ass off out there, Erica. My tables are covered, I'm taking a break." When Sawyer ignored the frustrated look Erica cast her, she rolled her eyes and walked away. "How do you work for her?" she asked Jori.

"She's a great boss."

"Yeah. Try being related to her. I think personal relationships interfere with supervisory ones."

"You're right about that."

Jori's tone piqued Sawyer's interest. "Are you speaking from experience?"

"It's a long story. Would you like to sample my lemon meringue torte?" She held up a plate she'd just finished garnishing. A square of lemon cake was topped with fluffy white meringue, the tips of the peaks tinged golden. A sprig of mint and a fan of thinly sliced lemon added to the visual effect.

"Ah, you're a quick study. You already know how to distract me." Sawyer took the plate, forked a bite into her mouth, and groaned. The tart lemon flavor that practically burst on her tongue was tempered by the lightest meringue she had ever tasted. "This is amazing."

"Thanks." Jori smiled and again rubbed her arm against her forehead. "I have a piece of hair that keeps getting in my eye. Could you push it back for me?"

"Sure." After setting down her plate, she studied Jori's face. A lock of dark hair rested close to the corner of her eye. Sawyer brushed it back and tucked it under the edge of her bandana, resisting the urge to rub the silky strand between her fingertips to determine if it was as soft as it appeared.

"Thank you," Jori said quietly.

Sawyer searched her eyes and noticed for the first time that her pupils were ringed with a halo of silver and the darkest gray irises she'd ever seen.

"Sawyer?" The question in Jori's voice made her realize she was still lightly touching Jori's temple.

She jerked her hand back and shoved it awkwardly in the pocket of her black slacks. "Sorry. I guess I zoned out for a minute there."

"I should get these orders done." Jori appeared as flustered as Sawyer felt.

"Yeah." She backed away from Jori. "I need to get out there before Erica comes looking for me again."

❖

Sawyer walked through the front door to her apartment and dropped her keys on the table by the door. After only two days at the restaurant she was exhausted, her feet ached, and her back felt tight. Her only thought was of sinking into a steaming bath.

"Honey, I'm home," she called as she walked into the living room. Her roommate, Matt, sat at one end of the sofa with a book open in his lap.

He glanced up from his book. "How was your day?"

"Very long." She dropped down on the sofa opposite him. His faded T-shirt and disheveled brown hair belied the smooth car salesman he portrayed during the day. She was always a bit taken aback to see the disorganized boy she'd met in college put on a shirt and tie, slick back his hair, and run his game. But he was actually very good, having garnered multiple awards for top sales. "Did you sell any cars today?"

"Two. My streak continues. How do you like working for your sister?"

"I don't know how long I can do this. Erica seems determined to treat me like hired help." She rested her feet on the oak coffee table in front of her.

"Well, she's probably under a lot of pres—"

"Don't you dare take her side, Matt. Erica has never been helpless a day in her life. Why, all of a sudden, does everyone want me to feel sorry for her because she's pregnant?" Erica was one of the strongest women Sawyer knew. Outside of their conversation earlier that day, Sawyer had never seen even the tiniest crack in her composure.

"I'm not taking sides, but you have to admit Erica is dealing with a lot right now. After your dad's heart attack and their retirement, then she found out she was pregnant and that deadbeat she was dating took off—"

"And I'm a heartless bitch because I don't want to run the damn restaurant," Sawyer finished for him.

"Come on, Sawyer, this isn't you versus the world. Besides, martyrdom doesn't suit you."

She didn't respond. It wouldn't do any good to argue with him now, even though she felt like he should have her back instead of being so rational. After all, he was her best friend and he'd been supporting her since that time, freshman year, when Misty Simmons had accused Sawyer of cheating on her, when really she'd been in a gay bar with Matt all night. As it turned out, Misty was much less interesting than Sawyer had originally thought anyway.

Chapter Four

Sunday morning, Sawyer pulled into Jori's driveway just as she was descending the steps of her apartment and allowed herself a moment to drink in the sight. Seeing her for the first time in something other than the boxy chef jacket and loose pants, she felt a flash of arousal. Jori's red polo shirt was tucked into khaki shorts riding low on narrow hips. Short, shiny curls were free of their usual bandana, and dark sunglasses obscured eyes Sawyer already knew she could get lost in.

"Good morning." Jori bent to smile at her through the car window, and when Sawyer saw a small gold four-leaf clover resting in the hollow between her collarbones, she fought the urge to reach out and touch it.

She stretched across and pushed the door open, took the foil-covered plate Jori carried, and held it until she got settled.

Jori glanced at Sawyer as she turned the car around and headed down the drive. She looked comfortable, steering with one hand draped over the top of the wheel. She wore baggy camouflage cargo shorts and an olive green T-shirt, and the baseball cap pulled low over her eyes shaded her face.

Sawyer glanced pointedly at the plate on Jori's lap.

"Double-fudge brownies." Jori laughed as she guessed the sudden look of desire on Sawyer's face was for the brownies, not her. "I know Brady said not to bring anything, but I figured everyone likes dessert, right?"

"Tell me they're frosted and you'll own me."

Jori was surprised by a surge of pleasure in reaction to Sawyer's words. An unsolicited vision of herself *claiming* Sawyer flew through her mind. "I'm sorry, no. They're not frosted."

"Well, I'm sure they're good, just the same."

Sawyer turned her attention back to the road, and Jori mentally jerked her mind back on track. She had no business thinking about Sawyer sexually; that would only lead to trouble.

❖

When Sawyer pulled the car up to the curb in front of a ranch-style home, Jori felt the familiar racing of her heart and questioned why she had agreed to this outing.

She'd been described as *shy*, but Jori thought the description a bit simple for the panic that bordered on debilitating. Her chest tightened and she struggled to keep her breathing even. After a lifetime of feeling this way, she should be used to the weakness in her limbs and her sweating palms, and she tried to talk herself out of her nervousness. It wasn't like she was a complete stranger, thank God, or she would be shaking and nauseated. "I know Brady, Erica, and Sawyer," she mentally chanted while she willed her heart to slow.

As she followed Sawyer to the backyard, she tried not to think about the other fifteen to twenty people Sawyer had said would be there. She forced herself to focus on the expanse of Sawyer's back and the set of her broad shoulders rather than the ball of fear forming in her stomach. Sawyer's T-shirt was tucked in, her shorts rode low, and a wide brown leather belt circled her hips. Watching Sawyer's arms swing slightly at her sides, Jori had the sudden urge to capture one of her hands and try to draw strength from her obvious social ease. Instead, she followed in Sawyer's wake as if she could blend into the aura of confidence that surrounded her.

At least a dozen adults stood in groups around the large

backyard talking and laughing, and nearly as many children zoomed around.

"Would you like a beer or some lemonade?" Sawyer asked as she led her toward a picnic table laden with food.

"Lemonade sounds great, thank you."

"Hey, Jori," Brady called from where he stood nearby expertly flipping a row of hamburgers. The smoky scent rising from the grill made her stomach growl.

"Hello, Brady. Something smells delicious."

"Yeah, Brady's the man on the grill," Sawyer said as she handed her a plastic cup. "But he sticks to that because he knows he can't compete with Erica's potato salad."

"Yes. It's true. I bow to my sister's culinary mastery." Brady laughed.

"See that you remember that. Hi, Jori," Erica said as she walked by carrying a plate of hamburger buns.

"Don't worry, I have him well trained." A tall strawberry blonde winked at Brady. She shifted the bags of potato chips she carried into one arm and with the other drew Sawyer into a hug. "You don't come around often enough," she murmured, then released her and smiled at Jori. "I'm Brady's wife, Paige."

"Jori." She had seen Paige at the restaurant a few times when she first started working there, but they'd never actually met. She did remember, though, being impressed by the level of respect Brady seemed to have for his wife, evident in the way he had talked about her and now in the way he looked at her.

"Ah, the pastry chef. I've heard good things about you. Welcome to our home."

"Thank you." She couldn't help but be taken in by Paige's friendly smile. Her green eyes were bright, and the dash of freckles across the bridge of her nose was the only hint of color on otherwise porcelain skin.

"You two go get some food. I'll bring these over in a minute." Brady began stacking the burgers and hot dogs on a platter.

Jori followed Sawyer to the picnic table, then—after they

filled their plates with potato salad, baked beans, corn on the cob, and hamburgers—to a couple of lawn chairs under a tree.

She took a bite of the potato salad and said, "You're right. The salad's great. I know Erica and Brady are chefs. What happened to you?"

"I'm the black sheep," Sawyer said lightly, and Jori wondered if she was being blown off. But then she continued. "Erica wants to be in the kitchen, not the office. That was always supposed to be my place."

"But you don't want it. Why did your parents choose to retire when they knew Erica didn't really want to take over?"

"They didn't exactly choose. My dad had a heart attack."

"Oh, I'm so sorry."

"He's fine. It was a mild one. But his doctor told him he was on his way to another if he didn't slow down. So they decided it was time to do what they always talked about doing and they retired."

"And Erica took over."

"Yes." Sawyer paused and bit into her hamburger, hesitant to reveal what she knew everyone else saw as selfishness on her part. "By the time they were in junior high, Erica and Brady knew they wanted to cook. They both waited tables at Drake's during high school. So everyone assumed I'd take Dad's place. And when it came time to go to college, I didn't feel passionate about any other subject, so I majored in business as expected. But when it came time to work at the restaurant I started feeling like I might suffocate."

"Why?"

"I don't know. It's like I was supposed to fit into a mold that just wasn't right for me." She hadn't wanted to step into the role her father had prepared. She wanted to find her own way, but, looking back, she hadn't been very successful at that either. "I had to try something else."

"What did you do?"

"What didn't I do? You name it and I think I've done it. Waited tables, worked at a law office and at the zoo." Sawyer ticked them off on her fingers.

"But you didn't stay at any of those places?"

Sawyer shrugged, unable to explain why she'd never felt settled. There was no great drama or deciding factor, but with each of those jobs she had suddenly become restless and had to get out. She'd hoped that if she found a career that fit, she might begin to feel more comfortable in her own skin. "So what about you, did you always want to be a chef?"

Jori considered the question, trying to decide how much to reveal. "Yeah, I used to cook a lot when I was younger. After high school I went to culinary school during the day and waited tables at night and on weekends."

As a child she'd begun planning early to be on her own. She had known since she was old enough to understand what it meant to be in foster care that she would someday have to survive alone. In the last of a string of foster homes she had been charged with caring for the younger children while both parents worked late every night. She quickly learned how to cook for them, and since the pantry was rarely well stocked, she also figured out how to be creative with few ingredients. So when it came time to choose a career, she'd gravitated toward food. It had taken some time and a lot of work for her to get there, but all the work had been worth it. She loved her job, especially since she had come to Drake's, and she constantly challenged herself to create new recipes.

"You worked full-time while you were in school?"

"Sure. I had to pay the rent somehow." When, the day after her eighteenth birthday, her foster parents told her she needed to find someplace else to live, she was prepared. She packed her few belongings, retrieved the money she'd hidden in a coffee can in the back of her closet, and found a tiny apartment in the warehouse district.

"My parents paid for our education, because they assumed

we would work at Drake's, and I guess they considered it an investment in the restaurant." Sawyer gave a self-effacing grin. "Two out of three ain't bad, huh?"

"You're there now."

"Yeah, but that's temporary. And don't think my mother didn't ask for a refund when she found out I got a job as a tour guide on a trolley after college."

Jori wasn't successful in smothering a laugh. "You were a tour guide? Did you have a uniform?"

"Yes, I did." Mischief flashed in Sawyer's eyes. She leaned close and lowered her voice. "And I looked damn cute in it."

"I'll just bet you did." Jori pictured her in a sharply pressed khaki uniform pointing out tourist attractions and thought her square-framed glasses would make her seem even more knowledgeable. She was probably popular among the guests, friendly and engaging.

Sawyer laughed and, taking Jori's empty plate, she stood. "Can I get you anything else? Another drink?"

"No, I'm fine."

"Okay, I'll be right back."

Jori watched as Sawyer disposed of their plates and strode confidently through the crowd, occasionally pausing to return a greeting. She was surprised at the slight clench of jealousy when Sawyer leaned close to a pretty young woman and smiled as they spoke. Sawyer laughed at something the woman said, then moved on.

She looked comfortable and relaxed, and Jori was envious. She'd never had that level of ease. Merely being there—sitting apart from the group—had her stomach in knots. She'd been fine while they were talking, but without Sawyer at her side she again felt nervousness build inside her.

"Miss me?" Sawyer asked with a grin when she returned.

"Oh, yes, terribly." Jori purposely injected false enthusiasm into her voice.

"Okay. You don't need to patronize me."

Jori held back her response as a blond boy, a miniature Brady, ran over.

"Aunt Sawyer, we're gonna play T-ball and we need an umpire." Sawyer barely kept from falling out of her chair when he yanked her hand. She glanced at Jori.

"Go ahead," Jori said as he continued to tug.

"Come on," he grumbled.

"Come with me. The boys could use a cheerleader."

"Maybe later," Jori hedged. She wasn't the cheerleader type.

❖

"They could be at it for a while. My kids have endless energy," Paige said as she approached Jori's spot under the tree. "Mind if I join you?"

"Please." Jori gestured to the chair Sawyer had vacated. "Which are yours?"

"That's my oldest, Daniel, playing first base." She pointed to the blond who had come to persuade Sawyer to join them. Paige searched the group of children before indicating a smaller boy wandering around in the outfield. "And there's Quintin."

Instead of paying attention to the action at home plate, he bent down to study something in the grass at his feet.

"He looks just like you." His hair was a halo of shiny strawberry curls, and Jori guessed if she were close enough she would see freckles dotting his pale skin.

"Yeah, poor kid."

"What are you talking about? You're beautiful." Jori had spoken without thinking, and as soon as she realized what she'd said, she felt her face flush. "I mean—I—"

"Thank you." Paige touched her arm fleetingly. But her easy acceptance did little to cool the heat in Jori's cheeks.

"Um, so, Erica said you're a stay-at-home mom," Jori said in an effort to draw attention from her embarrassment.

"Before the kids, I worked in an office downtown, but with

the hours Brady keeps it was sometimes hard to plan for child care. Eventually we realized it made more sense for me to stay home." Her eyes followed the action on the makeshift diamond. "It was the best decision I ever made."

They watched for a moment longer in silence. The teams had changed sides and Paige's face lit up as her younger son took a mighty swing with a bat almost as tall as he was. When the ball sailed past the pitcher, Paige cheered him on as he ran toward first base. Jori finally felt the warmth begin to drain from her face.

"So, how are you settling in at Drake's?"

"Very well."

"Erica and Brady don't drive you nuts with their bickering? And I imagine it's worse now with Sawyer there, too."

Jori shrugged. "I kind of like it." She wondered if Paige would understand the comfort of being around such a close family connection. Even when the Drakes didn't agree, the affection between them was still obvious.

"You an only child?"

"Yeah." Jori gave the simplest answer.

"Me, too. It took me a while to get used to them." Paige glanced around the yard, her gaze touching on each of the siblings. "But it's hard not to spend any amount of time around them and not fall in love with the whole family. They're so much fun to be around and, despite their differences, deep down they're very loyal to each other."

Jori only smiled in response. She'd certainly developed a fondness for Erica and Brady in the time they'd worked together. But as she looked at Sawyer, taking in her easy smile as she ran alongside one of the boys, she realized there was one member of the Drake family with whom she didn't want to fall in love.

Erica paused on her way into the house when she noticed Jori and Paige watching the kids play. One of the boys ran across home plate just ahead of a throw by the first baseman, and Sawyer called him safe with an exaggerated sweep of her arms. Immediately three boys ran up to her and argued the call, but she didn't back down.

Jori's eyes followed Sawyer, and Erica wondered if she was aware of the smile that brought out her dimple. She'd seen the way Sawyer looked at Jori and now it seemed the attraction might be mutual, which concerned Erica. If Sawyer got involved with Jori, things would be uncomfortable around the restaurant.

She debated talking to Jori, but when she saw Sawyer glance up and wave at Jori, she reconsidered. Jori had never talked about her relationships. In fact, Erica wasn't certain Jori was a lesbian, though the blush spreading over her cheeks in response to Sawyer's attention was definitely a strong hint. Jori was an employee, and she needed to be careful when broaching such a personal subject. Jori could misunderstand a request from her employer not to get involved with Sawyer. No, she decided, talking to Sawyer was a much better route.

When the game broke up, Erica crossed the lawn to intercept Sawyer before she could join the rest of the guests.

"Can I talk to you for a minute?"

"What's up?"

Erica waited until she was certain the children were out of earshot, then said, "*Please* don't make a move on my pastry chef."

Sawyer laughed, but Erica's expression remained serious.

"I'm serious. I don't want Jori—"

"Erica, you can't tell Jori what she can do in her personal time."

"I'm not telling her. I'm telling you."

Sawyer smothered her instinct to inform Erica she had no right to tell her what to do either. But she didn't try to deny her attraction to Jori; instead she tried to reason with Erica. "What's the big deal? If Jori and I want to hang out, who does it hurt?"

"Why her? Can't you find someone who doesn't work for

me? I just don't want things to be difficult when you get tired of her."

Sawyer flinched, but her sister's bluntness didn't surprise her. "Who says I'll get tired of her?"

"You always do. I don't want to watch you hurt Jori like that."

"I didn't intend to hurt anyone." Stubbornly, she didn't correct Erica's assessment of her personal life. She never did because Erica was going to believe whatever she wanted to despite any explanation on her part. Ever since Sawyer's failed relationship with Erica's friend, she hadn't wanted to hear her side of the story.

"I know you didn't mean to. But you did."

Sawyer looked across the lawn where Jori sat next to Paige. She was smiling politely, but to Sawyer she appeared a bit uncomfortable. Erica was right about one thing; she could get involved with plenty of other women. But though it seemed crazy, considering she barely knew Jori, something about her attracted Sawyer, something more than just her dark good looks and adorable smile. She recalled the one break in Jori's perpetually guarded expression, when they'd first met and Jori was describing the chocolate cake. She wanted to see that flash of confidence and bit of teasing again.

Erica interrupted her thoughts. "I'm serious. Promise me you won't hit on her."

If she didn't agree Erica would only continue to harp on the idea, and she'd be watching them both closely. Maybe she could satisfy Erica and still have a chance with Jori if *Jori* came on to *her.* "Okay. I promise."

CHAPTER FIVE

Late Monday morning Sawyer awoke with a new purpose. She rolled onto her back and stretched, enjoying the lingering arousal from the dream she'd been having when the alarm went off, one in which Jori had starred. Her stomach was pleasantly tight and the expensive sheets, a favorite indulgence, slid against skin left bare by a tank top and soft flannel boxers.

She showered and dressed quickly in black pants and a white button-down shirt. While pinning her hair back, she glanced in the mirror only long enough to scowl at her plain features. She looped her tie around her neck and shoved her wallet in her back pocket, suddenly in a hurry to get to the restaurant. She wanted to see Jori and she hoped the added challenge of getting Jori to fall for her would provide a nice distraction, because in only a week she was already tiring of waiting tables. If not for Jori, she would be ready to move on soon. Oddly enough, this restlessness was comfortable. She'd grown to expect it, so much so that she didn't know what she would do if she ever found someplace that held her interest, that challenged her.

Following the smell of fresh-brewed coffee, she headed for the kitchen. As she passed the hall bathroom she heard the shower running. She hadn't expected to see Matt before noon, considering she hadn't even heard him come in the night before.

She stepped into the kitchen and paused. Matt stood at the

counter wearing only boxers and a wrinkled white T-shirt and pouring himself a cup of coffee. With his hair sticking up and his features softened by sleep, he looked more like the boy she'd known than the man he'd become. He'd been so cocky and sure of what he wanted back then that Sawyer had envied him. He seemed to have no fear when he told his father he wanted to sell cars.

She crossed the room and lifted her own mug off a rack.

"Good morning." He moved aside so she could reach the coffeemaker.

"Who's in the shower?"

"I went to that new club on Church Street with some friends." He leaned against the counter and sipped from his mug. "I met someone."

"Details?"

"His name is Davis and he's really cute. Gorgeous blue eyes. He works out, has pecs I'd kill for."

Sawyer laughed. Matt had gone through a phase during which he lifted weights obsessively, but he couldn't build any bulk. His high metabolism burned all the extra protein he consumed, and he remained lean and lanky.

Matt was spared further interrogation when a soft voice called from the next room, "Matty, do I smell coffee? I don't think I need to tell you what I would do for a cup right—"

Davis bit off his words as he walked into the kitchen and saw her standing there. Dark wet hair fell across his brow. He wore a pair of old sweatpants Sawyer recognized as Matt's, and his broad chest was bare. The rapid blush that crept up his face left little doubt about what he'd been about to suggest in trade for caffeine.

"Hi," he said, clearing his throat. "You must be Sawyer."

"Yes. And you're Davis."

When he turned to take the mug Matt offered, Sawyer grinned at Matt behind his back and mouthed, "*Matty*?" He glared at her and wrapped an arm around Davis's waist to pull him close.

"Well, I'm off to work." She grabbed her keys from the counter and called over her shoulder, "You were right about the pecs, Matty."

❖

Sawyer strolled through the back door of the restaurant. Brady had a row of knives laid out and rasped the one in his hand over the diamond-stone sharpener. He was particular about his knives and insisted on sharpening them despite Chuck's repeated offers to do it for him.

"You better check on your sister. She didn't look too well," Brady said without slowing the rhythmic swipe of the chef's knife against the sharpener.

"Sure, all of a sudden she's *my* sister," Sawyer shot back sarcastically.

"You know I can't handle the pregnancy stuff."

"You're such a wimp, Brady. You have two kids."

"I know. And Paige will tell you, I was no help at all."

Sawyer rolled her eyes at him as she left the kitchen.

She found Erica in her office, sitting with her elbows propped on her desk and her head in her hands.

"Erica, what's wrong?"

She snapped her head up and, though it was too late for pretense, she shuffled the papers in front of her as if she'd been working. But her eyes were glassy and she looked as if she might drop out of her chair at any moment.

"Nothing. I'm fine. I was just going over some orders."

"Uh-huh." As Sawyer sat in the chair opposite her, she let her sister know she wasn't deceived. "You look beat. You should go upstairs and get some rest."

Erica shook her head, denial coming automatically. "I'm

fine." She was exhausted, but she refused to let that keep her from doing her job. She knew her complexion was pale and hoped Sawyer didn't notice the film of sweat on her face.

"Go. Brady and I can handle things here."

"I can't. We're already shorthanded."

"You'll just be upstairs. We'll call you if we need anything."

Erica knew once she left they wouldn't call and disturb her, and she wanted to protest further, but she felt weak and nauseated. Crawling into bed sounded good. "Maybe I'll just take a short nap and come back down in time for the dinner rush."

"The place won't fall apart without you for one night. You'll probably have to take at least one night off to have that baby, you know."

"You think?"

"So consider today practice. Go upstairs."

Aware that Sawyer wouldn't give up, Erica finally nodded and stood carefully to avoid the dizziness that came when she moved too quickly. She'd lost her share of sleep wondering how she would manage as a single mother and restaurant manager, afraid she wouldn't be able to balance the two roles as well as she should. She'd begun looking into child-care centers, but with her long hours at Drake's, her child would essentially be raised by a stranger. This type of thinking had led to the exhaustion she now battled. After making Sawyer promise to let her know if things got too crazy, she headed for the back stairs leading to her second-floor apartment.

Sawyer returned to the kitchen to find Brady seasoning a tray of thick steaks and Chuck peeling potatoes for dinner.

"Hey, guys, Erica's resting and we're down a busboy. We're working short tonight. I'll take fewer tables so I can keep an eye on the dining room. I'll pretty much stay out front. You can handle things back here, right?"

"Sure, we got it. Right, Chuck?" Brady nudged the sous chef.

"Yes, Chef. And if you get behind clearing tables, let me know and I'll come help."

"Thanks, Chuck." Sawyer was grateful for the offer. She would never have asked him to bus tables, though she might have bullied Brady into it.

Sawyer left them in the kitchen, confident that her brother had everything under control. Of course he did; they'd been getting along fine without her for years.

❖

An hour later, in the dining room, Sawyer wound among the rapidly filling tables. Apparently she wouldn't get her wish for a slow night after all. At the front of the restaurant she paused next to the hostess stand and waited while the young woman finished taking a phone reservation.

As the hostess hung up the phone, she turned to Sawyer with a friendly smile that was undoubtedly one of the reasons Erica had hired her. She had seemingly endless patience no matter how full the lobby got, and on more than one occasion, Sawyer had seen her talk a patron out of his irritation at having to wait for a table.

Sawyer reviewed the section assignments for the night's servers, including the cluster of tables she would be handling. Then she walked around the dining room, stopping to check on each table.

Her final stop was a full circular booth in the corner. A man with thick salt-and-pepper hair that feathered back from his forehead sat in the center, flanked by several young men in dark suits.

"How is everything this evening, gentlemen?" she asked. The men didn't look up from their plates, clearly deferring to the older man.

"Everything is wonderful as usual, miss. My compliments to the chef. If I may ask, where is Miss Drake this evening? We're here every Monday and I don't recall a single night she wasn't working." He waved his hands as he spoke and Sawyer noticed several gold rings pushed over thick knuckles.

"My sister is not here this evening," she answered politely, keeping her answer general in deference to Erica's privacy. The young man closest to her shifted slightly, and through the gap in his jacket she caught sight of a compact handgun tucked into a shoulder holster. Instinctively, she took a step back, and when she jerked her eyes back to the ringleader she saw that he'd noticed her reaction.

"Sister? Then you must be Sawyer," he said with a friendly smile. When she gave him a curious look, he said, "Erica talks about you. Please, tell her that Lieutenant Ames said hello." He casually eased his jacket back so she could see the flash of his gold shield.

She wondered if he could hear her sigh of relief. "I certainly will, Lieutenant. Well, I'll leave you to your meal. Let me know if I can get you anything."

"Certainly. And you can call me Derrick."

Laughing at her overactive imagination, Sawyer headed for the kitchen. She always loved that first moment when she entered the room. There was something nostalgic in the bustling energy of the various chefs rushing to plate appetizers and meals. Her mother said the kitchen was the one place that stimulated all the senses. Sawyer paused to enjoy the sizzle from the sauté pan and the cloud of steam roiling from a large pot on the range. She inhaled and envisioned Tia standing at the kitchen door and identifying the exact foods and spices that composed the mingled aroma.

❖

"Damn, no wonder Erica's exhausted," Sawyer said as she pushed through the kitchen door after closing. She'd just finished a final check of the dining room and bar area. She crossed to the table where Jori still worked. "What are you making?"

"Frosting for tomorrow's cake."

"Jori, I just closed everything up. It's late. Why don't you go home and do that tomorrow?" Secretly she was happy to find Jori here alone. There was something intimate about the nearly tangible stillness of the partially darkened kitchen. Jori had left on the row of lights closest to her, but the ones at the far end of the spacious room were unnecessary for her workstation. Her dark eyes appeared even more mysterious and the low light softened her features. It had been a busy day and she looked tired, but her beauty still made Sawyer's chest ache.

"I'm almost done. I'm making three other desserts tomorrow, and the cake is the only one that will keep until then. Besides, I love the peace of the restaurant when no one else is here. But I can go if I'm holding you up."

"You're not keeping me from anything." Sawyer pulled a stool close to Jori and sat. "I hope you don't mind the company."

"Of course not." Jori slid a stainless steel bowl of melted chocolate under the mixer, added sour cream, and turned it on.

"I thought you were making frosting," Sawyer said when Jori turned the mixer off and extracted the bowl.

"I am." Jori felt Sawyer's breath sweep across her forearm as she leaned closer to peer over her shoulder. She dipped a spoon into the thick frosting, testing the consistency.

"With sour cream?"

When Sawyer wrinkled her nose, she smiled. "A skeptic, eh?" She held up the spoon. "Taste."

Sawyer took the spoon, but her expression said she was still unsure. "You first."

The challenge in Sawyer's voice struck a competitive vein in Jori. This was her domain and if Sawyer wanted to test her, then she had to answer. When Sawyer would have handed the utensil back to her, Jori simply dragged one finger through the sweet concoction. She met Sawyer's gaze and sucked her finger into her mouth seductively, letting the rich icing melt on her tongue. Sawyer's eyebrows lifted and she gasped softly, which surprisingly made Jori's stomach tighten.

"Perfect," she rasped, unable to keep the trickle of excitement out of her voice.

"I think"— Sawyer paused and slowly ran her tongue over the back of the spoon—"you're right. It's heavenly. *And* I think *you* are secretly a tease."

"No."

"Not even if I want you to be?"

Jori smiled. "No." She wasn't a tease. At least, she never had been. But she hadn't been able to resist the attempt to fluster the normally confident Sawyer. What she hadn't intended was her own body's reaction or the fact that she could so easily shed her usual self-consciousness. The protracted drag of Sawyer's tongue over the spoon gave her time to imagine that tongue against her own skin, and the vividness of the vision shocked her. Their flirting, which had begun with a buzz of arousal, had ratcheted into full-blown lust in a matter of seconds.

"Hmm. Pity," Sawyer murmured.

Jori watched Sawyer deliberately place the spoon on the counter in front of them. Her slender fingers seemed to caress the arch of the utensil as she released it, and suddenly Jori wished she were braver, but her shyness reappeared. She could easily close the small space between them and— *What? Idiot.* What would she do with her boss's sister, who, from everything she'd heard, had the shortest attention span in the world?

Chapter Six

I'm ready," Jori called as she finished wiping down her work surface.

"Just let me set the alarm, then I'll walk you out." Sawyer waited for the series of beeps that signaled she could leave. "Are you in a hurry to get home?"

"Not really."

"Then how about a walk by the river?" The Cumberland River wound through the city like the curled end of ribbon on gift wrap, coiling around downtown and then doubling back to flow past the Opryland Hotel and into Old Hickory Lake.

"Sure." Jori waited while Sawyer whipped the tie from her collar and tossed it in the open window of her car. At some point during the evening, she had rolled up her sleeves. Now she freed the button-down shirt from her waistband, then took off her glasses and tucked them in her breast pocket. A strand of hair the color of dark honey fell across her cheek, and when Sawyer reached up and slipped it behind her ear the gesture seemed familiar. Jori realized she'd seen Sawyer do it often throughout the evening as she passed through the kitchen, and it was unsettling to discover how much she'd been watching her.

"By the end of the night I can't wait to get out of that tie." Sawyer led her across the street toward the park. The night air was warm and heavy and carried the scents of the city—exhaust mingled with the smell of fried foods wafting out from the bars that lined the street. The glow of neon beckoned patrons to the various establishments, and blues and reds bled into the orange halos of the streetlights.

Riverfront Park was comprised of a large swath of land between the river and First Avenue. At one end was a scaled-down replica of Fort Nashborough and, at the other, a large commercial dock where the General Jackson riverboat stopped during the dinner cruise.

Oversized concrete steps were etched into the grassy bank providing a place for people to sit during outdoor events. In the summer, a collection of the downtown businesses sponsored a free weekly concert series intended to draw people into the area.

As they approached the steps, Sawyer took her hand and said, "Be careful."

Jori tried not to flinch as Sawyer's warm fingers closed around hers. She knew Sawyer only meant to steady her on the steps, but it had been a long time since anyone had touched her, at least anything more than a handshake. An ache formed in the back of her throat. Essentially, she'd been alone for most of her life, so long that she rarely noticed the solitude. But every so often the bone-deep loneliness crept through. Still, it irritated her that she could get choked up from such simple contact with Sawyer.

"Everything okay?" Sawyer asked, and Jori guessed she'd felt her tremble.

"Yeah. Fine. Want to sit for a minute?"

"Sure." After Jori was settled, Sawyer sat beside her.

Sawyer glanced down at Jori's hand resting nearby. She hadn't wanted to release it when they sat, and now she fought the urge to reclaim it, feeling rough concrete beneath her palm as she curled her fingers around the edge of the step. Her new plan might be harder than she thought.

"It's a beautiful night," Jori said, gazing at the sky.

Sawyer stared at her and murmured, "Mmm, beautiful."

The hollows beneath Jori's high cheekbones were shadowed in the half-lit park. In profile, Sawyer could see a tiny bump in the middle of her nose and decided the flaw in otherwise stunning features only added to her attractiveness. Jori had the kind of natural beauty Sawyer had always wished she had. The desire to trace the line of her neck, to press her mouth against the softness just beneath Jori's ear overwhelmed her. Lord, how long had it been since she reacted this way to a woman? Had she ever? Certainly she'd seen gorgeous women before—she'd dated more than her share—but something else drew her to Jori. She possessed a sensitivity that she covered well with self-sufficiency, and Sawyer wanted to know the root of it. Even more, she wanted to soothe it. She stood and began to pace two steps below the one Jori sat on.

Her mind still on Jori's exotic features, she said, "Diamantina—is that Greek?"

"I have no idea." Not for the first time Sawyer saw a hint of sadness in Jori's eyes that made her want to protect her, though she didn't know from what. Just as their gazes touched, Jori glanced away. "I'm not close to my father's side of the family."

"Are you from a big family?"

"Nope. Just me."

"Lucky." Growing up, sometimes Sawyer had wished she was an only child. For instance, on her fifth birthday, when Brady took his first steps and her family spent her entire party fawning over the twins.

"Are you kidding? You're the lucky one."

"Ha. I bet nobody tells you what you *should* be doing."

"No one cares what I do."

"Come on, everyone has *someone* who cares." Despite the resignation in Jori's tone, Sawyer was certain she was exaggerating.

"There's no one." Now her voice was hard, making it evident she didn't expect Sawyer to press the issue.

But Sawyer wasn't willing to let it go. "What about your parents?"

Ignoring the question, Jori changed the subject. "I've never been down here after dark."

"Well, I wouldn't recommend you come here by yourself." Though the police chief bragged crime was down, like many other cities its size, Nashville still had its share. And despite the recent marked increase in police presence in the downtown area, Sawyer still wasn't comfortable with the thought of Jori on the street alone at night.

"I can take care of myself," Jori said, aware of the trace of defensiveness that crept into her tone. Her anxiety had increased as they talked about family, and she had tried not to reveal too much about her past.

"I wasn't implying you couldn't. But I'd hate to see you test your self-defense skills against a mugger with a gun." Sawyer continued to wander from one end of the step to the other. "Just promise me you'll be careful."

"I will," Jori said, telling herself it was ridiculous to think Sawyer might care about her. She was probably just being nice. "It's late. I should go."

"How are you getting home?" Sawyer asked as they walked back toward Drake's.

"By cab."

"Doesn't that get expensive?"

"Sure. But the bus doesn't run this late, and I keep putting off car shopping. I always feel like the salesmen are trying to rip me off."

"Well, come on. I'll take you home."

"You don't have to."

"I want to. So there's no use arguing," Sawyer said, pausing beside her car.

Jori relented. "Should you check on Erica before we leave?"

Sawyer craned her neck and looked at the row of windows

on the second floor. "There aren't any lights on up there. She needs her rest, and if she's sleeping I don't want to wake her. I'll look in on her tomorrow when I get here." She slid into the driver's seat of the Solara and looked at Jori expectantly through the open passenger window. "Get in."

❖

Sawyer climbed the steps to her apartment, feeling energized despite the late hour and a long day. She dropped her keys on the table by the door as she entered. From the muted glow and the murmured voices coming from the living room, she guessed Matt was still awake.

Hoping she wasn't interrupting anything, she headed that way. Matt and Davis were entwined on the couch watching television.

"Hey, guys." Sawyer dropped into the chair nearby. "What're you watching?"

"Nothing, really. We were just lying here talking about going to bed," Matt said.

Davis sat up and Matt seemed reluctant to let go of him. "I'm off. See you in a few." He gave Matt a quick kiss on the mouth before he left. They seemed very comfortable together despite the short amount of time they'd known each other. Matt fell in love easily, then seemed so content that she wondered if she was missing out on some secret. Her own relationships always seemed complicated in comparison.

"How's your used-car inventory right now?" she asked.

"We've got a bunch of stuff—a Camry with low miles and a couple of SUVs. Why? Do you want to trade the Solara?"

"No. It's not for me. I might bring someone by later this week."

"Okay." Matt's tone was saturated with curiosity.

"Jori's been taking the bus to work. I just thought you might be able to help her out."

"Jori's the pastry chef, right?" he asked as he stood to gather the empty beer bottles from the coffee table.

"Yeah." Sawyer grabbed the nearly empty bowl of popcorn and followed him into the kitchen.

"Is she hot?" He disposed of the bottles and took the bowl from her.

"Matt!"

He nodded. "She is."

Sawyer pretended to glare at him. "Yeah, she's hot. But that's not why I'm doing this."

"Uh-huh." She could tell he didn't believe her. "I'll be there Thursday morning. Why don't you bring her by before work and I'll show her what we have."

"I'll check with her and see if she's free." Sawyer told herself she was just trying to be friendly and help Jori out. After all, why should she have to deal with an untrustworthy salesman when Sawyer knew someone who would make her a good deal? Her generosity had nothing to do with her desire to see more of Jori.

❖

Sawyer turned onto Jori's street, admiring as always the sprawling lawns in front of each large home. The neighborhood contained mostly older houses, and the residents here had enough money to stave off the growth and overcrowding that had spread through much of the city. She pulled into Jori's driveway and circled the main house a few minutes early. She had told Matt to expect them around eleven, and then she planned to take Jori to a late lunch before they went to work.

She was debating where to go for lunch when Jori, her hair still wet, stuck her head out the door at the top of the stairs.

"I'm almost ready. Do you want to wait up here?"

Sawyer told herself it was her desire to get out of the beaming sun and not her curiosity about Jori's place that propelled her out of the car. She paused at the top of the stairs and called through the door Jori had left open.

"I'll be out in a minute," Jori answered from what Sawyer assumed was the bathroom.

She wandered around the apartment. It wasn't large, but with the natural light and the minimalist furnishings, it didn't feel cramped either. She thought about her own place. No one would walk in and say it looked like her. But even after the short time she'd known Jori, this space, with its rich colors and unassuming décor, felt like it fit. She could imagine Jori taking comfort in the warm stillness here after a long day.

Though the screen at the far end of the room only partially obscured the bed with its Asian-inspired duvet, Sawyer avoided circling it, fearing she would be intruding on Jori's privacy. Instead she moved around the room and touched the back of the futon and the maple end table. Candles sat on nearly every surface, as did several decorative vases, but something was missing. She carefully lifted one of the vases, a beautiful glass piece with a swirl of dark red around the neck that looked like a ribbon embedded inside. It was heavier than she expected, given its delicate appearance.

The bathroom door opened and Jori headed for the kitchen, carrying her uniform on a hanger. When she turned to open the refrigerator door, Sawyer noticed the navy bandana that would cover her hair when she got to work, but for now it looked sexy hanging out of the back pocket of her faded blue jeans.

"You don't have any pictures of your family around," she said, jerking her eyes away from Jori's ass before she could be caught.

"What?" Jori asked from behind the refrigerator door.

"Well, most people put family photos out."

Jori fought a streak of panic and forced a casual tone. "My place is small and I don't like clutter." Before Sawyer could press her, she rushed on. "Would you like something to drink?"

"No, thank you."

She grabbed a bottle of water. "Ready?" She crossed to the door and held it open for Sawyer.

After she followed Sawyer to the car, she was surprised when Sawyer held the door for her, and her arm tingled when it brushed Sawyer's as she got in. She leaned across to unlock Sawyer's door and saw her eyes dip. Confused, she looked down and realized that as she'd reached for the door, the V-neck of her shirt had gaped, giving Sawyer a view of her small breasts. She felt uncomfortable and knew she was blushing. She wished she'd put on a bra that morning, but once she got into the chef's jacket no one could tell if she was wearing one or not, so she often didn't bother. She realized Sawyer was still staring and cleared her throat. Sawyer jerked her eyes away and hurriedly climbed in, started the engine, and backed out without looking at her again.

Sawyer's observant inquiry about her lack of family photos had thrown her. She had dodged the question, reluctant to explain her lack of sentimentality about her family because she was afraid of Sawyer's reaction. As a young girl she'd seen pitying looks on the face of more than one social worker, and that wasn't what she wanted to see when Sawyer looked at her.

She much preferred the expression on Sawyer's face as she'd leaned across the interior of the car. The flash of heat as Sawyer's gaze caressed her made her wonder how she would feel if Sawyer were actually to touch her, made her long for the certain intensity. Her face flushed anew as she realized the direction of her thoughts, and she looked out the window so Sawyer wouldn't notice.

Sawyer steered into the dealership and parked in front. Waving at the man who strode through the front door, she got out and met him at the front of the car.

"Jori, this is my roommate, Matt."

"Hey, how are you?" Matt held out his hand.

Jori took it and was surprised to find his grip warm and enveloping. His smile was friendly, and when he released her hand he stepped back, leaving her a comfortable cushion of personal space. "It's nice to meet you."

She'd expected something a bit more aggressive from a car dealer. Of course, she didn't trust them as a breed, so she readily admitted she was already biased against him in spite of her initial reaction. He certainly looked the part, with his slicked-back hair, dark navy suit, and bright yellow tie. But the welcome in his eyes contradicted the glossy appearance.

"What can I help you find today?"

"I'm looking for a used sedan, nothing too expensive or flashy."

Sawyer smiled in encouragement when Jori glanced nervously at her. She'd already talked to Matt a bit about what Jori was hunting for, but she'd let them work it out from here. She trusted Matt not to screw Jori. So while he led her from car to car and pointed out the features as well as the flaws of each one, Sawyer wandered among the new vehicles nearby.

When she noticed Matt leave Jori standing next to a green Toyota Camry and head for the building, she strolled back to Jori.

"Did you find something you like?"

"I'm going to test-drive this Camry." Jori touched Sawyer's arm. "By the way, thank you. Matt is a good guy."

"Yeah, he'll take care of you." Sawyer smiled, enjoying the warmth of Jori's hand against her skin and the feeling of helping her.

"Did you find something?" Jori asked, nodding toward the row of shiny new SUVs Sawyer had been looking at.

Sawyer shrugged. "Nothing I'd consider trading the Solara for. Don't feel obligated to make a deal you're not comfortable with. Matt sells a lot, he doesn't need the commission. I only brought you here because I know you can trust him to shoot straight."

Jori nodded and before she could respond, Matt returned, jangling the keys to the Camry.

"Ready for that test-drive?"

❖

"Thanks again for hooking me up with Matt, and for going with me. I know you must have been bored," Jori said, picking up a slice of pizza.

"Nah, I like car shopping, even when I'm not buying."

"But even with Matt fast-tracking the paperwork, it still took an hour and a half to finish it. *I* got bored, and I'm the one buying the car."

Sawyer waved off Jori's concern before she bit into her pizza. The pizzeria was a popular lunch spot and the booths around them were quickly filling up. "I'm glad I could help. So, you pick up the car tomorrow?"

"Yes, it'll be nice not to plan my day around the bus schedule. I haven't been here in years. But the food is still as good as I remember."

"Did you grow up around here?"

"Mostly. In the area, at least. I moved around a lot when I was younger."

Sawyer waited but Jori didn't volunteer any more. I *moved around, not* we, *not* my family.

"So you must have changed schools a lot." From the little she knew about Jori's past, she guessed Jori hadn't gone to private school.

"Yeah."

"I bet it was tough to keep friends." Sawyer thought about her own circle of school friends. She'd been popular, with a number of loyal friends, and she'd never had a problem getting to know new people. In high school she hadn't dated much, because by that time she knew she was interested in girls but was far too intimidated by the ones she found attractive. It wasn't until college that she'd ventured into that arena, and by then she'd learned to rely on her outgoing nature rather than her looks.

Jori shrugged.

"Did your dad have to move for work or something?"

"No."

Jori set down the glass she'd been sipping from and shifted uncomfortably in her side of the booth. Sawyer could tell she should just change the subject, but she was curious about why the light went out of Jori's eyes when the conversation turned to her past.

"Every time I ask about your family, you avoid answering."

"No, I don't."

"Yes, you do. So I'm going to stop asking."

"There isn't much to tell, really. My father wasn't a very nice guy." When Jori stroked her knuckles over her own cheekbone, Sawyer didn't think she realized she was doing it.

Her father hit her. She fought back a swell of anger and remained silent, sensing Jori would speak again when she was ready.

"My mother was too busy trying to remember where she left her bottle to pay attention to what he was doing. I was eight when I was put in foster care."

"If you don't want to talk about this, we don't have to." Sawyer touched her forearm. She'd had no idea and realized she shouldn't have pushed Jori to talk.

"It's history." Jori's voice was distant—cold, now. "One day, she was passed out on the couch when he came home from work. I was in the kitchen trying to make dinner because I knew he would be mad if it wasn't ready and I couldn't wake her up." As Jori spoke, she stared at the white-and-black speckled Formica tabletop, but Sawyer could tell she was seeing the events of that day. Not wanting her to relive it alone, Sawyer covered her hand. Jori turned it over and slipped her fingers between Sawyer's. "I burned his dinner and he beat me unconscious."

The ease with which Jori uttered the statement made rage surge within Sawyer. "Oh, Jori."

"I woke up in the hospital with ten stitches in my head, a

broken arm, and three cracked ribs. The social worker came and told me I couldn't go home. I never saw either one of them again." She looked at Sawyer with tears shining in her eyes. "But when I was about thirteen, I overhead my case worker say that my mother finally got sober and left him."

"Did you ever try to find her?"

Jori shook her head. "When I turned eighteen the folks I was staying with told me I had to go. The state wasn't paying for me anymore. I had to work my ass off to get by, and I was angry at her because I blamed her for not protecting me from him. So, no, I've never looked for them."

"Maybe they—"

Jori shook her head. "I've heard it all before, Sawyer. She was my mother and that whole time I was in foster care she could have found me with one phone call, but she didn't. She never came to get me back."

"I'm so sorry."

"It's in the past. That's why I don't talk about it much. I can't do anything about the way they lived their lives. The only thing I can control is mine."

"Everything you've accomplished is all yours, Jori. They can't claim any of that and they can't take it away from you." Suddenly, Jori's withdrawal from those around her made sense. Sawyer complained plenty about her family, but she'd never faced any of life's trials alone. Thinking about all that Jori had accomplished entirely by herself made Sawyer respect her even more.

Chapter Seven

G ood afternoon, Jori," Sawyer called as she strolled through the kitchen door.

"Hi there," Jori said, not looking up from the Bartlett-pear torte she was making.

As the weeks passed, Sawyer had started hanging out in the kitchen on her breaks. She would drink a cup of coffee and drool over that day's dessert. Sawyer talked while she worked, and she rather liked the running commentary on whatever had Sawyer's attention that day.

Jori watched her pass through the kitchen picking up orders, often scowling or looking irritated. But by the time she pulled a stool close to Jori, she was smiling, relaxed, and chatting away. At first Jori had tried to keep up her end of the conversation and ended up distracted from her work. But she soon figured out that Sawyer liked to talk and didn't require more than the occasional remark to let her know Jori was still listening. Jori fell easily into the rhythm of her speech and responded when she sensed the expectant lull.

She smiled to herself as Sawyer talked about a movie that she, Matt, and Davis had rented the night before. Behind Sawyer, servers passed through the kitchen and called out orders. Brady and Chuck spoke to each other in the shorthand they'd developed over the years, plating food and setting it on the counter to be picked up.

"Have you seen it?"

She quickly recalled the name of the movie Sawyer had been talking about. "Yeah." Surprisingly, she'd enjoyed Johnny Depp as an eccentric pirate.

"Well, the sequel just came out on DVD. Davis rented it, if you'd like to come over tonight and watch with us."

"That sounds fun. I'd like to run home and change first."

"Great. I'll give you directions before we leave."

"Okay."

"Good. Well, I have to get back to my tables."

"Sawyer, service," Brady said as he slid three entrées onto the counter.

"Duty calls," she said with a sigh. She loaded the plates on a tray, then shoved open the swinging door.

❖

Jori worked steadily through the dinner rush, barely taking time to look up when another server came to pick up desserts or shouted a new order. But every time she glanced up to find Sawyer standing in front of her, she felt a thrill at the thought of spending time with her after they closed. She hadn't known she would agree to the invitation until she was already saying the words. But now she looked forward to the end of her shift.

She had just passed a large order to one of the new waitresses and returned her attention to the orders still pending. When she heard a loud crash, she jerked her head up to see a waitress standing amid a scattering of broken plates and ruined desserts. The slender redhead had been working at Drake's for only a week and evidently had little or no prior experience.

Erica and Sawyer burst through the kitchen door at the same time. Sawyer rushed over and stooped to help the woman clean up the mess. While she brushed broken bits into a dustpan, she smiled and talked with the waitress. Warmth infused Sawyer's murmuring voice and the waitress's eyes barely left her face. Her trilling laughter in response to something Sawyer said grated on Jori's nerves.

Erica crossed to Jori's counter. "Jori, I need—"

"Yeah, I've got it." Irritated, she began to fill the lost orders again.

"You okay?" Erica asked quietly.

"Has she ever waited tables before?" When Jori jerked a plate from under the counter and set it down with such force that she nearly broke it, she took a deep breath and forced herself to be gentler with the next one.

"I don't think so. She's trying to work her way through college, and I wanted to give her a break." Erica clearly hadn't expected Jori's burst of temper. "She dropped a tray, Jori. It happens. With or without experience."

"I know." With some effort, she reined in her frustration, only to have it flare up again when she heard the waitress giggle at something Sawyer said.

"Is anything wrong?"

"I admit the girl is cute. But she's barely legal. Does Sawyer have to flirt with every female in range?"

Erica laughed. "That? That isn't Sawyer flirting. She's just being *Sawyer.* Our father says Sawyer has never met anyone who after ten minutes is still a stranger."

"So, what? She's just being friendly?"

"Yes." Erica glanced at her, looking oddly disappointed. "Now, the way she looks at you—that's flirting."

"What makes you think so?"

"There's something in her eyes, and in her voice, when she talks to you."

As Jori pushed the new desserts across the counter, Sawyer came over to load up the tray. "Thanks," she said with a wink.

Jori watched as she handed the tray to the smiling waitress, then picked up her own entrées and followed her to the dining room. *There's something in her eyes.* The warmth Jori had felt when Sawyer winked at her supplanted the tension in Erica's voice. Sawyer naturally hummed with energy, and being the singular focus of that energy was a powerful feeling.

❖

Sawyer stood inside her apartment door and smoothed her hands over the front of her T-shirt. The doorbell rang for the second time, and she realized Jori was waiting in the hallway while she was worried about looking good in a T-shirt and track pants. It was just a casual night with friends. She had absolutely no reason to be this nervous. Jori was definitely not thinking of this as a date. Besides, she hadn't been this nervous about a woman since high school.

She took a deep breath and opened the door.

"Hi," she said, wondering if she imagined the tremor in her voice.

Jori smiled. "I picked up some wine. You don't have to open it tonight, but I didn't want to show up empty-handed."

"Thank you." Sawyer took the bottle and read the label.

"It's Shiraz. I thought you'd like it because it's fruity and spicy with a hint of mocha."

"Fruity and spicy? You're right. That does sound like me."

Jori had changed into blue jeans and a light pink polo that clung to her. The gold clover was once again nestled against the base of her throat, and Sawyer wanted to press her mouth to the skin there. When she realized she was staring and rudely leaving Jori standing in the breezeway, she flushed and moved aside. "Come in. The guys are in here."

She led Jori to the living room. Matt sat at one end of the sofa and Davis half-reclined against him.

"Jori, you remember Matt. And this is Davis. Guys, what would you like to drink? I'm having wine." She held up the bottle.

"Beer," Matt and Davis answered in unison.

"Jori?"

"I'll have a glass of wine with you."

As she went to the kitchen to open the wine, she heard Jori exchange pleasantries with Davis.

"Jori, how's the car?" Matt asked.

"It's great. Thank you again."

Sawyer returned and passed around their drinks, then moved to sit on the floor at the corner of Jori's chair, which was perpendicular to the sofa.

"Are we ready to start the movie?" Matt picked up the remote.

Two and a half hours later, as the credits rolled, Jori turned her attention to the woman whose shoulder pressed against the outside of her leg. Sawyer had settled back and her outstretched legs were crossed at the ankle. Her proximity had been distracting during the movie; she was so close Jori caught hints of her fresh citrus scent. She noticed the curve of Sawyer's neck where it met the worn cotton of her T-shirt and wondered if her skin was as soft as it looked. But she would never know since, other than some flirting and heated glances, Sawyer hadn't made any moves toward her, and Jori certainly didn't plan to pursue her. She wouldn't even know where to start. In the few relationships she'd had, she'd never been an aggressor and had always taken a long time to feel comfortable with a woman's advances.

Davis and Matt leaned close together in the darkened room. As they whispered, Jori noticed Sawyer watching them. Her shoulders sagged and Jori wished she could see her expression. In spite of the fear in the back of her throat, she casually dropped her hand on Sawyer's shoulder, intending only a comforting touch. But when she should have removed it she squeezed instead, then smoothed it over the back of her neck because the skin there was even softer than she'd imagined. What in the world did she think she was doing? She braced herself for the expected panic, but it didn't come. Instead of scaring her, touching Sawyer excited her.

Davis stood and gathered their empty glasses and bottles.

"Leave that, sweetie. I'll get it," Matt said, trying to pull him back down on the sofa.

"It'll just take me a minute." Davis dropped a kiss on Matt's head. "Be right back."

"So, Matt, how long have you two been seeing each other?" Jori asked.

"About a month."

"You guys are cute together." Her fingers slipped of their own accord into Sawyer's hairline and massaged the base of her skull.

"We clicked from the moment we met."

"I sure hope so, since you brought him home that first night," Sawyer teased.

"Well, what can I say? I'm irresistible," Davis said as he came back into the room. "From what I hear, Sawyer, we have that in common."

"Hmm, you're right about that," Sawyer said, trying not to moan under Jori's ministrations. Her touch was at once relaxing and arousing. Her fingers soothed away her tension, but when she raked her nails against Sawyer's scalp, neurons fired all the way down Sawyer's spine.

"And you're both so modest, too." Jori tugged on a lock of Sawyer's hair and Sawyer grinned at her.

"Ladies, thank you very much for joining us." Matt stood and pulled Davis toward the bedroom. "But this one has to get up early in the morning, so I need to put him to bed."

"Good night, boys," Sawyer called as they disappeared.

Jori and Sawyer sat in silence in the room lit only by the glow from the television. Sawyer didn't move to the now-vacated sofa.

Jori's fingers still played in her hair, almost absently, and she marveled that such a simple touch could turn her on so much. She let her head fall forward as Jori traced down her neck. She remembered watching Jori slice strawberries and wondering what it would feel like to have her agile fingers on her.

"You have amazing hands," she murmured, caught up in her memory. "I love watching you work."

"Why?"

"Your fingers are quick yet somehow still graceful. I don't know how else to explain it. Not to mention you do sinful things with chocolate."

"Well, you did let me know your weakness the first day we met. So now I could have you just where I want you with little effort."

"You think so?" *You have no idea how easily you could have me—any way you want me.* Sawyer's stomach fluttered at the thought.

"Sure." Jori twined her fingers in Sawyer's hair and pulled her head back. "I could just melt some chocolate and pour it…" She leaned close until mere inches separated their mouths. Sawyer's brain finished that sentence in a dozen different ways, and they all made her weak. Her heart pounded so loudly she swore Jori must be able to hear it. "…over some fresh fruit."

Jori released her and sat back. She wondered if Jori was simply a tease, but she saw the heat leak from Jori's eyes and decided that something had caused her withdrawal.

"I suspect you could do just about anything with melted chocolate and I'd enjoy it," Sawyer said, watching her face to gauge her reaction to the suggestive comment.

One corner of Jori's mouth lifted slightly, and her eyebrow arched. But her verbal response was at odds with the physical one. "It's getting late."

When she stood, Sawyer followed.

"I should go." Jori headed for the door, but Sawyer grabbed her hand and pulled her toward the kitchen.

"Come with me."

As they stepped inside the kitchen, Jori said, "What are we doing in here?"

Sawyer moved closer and Jori retreated a step. "I was thinking, nearly every other time you've flirted with me, we've been in the kitchen. It's where you're most comfortable—most confident." She closed the distance between them, backing Jori up. She rested a hand on the counter on each side of Jori's hips, lightly, not quite embracing her. She leaned close, her body nearly trembling with the effort of holding back.

"Sawyer, I really didn't mean to flirt with you." Jori's hands loosely clasped Sawyer's forearms.

When she lifted her eyes, Jori avoided them. "What did you mean to do?"

"I just couldn't help myself those times."

"Because I'm irresistible?"

Jori smiled. "Perhaps it's as you said, I'm comfortable in the kitchen—"

"You let your guard down."

"Yes," Jori whispered. She lightly caressed Sawyer's arms.

"So here we are." She leaned close until her lips were inches from Jori's ear. "In the kitchen. Where you're comfortable." She saw the sharp intake of Jori's breath in the quick rise of her shoulders and knew she was bending her promise to Erica, but since she hadn't touched Jori yet, she still considered her word kept. "Let your guard down, Jori."

Jori felt the feathered breath against her ear and realized she only needed to turn her head slightly to capture Sawyer's lips. She wanted to, but did she dare?

"I can't," she whispered. Since Sawyer's arms still trapped her, she rested her forehead against Sawyer's shoulder.

"Why?" Sawyer palmed her cheek.

"I can't get involved with someone I work for." Jori stopped herself before adding *again*. She'd been burned by mixing her professional and personal relationships, and she wouldn't allow it to happen again. She loved working at Drake's and she didn't want to do anything that could potentially jeopardize that.

"Well, luckily, you work for my sister." Sawyer trailed her fingers down Jori's neck and into the vee of her polo, toying with the gold clover.

"You know it's the same thing."

"I'll quit."

Jori straightened. "You'd quit your job so you could seduce me?"

"I'd quit my job so *you* could seduce *me*," Sawyer drawled.

"From what I hear, your interest in me wouldn't last much longer than your tenure at Drake's." She hadn't meant to state it so bluntly, but she was irritated that Sawyer didn't seem to take anything seriously and that she would have the gall to maneuver her into a situation like this, then try to blame it on her. On second thought, if she was blunt enough, she could keep Sawyer at a safe distance and not have to be brave enough to do what she'd really like to.

Sawyer jerked back and dropped her arms. Hurt flickered across her face before she brought it under control, and her short bark of laughter seemed forced. "Do you believe everything you hear?"

"Sawyer—"

"What else have you heard?"

"I—"

"Because whatever it is, I can assure you, at one time or another it was probably true."

Whatever Sawyer was really feeling was hidden behind a mask of indifference, and Jori was too unsure of her own emotions to attempt to sort through Sawyer's.

"I'm sorry if I gave you the wrong idea. I like you, Sawyer. But I can't get involved with you."

When Sawyer nodded and moved aside, Jori left before she could change her mind. She spent the entire drive home trying to convince herself that leaving had been the right thing to do. Her skin still burned where Sawyer had touched her, and she could still see Sawyer's wounded expression at her rebuff. But she did have some nerve to orchestrate that little seduction scene in the kitchen.

❖

Sawyer leaned on the balcony rail outside her apartment staring at the city lights in the distance, the empty wine bottle next to her elbow. She rolled a wineglass between her hands, occasionally sipping from the last of the Shiraz.

She mentally reviewed the scene with Jori, feeling an echo of pleasure when she remembered standing close to her, almost kissing her. Jori's arousal had been evident in her widened pupils and the cadence of her breathing, but something had held Jori back, and though she'd been quick to throw up Sawyer's reputation, she suspected there was more to her resistance.

She figured Erica had warned Jori against getting involved with her. Despite Erica's opinion, she'd never considered her lack of a long-term relationship to be a big deal. She had a nice-enough time with the women she dated. But when it became apparent something was lacking, wasn't it best for all involved to end it so they could move on? Was it her fault she often came to this realization more quickly than the women she was involved with? Early attempts at a relationship had taught her how easy it was to get hurt. She had learned to read the lasting potential of a relationship as quickly as possible to minimize the risk.

But that didn't mean she wasn't willing to give it a shot with Jori. She'd only just begun to get Jori to open up, to know her. But from the first day they met, something about Jori had attracted her. She would have been willing to go up against Erica, to stand up for her right to date Jori. But it seemed Jori didn't want that. Was she teasing her, was she shy, or did she have an altogether different reason for keeping her distance?

So where did that leave her? She didn't want to wait tables. Erica's constant need to control her decisions got on her nerves. Her younger sister had rarely had the chance to do that while they were growing up, so she was taking full advantage of her opportunity now. And now she'd have to face the inevitable awkwardness with Jori, not to mention the raging arousal she inspired.

Yeah, I'm in great shape, she thought, feeling the urge to flee beginning to claw at her as she quickly drained her glass. It always started like that, a subtle itch to move, soon followed by restlessness that made her feel as if she couldn't sit still, like marbles rolling beneath her skin. And she would find no relief until she made a change.

CHAPTER EIGHT

For the second time in a month, Sawyer found herself sitting in Erica's office wondering if she was about to make a big mistake. She wasn't a waitress, of that she had no doubt. So if this wasn't the job for her and Jori seemed intent on rejecting her, why should she stick around? She'd never had a problem walking away before.

Erica came in and, barely glancing at her, circled the desk. "Sawyer, you're not scheduled to work today."

"I know. How are you feeling?"

Erica seemed tired, but aside from that one afternoon, she hadn't missed a day at the restaurant.

"I feel fine." She twirled a pencil between her fingers and flipped through several sheets of paper. "What's up? I've got to finish the payroll."

"Do you need help with that?" Sawyer was stalling and she didn't know why.

"What I need is—" Erica glanced up and paused, then studied her more closely. "What are you doing here, Sawyer?"

"I wanted to talk to you about something."

She watched comprehension sweep across Erica's face. "No."

"I'm sorry."

"Damn it." Erica slammed her hand down on the desk.

"This just isn't what I'm supposed to be doing."

"I really needed you to be reliable for once in your life, Sawyer. What are you expecting me to offer you to get you to stay?"

"Nothing. It's not about you."

"No, of course not. Because it's always about you, isn't it? Because *you* always come first, no matter what else is going on. It's been that way as long as I can remember."

Erica stood and left the office.

"Shit," Sawyer muttered as she rose slowly. She stepped into the hallway and stopped short. Jori leaned against the wall just outside the door.

"I—uh, I didn't mean to overhear. I was coming to talk to Erica."

Sawyer didn't bother trying to excuse her behavior. She headed for the back door, passing Jori in the narrow hall.

"You're leaving?" Jori asked when she was just a few steps away.

She stopped, but she didn't turn to look at Jori. She didn't want to have this conversation, she just wanted to go. "It was always supposed to be temporary."

"Does this have anything to do with—what happened in your kitchen?"

"No."

"Are you sure? Because if it does, there's no reason we can't keep working together. I just won't let you put me in that position again."

"This doesn't have anything to do with you," Sawyer repeated, facing her.

"What are you going to do?"

She shrugged. "I'll find something. I know a guy who owns a limo service. He'd probably let me drive for him."

"You hate it here that much?" Though she knew it wasn't logical, Jori was hurt. She'd been fighting her attraction to Sawyer from the day they met, but more than that, she'd enjoyed getting to know her and had thought the feeling was mutual. And though she had put the brakes on Sawyer's advance the night before, it still stung that Sawyer could simply walk away.

"Jori, I'm not a waitress."

"But you're a chauffeur?"

"I don't know."

She looked so confused Jori almost felt sorry for her. But she didn't understand how someone who had such a supportive family could just abandon them. Sawyer had the one thing she had always wished for, and she thought nothing of tossing it aside on a whim. Sawyer was pouting, Jori realized, and she couldn't respect that behavior.

"You need to find yourself, so you just say 'screw you' to everyone who needs you?" Though not normally confrontational, she didn't give a second thought to calling Sawyer on her egocentricity.

"Jori." Sawyer reached for her hand, but she jerked it away.

"Erica is working herself sick."

"She's fine. She doesn't want my help. Brady will—"

"Why should it always be up to Brady to pick up your slack?"

"My slack?" Anger flashed in Sawyer's eyes.

"They're your family. It's not like you have something else pressing to do. You're *bored*, so instead of at least sticking it out until she has the baby, you're taking off. You're just being selfish."

Sawyer's expression hardened. "This is *family* business. I don't expect you to understand what that's like."

Stunned, Jori nodded slowly. "You're right. I don't understand. Because I've never had a real family."

"Jori, that's not how I meant it."

"Maybe not, but you're absolutely right. In fact, no one's ever given a damn where I was or what I was doing. So if I were in your place, I wouldn't be so quick to take what you have for granted."

Seething, and not interested in Sawyer's response, Jori walked away. She was hurt that Sawyer would use something so personal against her, something she hadn't shared with anyone else, and went directly to the kitchen, refusing to look back. If Sawyer wanted to take off, it shouldn't bother her. After all, Sawyer had just proved how little she thought of her.

❖

"Come on, damn it," Sawyer muttered as she inched through traffic. She slammed her palm against the horn as an oversized SUV cut her off, barely missing her front bumper.

As she drove, Sawyer reviewed her conversations with both Erica and Jori and wondered why she'd made such a mess of things. She was convinced she didn't want to be a waitress, even if it meant seeing Jori every day, but Jori's remark about her being selfish stung and she'd lashed out, using Jori's past to hurt her. Was it selfish to want to be in a job that made her happy? Was she always supposed to put everyone else first?

Jori seemed to think if she just stayed on until Erica had the baby, everything would be back to normal. But the truth, as Sawyer saw it, was that things would never be the same for Erica. Running Drake's was more than a full-time job; it was seventy-plus hours a week. Add a newborn to that and Erica was facing some major changes. Sawyer couldn't be expected to set aside her life indefinitely to help Erica manage hers. Could she?

She was so engrossed in her thoughts that she almost missed the turn into Aces Toyota. Though it probably pissed off the guy in the car behind her, she executed a sharp turn into the parking lot and whipped into a spot in front of the dealership.

Matt was rushing through the showroom as she stepped inside and pulled off her sunglasses. When he saw her, he detoured in her direction, skirting a family of four admiring a minivan.

"Lunch. Oh, man, Sawyer, I completely forgot we were having lunch today." He tapped two fingers against his temple. "It was your idea. You said you wanted to talk to me about something." That morning before she'd left to see Erica, he had asked her to meet him later. "I know, I know. But we're so busy right now." Sawyer glanced at several small clusters of people, some of whom it appeared were being helped already, but others looked around expectantly. "Forget it. I'll catch up with you at home." "Wait, I've got time for a cup of coffee. Come back to the lounge." Without waiting to see if she would follow, Matt headed down a long hallway to the left. They entered a room large enough for a kitchenette and two circular tables. "Sit," he said, indicating one of the tables.

He filled two Styrofoam cups, adding cream and sugar to both, and set one in front of her.

"I did want to talk to you about something." He seemed hesitant.

"I'll see you at home later, if you're busy."

"Davis is coming over, and I wanted to speak to you privately." He paused as one of his coworkers came in and got a soda from the vending machine. He waited until the man left before he spoke again. "You know that Davis and I are getting serious and—"

He stopped again as a woman entered, went to the coffeemaker, and filled a mug. He tapped his fingers impatiently on the table as the woman stood with her back to them adding condiments to her drink. Between his tapping and the woman's spoon clinking against the side of the ceramic mug, Sawyer was losing her patience.

"Whatever it is, Matt, just say it."

"I'm moving out," he blurted.

"Why?" Sawyer sighed, and when she caught the woman at the counter trying to look discreetly over her shoulder at them, she glared at her. She knew Matt wasn't out at work and imagined that the woman thought she was witnessing a lovers' quarrel. Caught looking, the woman blushed and rushed out of the room, no doubt to go spread the juicy gossip.

Sawyer returned her attention to a contrite-looking Matt. She'd argued with Erica, then with Jori. She needed her relationship with Matt to stay level, because she was running out of places to turn.

"Davis and I are getting an apartment together."

"You've barely been together a month."

He shrugged. "When it's right, you just know it."

Sawyer had heard him say he'd met the right one before and it never seemed to last. But that didn't keep him from trying again. He approached relationships with an optimism that Sawyer envied. So, though she didn't really believe this guy would be any different, she wasn't in the mood to argue. "No, you should stay there. That place is more yours than mine. I'll move out."

She wanted to be happy for Matt and Davis. But she'd been living with Matt for years and would miss him terribly. They'd moved in together fresh out of college, and she'd backed him up when he told his father about his career change. He'd been the friend who listened when she lamented her failures and stayed up late talking until she felt better. She knew they'd always be friends, but she couldn't help worrying that their not living together would change things.

"You were there first and I moved in. Davis and I made this decision, so it's not fair to expect you to leave."

Sawyer sighed. "Can we talk about this later? It's been kind of a long day."

"What's wrong?"

"What isn't wrong?" Sawyer replied sarcastically. "I quit my job. Erica's pissed at me, and Jori and I argued."

"Wow. You have had a big day. I can guess why you quit your job—"

"Why?"

"How long have you been there?" He stood. "Refill?"

She shook her head as he stood and filled his own cup. "It's been almost a month. What's your point?"

"Well, it's about time for you to move on, isn't it?"

Sawyer remained silent. She supposed she hadn't given anyone any reason to expect any more from her, but she wished just one person had faith in her.

Matt regarded her thoughtfully as he leaned against the counter and stirred his coffee. "So Erica's pissed because you're leaving her short a server again. But what did you and Jori argue about?"

Sawyer shrugged. "She seemed mad that I was leaving, too. Erica had just basically accused me of being selfish, and I wasn't in the mood to hear the same thing from her."

"So you flew off the handle and now you owe her an apology."

"Close enough."

He glanced at his watch. "Listen, I hate to do this to you, but I really have to get back to work before my sales manager comes looking for me. Can we talk more when I get home?"

"Sure." Sawyer followed him back to the showroom. He waved, then approached the nearest customer as she walked numbly toward the front door.

She'd been spoiled, Sawyer decided as she got into her car. While she'd been cruising through life, not looking for a bump in the road, the universe had been conspiring to blindside her. In one day, she'd thrown away her job, admittedly one she didn't like, but along with it, the chance to see Jori every day. And now her home was facing upheaval as well. *Jesus, give me a break. I've never been this dramatic.* Immediately she shoved her self-pitying thoughts from her head. She certainly didn't have things any worse than anyone else.

She started the car and steered out into the street, accelerating quickly as if she could outrun her circuitous thoughts.

❖

"That looks good, Jori." The words came from behind her, spoken softly so they wouldn't startle her.

"Thank you." She rolled the pipe in her left hand slowly and evenly against the large wooden arm of her bench. With her other hand, she maneuvered the jacks, a tool that resembled cooking tongs, to shape the bulb of glass clinging to the end of the pipe. Though the molten glass had the consistency of stiff taffy, too much pressure could throw off the symmetry. Instead of the traditional vase shape, Jori's design for this piece resembled an hourglass. She pressed the jacks against the bulb, gradually narrowing the center.

She was one of four students in the studio, all of whom worked intently on their own piece while their instructor, a willowy blonde, walked among them offering encouragement and advice. Each of the three furnaces in the room served a different function in the glassblowing process, and even with the protective outer shells, their combined heat pushed the temperature in the room over one hundred degrees. Sweat trickled down the back of her neck and under her collar, and she knew her bandana would be damp at her forehead.

Jori put the end of the rod through a small hole in one of the furnaces to soften the glass, heating it to over two thousand degrees. Then she blew into the mouthpiece in the other end of the pipe, watching the bubble of glass slowly expand. After returning to her bench she picked up the jacks again.

The meticulous work was a good distraction for her, and she'd been lucky to find a class at the Gaines Art Center offered on her day off. Here she had to use an entirely different type of sensory energy than she used in cooking. Glassblowing required visual and tactile skills.

Despite the concentration required, she still found her mind wandering to Sawyer and the changes at Drake's. She'd expected the ease between Erica and Brady to return after Sawyer left, but her presence and the tension she had brought along with it lingered. Sawyer's indifference regarding her family still baffled her. She seemed to expect everyone to fall in line with her plans, including Jori and her plan to seduce her in the kitchen. Or rather for Jori to seduce her. She recalled the arrogance with which Sawyer had made that statement. She had seen the expectation of compliance in Sawyer's eyes, then the jolt of rejection when she'd refused.

"Was this the color you wanted?" The instructor's voice momentarily silenced her thoughts. She'd filled a trough with powdered glass in preparation for adding color to Jori's piece. The fine powder was tinted in varying shades of green, and Jori was hoping to achieve a variegated effect.

"That looks perfect. Thank you."

She rolled the vase in the trough until it was evenly coated, then returned it to the furnace. When she removed it, a verdant monochrome shaded the outside.

"That's lovely. Your best piece yet."

Jori smiled, then resumed expanding the size and shape of her vase. The instructor moved on to check in with another student.

The striations of green stretched as she blew the vase out, and the shades reminded her of the color of Paige's eyes. Though it was months yet until Christmas, she decided this piece would make the perfect gift for Paige. She thought again about the situation with Sawyer and hoped she would still be working at Drake's by the time the holidays rolled around. Despite the fact that Sawyer had left the restaurant, she had the uneasy feeling that things weren't over between them.

❖

Sawyer drove through downtown and dreaded going to Drake's to return her uniform. In the week since she'd left, she'd put off going back. In fact, she'd put off everything. She still insisted that she would be the one to move out, but after a few halfhearted attempts to find a new place, she hadn't gotten any closer to leaving.

The freshly laundered vest and tie had lain folded on top of her bureau for several days. This afternoon she was going job hunting and had decided to stop by the restaurant while she was out. She hoped she could see Erica without running into anyone, namely Jori. She hadn't seen her since they'd argued but had thought about her often.

She parked near the loading dock and slipped through the back door. Immediately turning right, she avoided the kitchen and headed for Erica's office. But when she got there, it was empty.

"Damn it," she mumbled. So much for getting out quick. In the hallway she stopped a passing busboy. "Do you know where Erica is?"

"She was in the dining room last time I saw her."

Thanking him, Sawyer turned back toward Erica's office. She'd just leave the uniform on her desk and call her later. Then she heard a commotion from the kitchen.

"Miss Drake just passed out."

Sawyer rushed to the dining room and shoved through the crowd gathered near the corner booth, where she saw Erica lying on the floor, Lieutenant Ames crouching nervously next to her. Brady and Jori had already reached her, but she pushed past them.

"Erica," she said, gently nudging her shoulder. "Erica, wake up, sweetie." The lieutenant radioed a request for an ambulance.

"What happened?" she asked.

"She was standing here talking to us and just collapsed," Ames answered.

The moments until Erica's eyes fluttered open were the longest of Sawyer's life, but soon she began to come around. She moaned and reached for her temple, but Sawyer grabbed her hand.

"I think you hit your head when you fell." She brushed Erica's hair back from the lump forming at her temple.

"Help me up, Sawyer," she said groggily.

Sawyer glanced at the nearby crowd of patrons and guessed her sister was embarrassed to be there. But she hesitated to move her until help arrived.

"Be still for a minute. The paramedics are on the way."

"I don't need paramedics, just help to my office."

"Erica, you just passed out in the middle of the dining room. You need to go to the hospital."

"I'll be fine."

"Damn it, Erica," Sawyer burst out.

Brady knelt next to Erica, then met her eyes and touched her stomach. Sawyer watched, astonished, as the look in Erica's eyes changed and the rest of the room seemed to fade away, herself included. "You need to go to the hospital," he said calmly. The bond they'd shared since birth tethered them. His words inspired a trust that Sawyer's never would. She was quite used to feeling excluded, having been in this position her entire life, but she still felt the sting.

Erica nodded, and then the paramedics carted in equipment and began to push their way in. Sawyer and Brady stepped aside.

"Go to the hospital, I'll handle things here," she said without looking at him.

"You can go."

"She needs you more than she needs me."

He took her elbow. "She doesn't—"

"Brady, just go." She jerked her arm away. "Chuck can handle the rest of dinner."

"Okay." He relented. "Come to the hospital when you're done. She'll want to see you."

"Yeah," she murmured as she headed for the kitchen with Jori behind her. Chuck was keeping an eye on a béarnaise that Brady had abandoned, and the other cooks continued to fill orders.

"How's she doing?"

"The paramedics are with her now." Jori was standing just inside the door, the rest of the staff trickling in as well.

"Okay, guys, here's how we'll handle this. Wendy," she addressed the shift manager, "you and the servers keep doing what you do. If you need anything, let me know." She felt a pang in her chest at the concern in Jori's eyes but ignored it, needing to stick to business. "Jori, how are you set for dessert?"

"I'm in good shape. I just have to plate as the orders come in."

"Good. Help Chuck with dinner. And if I can do anything at all for the two of you, yell. I'm not up to your standards but I take direction well, so just make sure it's a simple task."

As the staff dispersed, Sawyer paused to whisper a prayer for Erica and the baby, then got to work.

Chapter Nine

Sawyer headed for the nurses' station, but before she could ask for Erica's room number, she spotted Paige.

"Sawyer, I'm so glad you're here. You need to go talk some sense into your sister."

"Me? She doesn't listen to me." Her pride still stung from the moment at the restaurant. Paige drew her to the side of the hallway. "What's going on?"

"Her doctor says she needs complete bed rest. But she says she won't leave Brady with all the work for the next month."

"We can't make her—"

"Sawyer Drake," Paige said, her green eyes flashing. She was using her mommy voice, and Sawyer was surprised she didn't throw in her middle name. Then Paige's expression softened. "She could lose the baby."

Sawyer remembered the day Erica had told her she was pregnant. She'd been scared and wasn't even sure she wanted to keep it. They'd talked extensively about her options, and for a time she thought Erica would decide on adoption. But over the months something had changed. Erica had blossomed in her pregnancy and glowed with love for her unborn child. Sawyer couldn't let anything happen to her first niece.

"What do we need to do?"

"She can't go back to work until after she has the baby."
Which means I'll be back at Drake's. "Should someone stay with her?"
"It might be better if she spent the month in our guest room. She'd have to deal with the stairs at her place. And I'm home all day with the boys, so if she needs something I'll be there."
"Okay. I'll take care of it," she assured Paige. "Did Brady call Mom and Dad?"
"Yes. Erica insisted he tell them they didn't need to come right now."
"I agree. It sounds like she'll be okay, if she'll follow instructions."
"Knowing Erica, that's a big if."
Sawyer had to agree. "Where's her room?"
Erica had been admitted and was staying overnight so they could monitor the baby. She lay in bed partially reclined, fatigue etched on her pale face. Lines snaked from beneath the sheet and ran to a machine that Sawyer guessed monitored the baby's heartbeat. Brady sat in a chair next to her bed.
"Hey, sis." He stood and offered her the chair.
When he started to drag another chair over, Paige said, "Brady, I'm going to the cafeteria for some coffee. Would you come with me?"
"Sure." He touched Erica's hand and met Sawyer's eyes. "We'll be back in a bit."
"How are you feeling?" Sawyer asked after they were alone.
"I'll be better when I can get out of here and back home."
"Yeah, about that—"
"The doctor said I could leave tomorrow."
Sawyer hesitated, knowing Erica wouldn't like her suggestion. "He also said you needed bed rest."
Erica dismissed her words with a wave. "Sure, I'll take it easy. But I've got a business to run."

"I'll take care of things at the restaurant. You just do as the doctor ordered."

"But you don't know the first thing about—"

"I've worked there for a month. Brady and I'll manage. If we need help, you can advise us from your bed. Also, Paige and I discussed it and decided you should stay with them."

"I haven't lost the ability to make my own decisions, you know."

Sawyer went on as if she hadn't heard Erica. "Paige and the boys will be home all summer so you won't be alone."

"But—"

"No arguments, Erica." She was beginning to see why her mother favored not letting her children finish a sentence. It was quite effective. And an idea occurred to her that might solve more than one problem. "The traffic has been making me crazy, so I'll stay at your place. I'll be close to the restaurant and won't have to drive to work."

❖

In the waiting room, Jori watched Daniel and Quintin flip through a children's book. She'd told Paige she would wait with the boys while she and Brady went downstairs.

She had overheard Paige tell Brady that Sawyer was coming back to Drake's. Though she knew it probably wasn't what Sawyer wanted, she was glad. If Sawyer had refused to help her family under these circumstances, Jori would have considered her actions unredeemable.

After Brady had left to follow the ambulance to the hospital, Sawyer had automatically taken charge. She had directed the staff and pitched in wherever needed to keep things running smoothly. Jori had been helping Chuck get the last of the entrées ready when several dessert orders had come in. Sawyer had covered her slacks and button-down shirt with an apron and, while Jori directed her from nearby, had plated and garnished servings of caramel pie and double-fudge cake.

"Aunt Sawyer," Daniel called as Sawyer entered the waiting room. He rushed over to her and Quintin followed.

Sawyer knelt and draped an arm around each of their necks. "Hey, boys."

"Is Aunt Erica sick?" Quintin asked.

"A little bit, pal. But she's going to be just fine. In fact, she'll be staying with you guys for a while." Sawyer glanced at Jori, but her expression was unreadable. "Thanks for watching them. Guys, you remember Jori, don't you? She works with your dad and Aunt Erica." She ruffled Quintin's red curls.

"Do you make supper, too?" Quintin asked, clearly not satisfied with her explanation.

"Better." Jori leaned closer as if she was about to tell him a secret. "I make the dessert."

"Cool."

"Do you make hot-fudge sundaes? They're my favorite." Daniel bounced on the balls of his feet.

"I don't make them in the restaurant. But I do make them every once in a while for very special kids."

"We're special."

"Yeah, we are."

Jori smiled at them. "So I've heard."

Paige and Brady returned minutes later, carrying cups of coffee.

"Did you get her to agree?" Paige asked.

"After some discussion, yes."

"Good. Tomorrow after we pick her up here, Brady and I'll help her get some things from her apartment."

"I'm going to stay at her place while she's with you."

"Why?"

"Matt and Davis need some space. This way they can have it, and I can be closer to work."

"Admit it, sis," Brady teased. "You've always been jealous that she got the loft."

"I have not."

"Don't pay any attention to him, Sawyer. He's just trying to rile you." Paige took the role of peacekeeper.

"Come on, boys, it's past your bedtime." Brady corralled them toward the door. To Sawyer he said, "I'll see you tomorrow at work."

Sawyer nodded and accepted Paige's hug and her whispered "Thank you."

When they'd gone, Jori and Sawyer stood in awkward silence. Jori shifted from foot to foot and wondered how best to excuse herself from the room.

"Jori, I—"

"Sawyer—" They spoke at the same time.

"I guess I'll be seeing you at work." Sawyer's voice was hesitant.

Jori took her words as an offer of truce. She knew Sawyer was trying to avoid apologizing, but knowing Erica's health was Sawyer's foremost concern, she decided to let it slide.

"I want to say hello to Erica before I go," Jori said, avoiding her eyes and carefully keeping her tone neutral. She could be professional despite the tension that still wound tight between them.

❖

Early the next morning, Sawyer climbed the flight of stairs at Drake's, the thick soles of her boots echoing on the steps. At the top, she dropped the suitcase she carried long enough to dig Erica's key out of her pocket. She shoved open the heavy metal door and pushed the bag inside with her foot, leaving it just inside to deal with later.

Erica hadn't changed much in the apartment since Sawyer

was there last. Gleaming honeyed hardwood floors stretched from the front door to the far wall, where a large window looked out over Riverfront Park and the Cumberland River. Considering the downtown locale and the view, if they ever decided to lease out the apartment they could ask a fortune.

Erica, favoring a modern touch, had chosen bright colors throughout the open space. As in the office, she had apparently chosen the red sofa facing the window for its dramatic lines rather than for comfort. The boldly patterned accent chair sitting perpendicular to the sofa was the one piece of furniture Sawyer could actually get comfortable in. She wasn't entirely sure she could live there for even a month. But she had decided by the time Erica had the baby and was ready to move home, she would know what she wanted to do. If everything worked out between Matt and Davis, and she hoped for Matt's sake it did, she would be looking for a new apartment.

As she circled the counter that divided the kitchen from the main living area, she remembered how she'd teased Erica the first time she'd seen the renovation. Despite the full professional kitchen just a floor below, Erica had kept things top-of-the-line in her personal space as well. The kitchen was laid out in an efficient manner, with stainless-steel Pro-Series appliances and a wooden block housing her favorite set of knives.

The dark granite countertop accented the light maple cabinets with frosted-glass door inserts, but Sawyer grimaced at the kiwi-colored walls. She and her sister had completely different taste. *Well, I can't criticize her for at least making an effort to decorate. My beige apartment doesn't exactly scream "me."*

Now that she thought about it, she hadn't lived anywhere that felt like home to her in years. The last place that inspired any nostalgia in her was the house in the suburbs she'd grown up in. When she sought the comfort of sepia-toned memories, she recalled the home her parents had provided. While she would admit her childhood hadn't always been idyllic, it had been good. She suddenly remembered how Jori had trusted her with the story of her own less-than-perfect upbringing and was ashamed of how she'd flung it in her face the first time Jori challenged her.

Since she'd moved out of her parents' house, she had floated from one apartment to another, rarely staying longer than the length of her lease. And with the exception of a fireplace or washer and dryer here or there, they were all pretty much the same. She'd spent all of that time transferring her belongings from one cookie-cutter box to another.

❖

"Did you get Erica settled?" Sawyer asked Brady as she walked into the restaurant kitchen. She'd spent some time getting settled upstairs, then worked in Erica's office for a while. When she'd heard the sound of rattling pots and pans that signified life in the kitchen, she had come out.

"Yeah. She wants you to drop by tomorrow so she can go over things with you," Brady said, smiling.

"She's miserable already, isn't she?" She smiled at Jori over Brady's shoulder, but the pastry chef was either too engrossed in the chocolate she was shaving or purposely avoiding Sawyer's eyes.

"You know she hates not being in control." Brady dipped a spoon in one of the pans on the stovetop and handed it to her.

She tasted the savory reduction. "Red wine, shallots, and garlic," she guessed, falling easily into a game their mother had played while they were growing up. Though only Brady and Erica worked in the business, all three of them owed their practiced palates to Tia Drake.

"And chicken stock." Brady tested the sauce and added more wine. "She's already made a list of things she wants to tell you about running the place. Just go over there and humor her."

"I'd planned to stop by tomorrow anyway. I have a few questions myself."

"Please, don't give her a hard time."

"Why would you assume I'd give her a hard time?"

"Because you're the two most stubborn women I know." He handed the saucepan to Chuck.

"You mean besides Mom, right?"

"Well, I guess we know where you both get it from. It's a damn good thing I inherited Dad's tolerance."

Sawyer glanced at Chuck in time to see him smother a smile. She narrowed her eyes and he pretended to look chagrined, but she knew Chuck saw right through her mock sternness.

"Don't worry, little brother, I'll play nice tomorrow." She watched Chuck pull one of the perfectly seared steaks from the grill and place it on a plate, then spoon some of Brady's reduction over it. She separated a sprig of parsley and garnished each plate as Chuck slid it in front of her.

"See that you do."

Brady's attempt at peacekeeping annoyed her. As usual he focused on keeping Erica satisfied, which always made Sawyer feel like an outsider in her own family. "Your wife is rubbing off on you, Brady."

"I'm going to take that as a compliment, even though I know you didn't mean it that way."

When Sawyer stalked back to the dining room without responding, Jori watched her go. She'd carefully avoided looking at her while she was talking to Brady, though several times she thought she'd felt Sawyer's eyes on her. She probably shouldn't hold on to her anger about the way Sawyer had handled things when she'd left. That had been over a week ago, and so much had happened since then it seemed silly to cling to those hurt feelings.

She wondered if she'd read too much into the situation. She had taken Sawyer's leaving personally when, as Sawyer had so cavalierly told her, it had nothing to do with her. Why should Sawyer consider Jori's feelings when deciding whether to quit her job? Aside from an incredible attraction, what was really between them? The beginnings of a friendship...maybe. But that wasn't reason enough to keep Sawyer at Drake's.

Whatever her personal issues, Jori knew she would set them aside in deference to Erica's condition. The Drake family needed to focus on her health and the safe delivery of the baby. So she and Sawyer would have a truce by way of avoidance, even if that was all they could manage.

Chapter Ten

One of the servers caught up with Sawyer as she circled the dining room. "The guy at table twenty-three wants to speak to the manager."

She sighed. "I'll be right there."

They were halfway through the evening and she hadn't had even a few minutes of downtime. She had developed a circuit of sorts between checking in at the hostess stand, making the rounds of the dining room, and sticking her head in the kitchen. But she didn't have time for more than a quick exchange with Brady and a glance in Jori's direction. Often Jori continued to work, her head bent over the plate in front of her. But when she did look up and their eyes met, Sawyer immediately lost her concentration. Once she stopped right in front of the door and one of the waitresses hurrying to pick up an order nearly ran over her.

She smoothed her hand over her hips and focused on adopting a professional air as she wove through the tables. As she reached number twenty-three she pasted on a polite smile. "I'm the manager, sir. Can I help you with something?"

"You certainly can." The rotund man puffed out his chest and glared at her from under heavy gray brows. "This is overcooked." He handed her his plate. The goat cheese and arugula ravioli was one of Brady's most popular pasta dishes.

"I'll bring another right out for you."

She crossed the dining room, pushed through the swinging door, and slid the plate in front of Brady. "I need another ravioli. The customer says this one is overcooked."

Brady glanced at the plate in disgust. "It was perfectly cooked."

"I'll take care of it, Chef," Chuck jumped in, obviously knowing that Brady hated complaints.

Sawyer had learned that he refused to believe that either he or his staff could make a subpar entrée. Before coming to work at Drake's, she hadn't known her brother was such a temperamental chef. Erica was the same way, and Sawyer understood that, considering her sister's need for control. But she'd always thought of Brady as easygoing in the kitchen, so she was surprised to find him so stubborn when it came to critiques of his food. She was getting to know her family members better than she wanted to.

"Better make it al dente, Chuck," she suggested, glancing at Brady to see if he would protest. He ignored them both.

Her phone vibrated against her hip and she glanced at the display. Grimacing, she took several steps away from the chefs before she answered. "Erica, what a surprise. It's been more than an hour since the last time you checked up on me."

"Paige yells at me every time I get off the couch. What else am I supposed to do?"

"Make a list of books you want to read and I'll go to the library for you."

"I wouldn't know where to begin. Do you know how long it's been since I had time to read?"

"Come on, Erica. You can find something to do besides bugging me when I'm trying to work." She paced the far end of the kitchen, stepping quickly out of the way when Jori walked into the cooler.

"Sawyer, that place is my life. I rarely have time for anything else."

"Well, now this baby is going to be your life, too. So you may as well learn now how to give up some of the control here."

"What's the big deal? I just want to make sure things are running smoothly."

"And you don't trust me to do the job." She paused as she heard Chuck call out from behind her that the ravioli was ready. "I don't have time for this now. Everything's fine here. I'll stop by in the morning. Don't call again tonight."

Irritated, Sawyer flipped her phone closed and stowed it. As she spun around she nearly ran into Jori, who was emerging from the cooler carrying a carton of cream. She caught Jori's upper arms and held her just inches shy of crushing the carton between their bodies.

"Sorry," Jori murmured.

"No. I'm—sorry." Sawyer was sorry for more than just the near collision. She fought the urge to slide her hands across Jori's shoulders and up the sides of her neck. She could cradle Jori's jaw and kiss her before she even had time to react. Jori made no attempt to move away, so Sawyer held her there for a moment. Judging by Jori's sharply indrawn breath, Sawyer wasn't the only one affected by their nearness. Even though they weren't alone, she was confident if she leaned forward, Jori wouldn't resist.

"Ravioli's up," Chuck repeated from behind her, fracturing the connection. Sawyer dropped her hands, stepped backward, and waited for Jori to pass.

She returned the new entrée to the dissatisfied customer and waited patiently while he sampled it. When he nodded his head in approval, she smiled politely, then stopped his waitress and told her to comp the entire table. The young woman looked surprised but didn't argue.

As Sawyer turned away, she noticed a group of men clustered around the hostess stand. She quickly placed the tall man in the charcoal suit and, pleased to see him, crossed the dining room in time to hear him give his name to the hostess.

"Well, hello, Lieutenant. Is it Monday already?"

"Miss Drake." He took her outstretched hand, turned it over, and touched his lips to the back of it. Gesturing to the nearly full dining room, he said, "It looks you have things under control in your sister's absence."

"Yes. I hear you've visited her."

"I checked on her when she was in the hospital and she invited me to stop by your brother's place." He looked hesitant.

Sawyer studied him, finding sincerity in his kind eyes. "Good. She's getting bored over there. She must enjoy the company." She narrowed her eyes as guilt slid across his expression. "She asked you to report back after dinner tonight, didn't she?"

"As a matter of fact, she did." When he smiled, the warmth lit up his eyes and Sawyer could see why Erica liked him. "And I plan to tell her that while her presence is surely missed, you have everything well in hand."

"Very diplomatic."

He nodded in return before following the hostess to his table. Sawyer watched him go, contemplating her sister's interest in the lieutenant. Paige had reported the visit to her house and, she'd added with a grin, he seemed to be quite taken with Erica. Certainly he was charming, but he exuded a solid confidence that Sawyer guessed made Erica feel safe, especially after her last boyfriend had proved so unreliable.

❖

"Are you coming, Jori?" Brady asked after he finished cleaning up for the night. He paused on his way to the back door.

She closed the lid on the bakery box she had carefully filled with tarts. "I'll be a bit longer."

"See you tomorrow, then."

Jori stowed the box in the cooler and went into the employee locker room, stripping off her chef's jacket as she crossed to her locker and retrieved her keys. As she stepped back into the hallway, she noticed a light glowing at the far end.

She hesitated, clinging to hurt feelings over her confrontation with Sawyer. But she'd seen the apology in Sawyer's eyes when they'd nearly collided earlier. So, deciding to extend an olive branch, she returned to the kitchen and pulled down two ceramic mugs.

Ten minutes later, she headed down the hallway again. She braced her shoulder against the office doorjamb and, unnoticed, watched Sawyer as she leafed through a pile of papers. Every few moments she sighed and shoved a hand through her hair. The quiet concentration with which she worked was incongruent with the energy that usually emanated from her.

"Staying late?" Reluctant to disturb her, Jori kept her voice just above a whisper.

Sawyer glanced up. "For a bit. I'm trying to streamline Erica's system."

"How about a cocoa break?"

"That sounds great. Come in. Sit." Sawyer waved toward one of the chairs opposite her desk. She took off her glasses and dropped them on the desk, then rubbed her eyes.

Jori handed her one of the mugs of cocoa topped with miniature chocolate chips clinging to a cap of whipped cream. "It's hot."

"Thanks." Sawyer sipped carefully and Jori couldn't tear her eyes from Sawyer's lips as she ran her tongue along them to catch an errant bit of cream. "Mmm, that's good."

"Is something wrong with Erica's bookkeeping?"

Sawyer pushed aside a stack of invoices and bit the end of her pen. "She put a brand-new computer in here last year, yet she uses the same accounting system my dad used for years. It's all on paper when it would be much more efficient to go electronic."

"It must work for her. She keeps up with everything so well."

"She'd have a lot more hours in her day if she did things my way."

"Can you fix it?"

"Sure. I could have everything computerized within a week."

"So, why don't you do it? When Erica comes back you can show her what to do. There's no reason not to make both of your lives easier. Is there?"

"I guess not." Sawyer set her mug on a coaster and pulled the paperwork back in front of her. "Listen, the other day, I was frustrated with Erica. But that's no excuse for taking it out on you. So—I'm sorry."

Jori guessed from Sawyer's expression that she expected to be forgiven quickly. And perhaps that would have been easier, but she had opened herself up to Sawyer, which she didn't usually do, so to have Sawyer twist her words and stab her with them had hurt, and she wanted Sawyer to fully realize what she'd done. "I don't share my past with just anyone."

"I figured."

"So when you used what I told you to hurt me—"

"I didn't mean to." Sawyer reached across the desk and covered her hand. "It won't happen again."

Jori nodded. "It's late. You should start fresh tomorrow."

For three nights in a row, Sawyer had still been at work in the office when Jori left and was there before anyone else the next day. It had never bothered Jori to know that Erica kept nearly the same hours.

Sawyer glanced down at their hands. The jolt she'd felt when she first touched Jori had settled into a pleasant hum as she stroked her thumb over the back of Jori's hand. Jori turned it over and laced her fingers with Sawyer's.

Then Jori rose, not releasing her hand. "Come on. Walk me out."

Sawyer allowed Jori to draw her around the desk. They stood close, hands still clasped, and she stared at the hair curling over Jori's right ear, because she was afraid if she looked in her eyes she wouldn't be able to keep from kissing her. In Sawyer's kitchen when she had asked Jori to give in to the attraction between them, she'd said she couldn't get involved, and so soon after their renewed truce, Sawyer knew she should try to respect that. But while her apology was sincere, part of her wanted to push Jori's boundaries, if for nothing else than the pleasure she knew they could give each other.

"I need to grab my things from the kitchen." Jori's voice was low and a little rough.

"Okay." Sawyer didn't move and for a moment she wondered if Jori was going to.

Finally, Jori turned away, breaking the spell, and headed down the hallway. She went to the cooler and came out carrying a white box.

"Are you going to see Erica?"

"In the morning."

"Take these." Jori gave her the box. "Key lime tarts," she explained when Sawyer gave her a questioning look.

Jori gathered her jacket and keys from the counter, her fingers still tingling from holding Sawyer's. When Sawyer had touched her hand, Jori's mind had told her to pull away, but her body had been in charge when she'd laced their fingers together. She forgave herself the moment of weakness while steadying her resolve to avoid involvement.

"Trust me. She craves them. And if she's feeling generous, there are enough for Brady, Paige, and the boys."

"What's the deal, everyone gets a treat but me?"

Jori immediately conjured up a treat for Sawyer but stopped short of verbalizing it. *Damn, can I possibly be around her and not want to flirt with her?* "Be nice to your sister and maybe she'll share."

"Oh, that's too cruel," Sawyer said with a chuckle as she followed Jori to the back door. Jori glanced up as she got in her car and saw Sawyer closing the door. She hoped Sawyer would lock up and go upstairs to Erica's apartment instead of going back to work in the office. And she hoped she could figure out a way to stop thinking about how Sawyer was spending her time.

❖

"Here's the delivery schedule and some notes on payroll and suggestions for staffing," Erica instructed from Brady's sofa. She tore the top sheet from the legal pad in her lap and handed it to Sawyer.

"Who gave you paper and a pen, anyway?" Sawyer grumbled. "Aren't you supposed to be resting?" While running some errands, she had stopped by Brady and Paige's house to check on Erica.

"I'm delegating," Erica shot back.

Sawyer shifted in the arm chair and scanned the paper. "Erica, some of these deliveries are at seven a.m. Do you really get up that early after staying to close the night before?"

"You only have to go upstairs after you close. It's not like you have an hour commute."

"Seven in the morning?" Sawyer couldn't remember the last time she was awake and presentable at seven a.m. She calculated and decided that if she threw on some sweats and went downstairs she could sleep until a quarter till.

Sawyer's continued refusal to take her job seriously irritated Erica. But though she knew Sawyer was definitely not a morning person, she didn't feel guilty. Maybe now she'd learn to appreciate how hard Erica really worked. "It's important that you check the order against the invoice. Once you accept the delivery we have to pay for the full order whether it's correct or not."

"Okay."

"I mean it. Don't sign off if it's not right."

"I got it, Erica. I'm not an idiot."

"I didn't say you were."

"You're talking to me like I can't handle the simplest task." Sawyer's voice rose. Erica matched it. When it came to Drake's, she wouldn't back down. "I'm handing my restaurant over to you. I think it's understandable that—"

"*Your* restaurant? Yours? I wonder what Brady would think about that." Sawyer stood and backed away from her.

"Brady doesn't have anything to do with this."

"No? Because the last time I checked, this was still a family business."

"It is. But you're so damn selective about when you want to be a member of this family, it's hard to keep up."

"I don't have time to argue with you." Sawyer folded Erica's list and stuffed it in her pocket. "I have to go run *your* restaurant."

❖

"What'll it be?" Sawyer asked from behind the mahogany bar she'd just finished wiping down. Their bartender had gotten a call about a family emergency, and since it was only an hour until closing time, Sawyer had told him to go and had finished his shift. By the time Brady, Chuck, and Jori finished in the kitchen and found her, she'd closed out the register and cleaned up.

"Give me a beer," Brady said, sliding onto a stool at the bar while Jori took the one next to him.

"Coming up." Sawyer slipped the beer into the opener under the bar and smoothly uncapped it. She passed it to him, then opened one for herself and held up a bottle to Jori, questioning.

"Just water, please. Let me guess, you used to be a bartender, too," Jori said sarcastically as Sawyer handed her a bottled water. She followed the quick, competent motion of Sawyer's hands.

"Just one of my many talents," Sawyer quipped with a wink

and a teasing grin. Jori looked away, fighting curiosity about the nature of Sawyer's other talents. "Chuck?"

"Nothing, thanks."

Sawyer took a long swallow, then pressed her palms to the bar and leaned forward, her forearms flexing as they took her weight. "Countryfest starts this week. I expect business will pick up a bit with the swell of tourists in town."

"We usually don't get the crowds that the bars down on Broadway do," Brady said.

"I talked to a friend on the fund-raising committee and have arranged for us to be one of the sponsors for the main stage," Sawyer said. "We're having a banner made."

"And you think that's going to bring the crowds in?"

She shrugged. "Couldn't hurt to get our name out there. After all, maybe they'll get sick of beer and bar food and want a real meal."

"Sick of beer?" Brady punctuated his question with a swig from his own bottle.

"Maybe not," Sawyer admitted. "But we need to be more active with advertising and promotion. They gave me tickets to Friday's concert. Who wants them?"

Chuck shook his head. "I'll pass. I'm not a big country fan."

"Brady?"

"Yeah, give me a pair. I bet Paige would like to go."

Sawyer slid the tickets out of the envelope and handed over two. She fanned out the remaining pair and looked at Jori. "I've got two left. Want to join me?"

"Sure." Though Jori was uncertain if she should go with Sawyer, she told herself it wasn't really a date since Brady and Paige would be sitting next to them. In fact, it was really more of a work function. She wondered if the lie became less potent if she was aware of it.

CHAPTER ELEVEN

Friday morning, Jori parked in front of Brady's house and saw Paige kneeling next to the porch weeding a bed of daylilies. Her red-gold ponytail was pulled through the back of a baseball cap that shaded her eyes from the bright sun. The tops of her shoulders, left bare by a navy tank top, were turning pink. As Jori got out of the car, Paige looked up and waved.

"Good morning," Jori called as she walked over. "I just stopped by to check on Erica." She hadn't had time to visit since Erica had come home from the hospital.

Paige pulled off her gardening gloves and sat back on her heels. "She's inside. She's supposed to be resting, but I'd bet money she got off the couch the minute I came out here."

"She's not used to inactivity," Jori said diplomatically. "I need to go to work in an hour, so I'll run in and say hi."

"She's in the family room." Paige turned back to the flower bed. "Hey, will you tell her I'm leaving in fifteen minutes to pick the boys up from their friend's house?"

"Sure." Jori entered the house and passed through the living room to the family room. While Paige kept the rest of her home meticulously clean and organized, she seemed to have given up the cause in here. An assortment of toy guns, blocks, and cars and trucks of all sizes spilled out of a camouflage toy box and across the floor. Under the plasma television mounted on the far wall, a low table held a video-game console. This was clearly the room where the family played.

Erica reclined on a large dark green sofa leafing listlessly through a *Gourmet* magazine. A stack of crossword-puzzle books and other publications sat on one corner of the coffee table in front of her.

"Hey," Jori said from the doorway.

Erica laid the magazine down in her lap. "Hi. Thank you for the tarts."

"I'm glad you enjoyed them." Jori settled into the nearby chair.

"Very much." Erica barely paused before changing gears. "So, how's Sawyer really doing?"

"What do you mean?"

"At the restaurant. She tells me everything's under control. And here I sit, not allowed to do anything but ring this damn thing when I want something." Erica pointed at a small bell sitting nearby.

"She comes in early and she's still there when we close. She does the paperwork and works the dining room all night. She's amazing."

"Yes. She can be quite impressive."

Jori felt her face flush. She'd been raving about Sawyer and Erica seemed amused. She knew Sawyer was only doing what Erica had been doing for years. "I didn't mean—well, of course we miss you. I only meant she's really stepping up."

"I'm not offended, Jori. I just hope she sticks with it."

"What do you mean?"

"Time has always been Sawyer's enemy." Erica shifted and adjusted the mound of pillows behind her back.

"Maybe this time is different."

Erica smiled. "I'll bet Sawyer would appreciate your optimism, but I've known her longer than you have. Trust me, she'll leave. It's just a question of when. She's been doing it since she got out of college. She hops from one job to the next as soon as she gets bored."

"I hope you're wrong." After Jori spoke, she realized how telling her words must be.

"Jori, I know you work for me, but I'd like to think we're friends, too."

"We are."

"Ah—this is awkward. I don't know that much about your lifestyle, but I get the feeling I should warn you. Sawyer isn't known for her longevity." Erica watched Jori's earlier blush deepen.

"If you're trying not to ask if I'm a lesbian, the answer is yes. I am."

"I know you're a private person, Jori. And I'm not trying to pry into your life. But I don't want to see you get hurt." Erica wasn't certain if Jori would think she was butting in, but she was genuinely concerned. Sawyer was her sister and she loved her, but more than once, she'd seen Sawyer run away without worrying about what kind of mess she left behind. In fact, it was her signature move—rather similar to that of the men Erica usually dated, come to think of it.

"If it makes you feel any better, I've already turned her down."

"Oh." Erica would have been impressed if Sawyer had stood firm when Jori rejected her. But she now understood that Jori's refusal had likely been part of the reason she'd quit her job. *Typical.*

"What about you? How are you doing? Going stir-crazy?"

Erica easily accepted the subject change. "Absolutely. I'm not used to this much inactivity. Watching so much daytime television makes my brain feel like mush. Do you have any idea how many semicelebrities have their own talk shows now?"

Jori laughed. "I have no idea."

"I really don't know how I'll stand it." She couldn't keep the crankiness out of her voice. She hated to unload her frustration on everyone she talked to, but they all kept asking how she was doing, and sometimes she was too exhausted to pretend.

"It'll all be worth it when you're holding your child. Don't you think?"

"That's what everyone keeps telling me."

"Is something wrong?"

"Sometimes I wonder if keeping this baby is the right thing. Maybe I should have thought more about adoption."

Erica couldn't have known the emotions her words brought up for Jori. She was relieved that at least Erica hadn't been contemplating abortion. Jori's stance on that particular subject was solid and not the least bit politically based. Her most vivid memories included her mother screaming at her more than once that she wished Jori had never been born. She shivered and shoved the image aside. "Is that still an option?"

"I guess it is. But I'm past that point." Erica rested her hand gently on her rounded belly. "I just don't know if I'll be a good mother. I want her to have the best."

"She will."

"But am I being selfish to try to raise her alone? Doesn't she deserve a mother *and* a father?"

Jori could hear the indecision tearing at Erica. She slid to the edge of the chair and covered Erica's hand with hers. "Do you love this baby?"

Erica slipped her hand from beneath Jori's and caressed her stomach. "I really do. It's amazing how much."

"That's all she needs. Besides, you're not alone. She'll have lots of family around her—Sawyer, Brady, Paige, and the boys." The jolt against her palm surprised her and she quickly sought Erica's eyes.

Erica smiled. "Did you feel it?"

"Was that a kick?"

"Yeah. She's an active girl."

"That's amazing." Until then Jori hadn't considered what it might feel like for a child to grow inside her. She'd always known she wanted a large family, but she didn't feel ready for children yet. Because of her own screwed-up childhood she'd often thought she shouldn't have kids. But the movement beneath her hand happened again and she suddenly imagined the tiny foot that caused it.

❖

"Come on, Sawyer. We're going to be late," Brady said for the third time in fifteen minutes.

Drake's was packed with patrons, every table in the dimly lit dining room filled to capacity, and several small clusters of people waited near the front door. Sawyer strode through the dining room to the bar and picked up a tray full of drinks. Brady trailed her, stepping quickly out of her way as she spun and headed for a nearby table. He took the tray from her and held it while she served the drinks. "Maybe you guys should go on without me," she said and nodded politely in response to each murmured "thank you" as she placed the glasses in front of the diners.

"No way. Paige is waiting in the kitchen and Jori is getting ready. You're going with us." He slid the empty tray onto the bar, then, taking her shoulders, directed her toward the kitchen.

"We're slammed, Brady. I can't leave them like this." Sawyer was pleased that they'd been getting a lot of traffic the past two nights, which she attributed to their advertisement at the music festival.

"Wendy has handled worse."

"I know."Their shift manager was competent and smart. She didn't often get as much responsibility as she'd earned because Erica wouldn't relinquish much control.

"Besides, the rush has already started to ease. They're

catching up. And in an hour when the concert starts, it'll be even slower." He pushed her through the swinging door. "Now go get dressed."

"All right, all right. Give me ten minutes."

"You have five," he called as she headed for the small locker room.

"Geez. Impatient," she grumbled as she rounded the corner of a row of rusty gray lockers, already unbuttoning her shirt. She jerked to a stop as she saw Jori, bare from the waist up, standing near her locker. "Uh—sorry, I—" *Jesus, I should have gone to the office to change.* Sawyer had only that one rational thought before her brain slid out of focus. She knew she was staring but couldn't drag her eyes from smooth shoulders and ridges of collarbones that met in a hollow at the base of Jori's neck. She thought she might lose her mind as she roamed lower to Jori's breasts and the rose tips that tightened beneath her gaze.

"Sawyer, you have to stop looking at me like that." Jori's voice was gravelly and, Sawyer thought, a bit beseeching.

Jori clutched her T-shirt to her chest, and the dark blue cotton obscuring Sawyer's view was enough to break the thread that held her attention. But when she raised her eyes guiltily to Jori's face, she discovered flushed skin and eyes round and liquid with…was that desire?

"Why?" Sawyer stepped closer. Another two seconds and she would have to touch her.

"Because Brady and Paige are waiting for us." Jori blinked once, then again, and the heat faded slowly from her eyes.

Brady and Paige are waiting. She didn't say because she didn't want me to.

"Of course."

With some effort, Sawyer turned away, opened her locker, and pulled out a pair of jeans and a plaid camp shirt. Keeping her back to Jori, she quickly stripped off her slacks and blouse and dressed in the more casual clothes. She swung her locker closed, turned around, and saw Jori now completely covered, leaning against the door watching her with unguarded lust. Arousal slammed into Sawyer's stomach, and the air in the small room grew heavy and so hot it seemed to sear her lungs as she dragged it in.

Jori quickly straightened. "Sorry," she mumbled, averting her eyes, and pulled her lower lip between her teeth.

"Don't be." Unable to ignore her thudding heart, Sawyer crossed the room in three quick strides. Before Jori had time to react, she pinned her against the door and shoved one hand into her hair, holding her captive. She allowed her mouth to hover a whisper from Jori's for several seconds, enjoying the anticipation of the kiss, the reflexive grasp of Jori's hand on her forearm, and her unsteadily indrawn breath.

When she couldn't stand it anymore, she closed the distance between them and met Jori's unexpectedly hungry mouth. Jori matched each stroke of her tongue and nip of teeth against her lip. Sawyer drank her in, infused with thrumming pleasure and the sweet exhilaration of a first kiss.

When she finally registered Jori's hands pushing against her shoulders, she drew back.

"Something wrong?" she asked softly. *It certainly felt right to me.*

"We should go." Jori stared at the floor between them.

Sawyer touched Jori's chin, drawing her head up so she could see her face. Her eyes were soft and hazy, her lips dark pink. Sawyer longed to kiss them again, and having felt the abandon in Jori's response, she knew she could. But she wouldn't want to stop, and Brady was waiting. So instead, she said, "We have a minute. Did I upset you?"

"No. I—um, it was nice."

"Nice?" Sawyer chuckled. Such an inane word to describe the exchange that had left her breathless and nearly shaking.

"Very nice."

"Okay." Sawyer smiled to herself and took another step away from her. She picked up her light jacket from the nearby bench. "Let's go."

As they came down the hallway Sawyer heard Paige say, "Sweetheart, we have plenty of time. The concert doesn't start for another hour."

Brady was unconvinced. "Well, how long does it take to change clothes?"

"Hey, it takes time to look this good," Sawyer called out as she strutted into the kitchen, purposely calling attention to herself and away from Jori's flushed face and freshly kissed appearance.

"About time," Brady grumbled. He hated to be late for anything, so much so that it actually stressed him out if he wasn't early. He hadn't inherited the trait. Unless it pertained to Drake's, both their parents were more likely to be tardy. Sawyer wondered if Brady's obsession with being on time stemmed from growing up with their lax idea of schedules.

As Brady headed for the back door, Sawyer let Jori precede her. She touched her lower back lightly as they stepped outside, but Jori's continued avoidance of eye contact worried her.

"It's a nice night. Would you like to walk?" Brady asked. Sawyer knew he would relax now they were on the way. She briefly wondered if twins were more complex than singles like her.

The sidewalk was still damp from a brief shower earlier, but the clouds had passed quickly and the clear, orange-tinged sky was streaked with red as the sun set behind the skyline.

Countryfest drew over a hundred thousand fans to Nashville each year, so the sidewalks were more crowded than usual and they were swept along in the rhythm of the throng. As dusk approached, neon glowed in the windows of the bars lining Broadway. Live music and the smell of fried food emanated from open doors, but nothing could entice the flock. Aside from the occasional stragglers who ventured inside, most of them continued to flow toward the Sommet Center seeking big-name country stars.

Sawyer smothered a curse as a particularly zealous fan rushed past, slamming his shoulder into hers. "When you live here, it's easy to forget people actually come here on vacation, isn't it?"

"This is the first thing I've done that is remotely touristy," Jori said.

"Really? But didn't you grow up here?" Paige asked.

Jori shrugged. "I guess I've never had the time."

Her slightly sad tone tugged at Sawyer's heart, and she sensed that Jori's neutral expression took some effort. She could imagine that such luxuries had never been a priority or even a possibility for Jori. Though Sawyer sometimes resented her family's intrusion into her life, she couldn't imagine being completely alone in the world.

Swamped by a wave of empathetic loneliness, she tucked her hand in the crook of Jori's elbow and drew her nearer.

"Stick with me. I'll show you all kinds of new things," she murmured, leaning close as they walked.

Jori couldn't help but smile at Sawyer's mildly flirtatious tone. She had to admit she liked the warm feeling of Sawyer's fingers wrapped around her arm. It amazed her that the same woman who could make her senses go haywire with a kiss could also so totally anchor her with a touch. *And what a kiss.* It had taken a good part of Jori's willpower to draw back from Sawyer's embrace. She could easily have lost herself in the softness of Sawyer's breasts pressed against hers and Sawyer's hips pushing her insistently against the locker-room door.

She hadn't reacted this way to anyone before. Her few relationships, though pleasant, had been tame. Never before had she been unable to resist the magnetic pull of another person. And it had been years since she'd believed someone could fill the hollowness in her heart, but she closed out those sensations in favor of the alarms ringing in her head. The last thing she needed was to start thinking Sawyer Drake would be the one to occupy real estate in her heart. She was either too self-centered to care about those around her or too lazy to put forth the effort. Either way, Jori didn't need to waste her time. Besides, Sawyer had proven how little respect she had for her when she'd kissed her just now, even after she'd made it clear that night in Sawyer's kitchen that wasn't what she wanted.

When they reached the Sommet Center, Sawyer dropped her hand long enough to open the door for them. As Jori followed Brady and Paige inside, she felt the brush of Sawyer's hand on her back and wondered if, in time, she would become less aware of her. She read too much into every touch, every look, but she couldn't deny the tingle along her spine when Sawyer's fingers brushed the bare skin of her arm. Surely if she felt it, Sawyer did, too, though nothing could come of it. She refused to let it.

❖

A slender blonde dressed in tight black jeans and a black tank top strode across the stage. Her unrestrained long hair feathered wildly around her face and over her shoulders. She strapped on a bright pink guitar, cradling its body against her hip, and a collection of silver bangles at her wrist failed to hide the tattoo that crept up the inside of her forearm.

The band behind her immediately launched into a rocking country tune, and she stepped up to the microphone. As the volume increased, she tapped a steady rhythm on the stage floor and her fingers flew over the strings, driving the music up until everything exploded in a burst of drums and guitar.

"Country music ain't what it used to be," Brady said between songs. The appreciation in his eyes earned him an elbow in the ribs from Paige. His grin in response didn't show a trace of remorse. "How come you didn't elbow Sawyer? She was looking, too."

"She's not my responsibility," Paige countered, slanting Sawyer a look anyway.

"Who are you kidding, Paige? I saw you checking her out, too," Sawyer teased.

"I was not," she protested, but Sawyer thought she saw her color slightly.

"Even if you were, it doesn't mean you're gay," Sawyer deadpanned.

Paige laughed and gave her a shove. "Thanks."

Sawyer glanced at Jori, who was smiling wide enough to display the dimple in her right cheek. Sawyer *had* been checking out the blonde. A study in sensual energy and confidence, the singer had captivated every person in the audience. But looking at Jori now, her eyes sparkling and sheer enjoyment lighting up her face, Sawyer thought, *What blonde?* In that moment, she couldn't think of anyone she'd rather be looking at, couldn't imagine anyone more breathtaking. When Jori gave her a questioning look, she forced herself to smile, then look away.

"Come on, Jori, back me up here," Brady said, leaning to look past Sawyer and Paige. "Shouldn't Sawyer get in trouble, too?"

"I'm not married," Sawyer declared.

When Brady looked at Jori expectantly, she merely shrugged. "She has a point. There's no one to stop her."

Sawyer gave Brady a smug smile, then turned to blatantly leer at the woman on stage. Though Jori knew Sawyer was trying to annoy her brother, she was surprised by a stab of jealousy. She didn't have any claim on Sawyer just because an hour ago in the locker room Sawyer had acted like she wanted to rip her clothes off. *Now there's a bad idea.* In fact, she'd just finished reminding herself why she wasn't worth her time.

When the music began again, Brady and Paige concentrated on the stage again. "So, is she your type?" Jori asked close to Sawyer's ear in order to be heard.

"What?" Sawyer turned and suddenly their faces were inches apart. Sawyer arched a brow and the depths of her eyes, enhanced by the sable flare in her warm mocha irises, distracted Jori.

"That singer. Blonde, tight body. Is that your type?" She shouldn't care.

"There's really no right answer to that question, now, is there?" Sawyer smiled, a lazy lifting of the corners of her beautiful mouth that Jori wished she didn't find so damn attractive.

"Chicken?" Jori challenged.

"Oh, you want to go there? You really want to know?"

Jori nodded.

"Right now, my type is an exotically beautiful brunette with dark eyes and a dimple," Sawyer said boldly as she touched the dimple in question, then brushed Jori's chin.

"Smooth." Jori didn't expect anything less from Sawyer. Still, mesmerized by the sensation of Sawyer's fingertips on her skin, she swayed closer, not caring if anyone noticed. For once she didn't mind the crowd pressing in around them and felt oddly cloaked instead of smothered.

Chapter Twelve

Sawyer rushed through the hallways of Baptist Hospital, trying to follow the signs to the maternity ward. She cursed under her breath. Erica would kill her if she missed the birth. *Every freaking hallway looks the same.* Finally she turned a corner and rushed into the waiting room.

Grabbing her upper arms, Brady halted the forward progress that would have otherwise flattened him. "It's about time."

"She just had to go into labor a week and a half early and at one in the morning," Sawyer grumbled. She'd been asleep for only an hour when the phone rang. Thirty minutes later, after slipping on a pair of jeans and a rumpled T-shirt, she'd been in the car on her way to the hospital. "How's she doing?"

"Paige is with her now. The doctor says she's progressing quickly."

Sawyer slouched in a nearby chair and tried to get comfortable. She knew *quickly* didn't mean anything when referring to childbirth. Her new niece probably wouldn't show herself for hours.

"Mom and Dad are driving up." Brady sat next to her. "I called Wendy, too. She'll take care of the morning delivery. I told her one of us would get there when we could."

"Good. Thank you." Sawyer had planned to run back downtown to meet the truck.

They sat together quietly in the sterile-looking room, hearing only the distant beep of some piece of machinery and the occasional squeak of rubber-soled shoes on the polished hallway floor.

"Do you think you guys will ever do this again?" Sawyer asked, elbowing Brady.

"Probably not. Paige wants a girl, but neither of us can handle her being pregnant again. What about you? Do you think you'll have kids?"

She shrugged and remained silent.

"You don't know?"

She considered and discarded several white lies. "What if Erica is right about me? What if I really can't commit to anyone? I don't know if it's fair to bring a child into a relationship that may not last."

"There's no guarantee any relationship will last, no matter who's involved."

"Give me a break, Brady. You and Paige are perfect."

"We're really not. We have problems just like anyone else. Relationships are work. There's no magic formula."

"I know. But if you believe Erica, I have even less chance."

"Do you believe her?"

"She knows me pretty well."

Brady laughed. "That's ridiculous."

"What?"

"Don't worry about what Erica thinks. Do you want to love someone completely and be committed?"

Sawyer hesitated. "I want to."

"Okay. Then why worry about what anyone else thinks?" He yawned and stretched his arm along the chair behind her. "What's stopping you?"

"The only times I've really tried, I failed." Sawyer recalled her early naïveté in love. She'd been a freshman in college the first time someone broke her heart—crushed was probably a more accurate description. In hindsight, she blamed herself for falling for her roommate, though certainly the woman should have told her she was straight from the beginning. She was completely in love by the time her roommate told her it was just a fling. Sawyer even remembered her exact words. "You didn't really think this was serious, did you? It was just a bit of fun, before I settle down and get married." Sawyer had moved to another dorm and a few months later heard that her former lover was engaged to a football player.

She could probably have gotten over that incident if it had been the only one. But each of her subsequent attempts ended similarly until she finally decided she was just the type that other women stayed with until something better came along.

"You're not still hung up on that, are you?" Brady's voice tugged her back to the present before she could dissect her other failed relationships. After Sawyer had ended things with Erica's friend and Erica wasn't speaking to her, she had confided in Brady about her insecurities.

"Maybe I'm just not meant for love. The truth is, most of the time I bail before I start to care because I expect them to eventually move on. So I do it first."

"You just need to find the right person." Brady dismissed her concerns with the same phrase her mother often used. In fact, they were the exact words her mother had used when Sawyer came out to her, only then she hadn't met the right man. Since that day, Tia had accepted that Sawyer was a lesbian and had amended the phrase. "Just think, someday you'll have someone to nag you about picking your towel up off the bathroom floor, and a couple of kids leaving Matchbox cars on the floor for you to step on." He rubbed a hand over the stubble on his jaw. "Man, those things really hurt."

Sawyer laughed. "You make it sound so appealing."

"It is. I mean, sure, there are days—but most of the time it's good. Knowing she'll be there when you wake up. Having someone to talk to over the dinner table."

"I've had that." *Albeit briefly.* She and Deborah had

practically lived together for one intense week. Of course, it hadn't lasted past the following weekend.

"I'm not talking about Matt."

"Very funny." She tried to shove him away, but he squeezed her shoulder.

"Seriously—"

"You're never serious."

"As I was saying, seriously, it's different when you're married."

"Yeah, well, until the laws change, I'll have to take your word on that one."

"You know what I mean. It's different when you know that person will be there no matter what stupid thing you might do or say. Why do you have such a hard time envisioning this? Our parents are still together, Paige and I are going strong. Can't we be your role models?"

"I'll work on it," Sawyer said, more to stop this conversation than to admit her desire to pattern her life after his. She didn't really believe she'd have anyone who would stick around no matter what she said or did. Others might have that kind of life, but she had finally accepted that she might never achieve her version of the fairytale. Still, she secretly envied her friends who had been coupled for more than a decade.

❖

Sawyer eased the door open and peeked inside the darkened room. The amber glow of the streetlight outside the window slashed through the space between the vertical blinds and fell across the sleeping form in the bed.

But when she started to close the door she heard Erica whisper, "I'm awake."

She tiptoed halfway in before she realized the other bed was vacant. "How are you feeling?" she asked as she sat in the chair next to Erica.

"I'm still pretty tired." Using the nearby control, she raised the back of her bed a bit. "I bet you're getting sick of visiting me in the hospital."

"Well, hopefully this will be the last time for a while."

"Did you see her?"

"She's beautiful." Through the nursery window, Sawyer, Paige, and Brady had watched the pink-skinned baby cry and wave her fists. The tiny knit cap covered her head, but Paige said she had a thick head of white-blond hair. Taylor Ashley Drake. Sawyer remembered how fragile her nephews had looked when they were born, but somehow her first niece seemed even more delicate.

Erica grinned. "I might be biased, but I think she's gorgeous."

"Yeah, well, luckily she looks like her mother."

Erica's smile faded a bit. "She has his chin."

"Have you called him?" Sawyer regretted reminding her of Taylor's loser father.

"No."

"Do you—want me to?"

"No. He knew I was pregnant and never bothered to get in touch. There's no point now. I don't need him. I've got you guys."

"That's right." Sawyer squeezed Erica's hand. She hadn't always had such a positive attitude. The first four months Erica was pregnant, her anger had been palpable. Sawyer had been worried until the first time Erica felt the baby kick; then love pushed out her rage. Now Erica seemed to experience only brief glimmers of hurt, which she clearly tried hard to hide.

"I'm going to stay at Paige and Brady's for a couple more weeks, and then Taylor and I are going home. But you're welcome to stay as long as you want, provided you don't mind a newborn crying in the middle of the night."

"We'll work that out when the time comes." Sawyer hadn't expected to miss Matt so much. Every day after work, she went upstairs and flopped down in the chair and stared at the empty sofa. She was still adjusting to living alone and hadn't yet considered what she would do when Erica returned.

"Mom called this morning. She and Dad are on the way up and should be here this afternoon. Are you going to Drake's?"

Sawyer laughed. "Can you ever stop thinking about work?"

Erica's expectant silence was answer enough.

"Yes, I'll be at the restaurant, but first I'm going home and try to grab a power nap, since I was up all night waiting for Miss Taylor to appear."

"Up all night, my ass. Paige said she saw you and Brady sleeping in the waiting room."

"We were resting our eyes," Sawyer shot back.

"Brady was drooling."

Sawyer smiled. "He's been taking pictures of Taylor through the nursery window to show everyone at the restaurant."

"Will you tell Jori and Chuck I expect them to come by Brady's and visit?"

"Sure."

"And if you see Derrick Ames, please tell him—well, never mind."

"So, you and the lieutenant, huh?"

"I don't know what I'm thinking. I mean, look at me." Erica fluttered the edge of the sheet covering her.

"What are you talking about? You just had a baby. No one expects you to be a beauty queen."

"Gee, thanks, Sawyer."

"Oh, you know what I mean."

"That's my point. Even if I'd let myself believe he could be interested in a pregnant woman, now I'm the mother of an infant. How sexy is that?"

"He asks about you every Monday. And I got the impression you two had been in touch."

"We have."

"Obviously he was into you before, and so far the idea of a baby hasn't scared him off. So why not give him a chance?"

"You're probably right."

Sawyer feigned shock. "Could you say that again?"

"Okay, I said you're probably right. Enjoy it, because who knows when it'll happen again. Why are you so smart about my life, but when it comes to your own—"

"And that's my cue to leave." They'd been getting along and Sawyer didn't want to ruin that. "I'm heading home for that nap."

❖

Jori pressed a ball of dough against the floured metal counter in front of her, then picked up a solid maple rolling pin and began to flatten the ball. She had already prepared the filling for the blackberry cobbler.

"Hi, Jori," Chuck called as he entered the kitchen. He pulled an armload of vegetables from the subzero and carried them to his station, whistling as he began to prepare them for the day's menu. "You hear about the baby?"

"Yeah, Paige left me a message this morning. Do you have any kids, Chuck?" Jori realized that in the months she'd worked at Drake's, she hadn't learned much about her coworkers. Brady and Erica were easy to know, because they shared a bit of the same outgoing nature that Sawyer had in abundance. They brought their family life into the kitchen and Jori couldn't help but learn about them. But Chuck was more reserved.

"One daughter. She's fourteen. She lives with her mom."

"Do you see her much?"

"Every other weekend, although lately she's more interested in going to parties with her friends than hanging out with her dad."

Having never done much of either, Jori didn't know how to respond.

"Ah, I guess that's just part of growing up." He shrugged and started whistling again. "I'm going out back for a cigarette before Brady gets here." Brady had been after him to quit, and while he showed no signs of doing so, he had cut back and tried to get them in when Brady wasn't around.

Jori smiled and continued to work the dough. She loved the bustle and din of the kitchen during service, but she also savored these quiet times before the rest of the staff and the customers arrived. She did some of her best thinking during the peaceful pre-open period. And today her thoughts were firmly on Sawyer Drake. If she was being honest, Sawyer had been logging a lot of hours in her mind lately.

During the concert and later that night at home alone, she had rehearsed how she would let Sawyer down easily. She simply couldn't get involved with someone she worked with. But Sawyer wouldn't hear it; every time she tried to bring it up, Sawyer suddenly got busy or just flat-out left the room.

The memory of past mistakes still stung. Once before, she had ignored the voice that told her a relationship with her boss was a bad idea. She'd vowed not to put herself in that situation again. And until she'd met Sawyer, she'd had no problem keeping that promise. But the constant arc of energy that surrounded Sawyer drew her in. Being in the spotlight of that energy was exhilarating, electrifying, and dangerous. Sawyer could almost make her forget her resolve, and losing Drake's would be even more painful than losing the last job. Jori had to admit, though, if she hadn't already been burned once, she probably wouldn't be trying so hard to avoid her growing feelings for Sawyer.

In addition to their attraction, she was beginning to respect Sawyer's burgeoning work ethic. She was much easier to resist when she was just a slacker. But now Sawyer was spending long hours in the restaurant, often not going upstairs after the morning deliveries. Instead, Jori found her in the office when she arrived every day. Sawyer had made the accounting changes they'd discussed and had also instituted a computerized scheduling system for the employees to replace the handwritten ones Erica used to post.

She wondered why it pleased her so much to see Sawyer investing her time in Drake's, though it certainly didn't take a rocket scientist to figure that one out. She was obviously hoping Sawyer would stick around after Erica returned. As much as Jori wanted to ignore the thought, she couldn't deny its truth. She wanted Sawyer to stay. She enjoyed seeing her every day. And even though she wasn't ready to admit that she wanted more from their relationship, she wanted Sawyer to want more. She'd never met anyone who could excite her with just a wink or a smile.

Sawyer shoved through the swinging door, as if Jori's thoughts had conjured her. When she saw Jori, she smiled widely. "Hello."

"Hey. You look tired." Fatigue smudged Sawyer's eyes, and Jori suppressed the desire to touch her cheek.

"I just took a nap." Sawyer tugged on her earlobe. "I thought I looked better. You should have seen me in the middle of the night."

Jori could imagine how Sawyer would look if awakened in the early morning hours for one more round of lovemaking. Desire would flare behind the sleepiness in her eyes, and Jori's body warmed at the thought of that desire focused on her.

"Did you bring baby pictures?"

"Brady's got them. Erica will be going home tomorrow or the next day. Well, actually, she'll be staying with Brady and Paige for two more weeks. But she expects you to stop by and see the baby."

Jori nodded.

"Okay." Sawyer rubbed a hand over her face. "I guess I better get to work." By the time she'd got back to Drake's she'd managed only a thirty-minute nap. But despite her sluggish mind, her body was still sharp enough to react to Jori, and she didn't rein in the impulse to touch her. She brushed her hand down the outside of Jori's arm and tangled their fingers.

When she didn't pull away, Sawyer was encouraged. Certain she could make Jori forget her reservations, she drew her close and kissed her. Heat flashed through her when Jori allowed her tongue to possess her, then tentatively stroked back. How was it possible that she'd missed the taste of Jori's kiss after only one? She held Jori's face in her hands, then slid them behind her neck. When her fingers encountered the knot of her bandana she worked it loose, balled the fabric in one hand, and buried the other in the back of Jori's hair.

Jori leaned against her, grasping her collar almost desperately, and one of them moaned. While Sawyer was losing her mind, Jori must have been gathering herself, because in the next instant she tried to jerk out of Sawyer's embrace, but Sawyer caught her around the waist.

"I can't do this."

"Sure you can." Expecting no resistance, Sawyer trailed a line of kisses along her neck.

"No," Jori insisted, and this time when she stumbled back, Sawyer let her go. "I thought I was clear. I won't get involved with you."

Sawyer bristled at the accusation in her tone. "I didn't imagine your tongue in my mouth. You're sending some pretty mixed signals. Or are you really just a tease?"

Jori flushed but Sawyer didn't know if she was embarrassed or angry. Her jaw was tight and she avoided Sawyer's eyes.

"I've got baby pictures," Brady called as he strode into the kitchen, followed by Chuck.

Sawyer stepped back, giving Jori room so she and Chuck could ooh and ahh over the photos. Brady handed over the stack, then went to the sink to wash his hands.

The door to the dining room opened and a female voice said, "What does a person have to do to get service in this place?" "I'm sorry, ma'am. We're not open yet." Sawyer turned and grinned at her mother. "That explains why the front door was still locked. Luckily, I have a key."

Tia's hair, the same shade as Erica's, fell in waves to her shoulders, brushing against the flowered dress that flowed around her slight frame. Sawyer's father, Tom, towered behind her. His dark hair was liberally peppered with gray and had begun to recede years ago. His neat mustache and wire-rimmed glasses made him appear academic.

Brady wiped his hands on the towel at his waist and crossed to her. "Hello, Mom. Dad." He kissed Tia's cheek and hugged Tom. "Have you been to the hospital yet?"

"We just came from there. Erica was resting so we decided to stop by here before we check into the hotel. Come give me a hug, Sawyer."

"Hi, Mom." Sawyer accepted Tia's embrace. "You guys can stay upstairs. I'll sleep on the couch."

Tia waved off the suggestion. "No one could sleep on Erica's couch. You wouldn't be able to walk in the morning."

"That's true," Brady said. "But you don't have to stay in a hotel. We've got room at our place."

"Okay, dear."

"It's settled, then. I'll call Paige and let her know to expect you."

"I understand you've been making some changes to my restaurant." Tia looked around the kitchen as if she would be able to see the difference.

Sawyer laughed. "You and Erica should get together and

decide whose restaurant it really is, because I can handle only one possessive woman at a time."

Tia ignored Sawyer's comment. "Show me what you've done."

"Okay. But first"—hesitantly, Sawyer touched Jori's shoulder—"let me introduce you to our pastry chef. Jori Diamantina, Tia Drake and my father, Tom."

Jori smiled. "It's nice to meet you, Mr. and Mrs. Drake."

"Please, call me Tia. My daughters rave about your desserts."

Jori blushed.

"Jori makes an awesome lemon-meringue torte." Sawyer rested her hand at the small of Jori's back, but her posture remained rigid and she didn't meet her eyes.

"A great pastry chef is hard to find." Tom smiled at Jori. "Please, don't let my children run you off."

"Oh, don't worry, Dad. We don't plan to let Jori get away. Do we, Sawyer?" Brady said with a wink.

Tia looped her arm around Sawyer's. "I'd like that tour now, dear, before you get busy with opening."

"Okay, Mom."

Sawyer allowed her mother to lead her away, glancing back at Jori as they headed down the hall to the office. *We don't plan on letting Jori get away.* Brady had purposely been trying to pique Tia's interest with the comment, but their mother had been too distracted to notice. Thank God. Because if Tia caught on to Sawyer's interest in Jori, she wouldn't hear the end of it. Tia had always fancied herself a matchmaker for her children, and Sawyer was no exception.

Every time she split up with someone, Tia told her she was going after the wrong type of woman and that she should just let her find her a suitable mate. And when Sawyer implored Erica to stop telling their mother who she was seeing or not seeing, Erica only argued that it was Sawyer's own fault for going through women as if they were disposable.

Well, it served them both right that Sawyer hadn't dated anyone new in more than three months. Had it really been that long? Yes, she'd been at Drake's for almost two months, and since she'd met Jori, she hadn't looked at another woman.

Chapter Thirteen

Sunday morning, Jori mounted the steps to Brady's house and rang the bell. She was hoping she would run into Sawyer here, but she didn't see her Solara in the driveway. Between Sawyer's responsibilities at Drake's and visiting with her parents, Jori hadn't spent much time with her in the past two days. But the distance didn't have the desired effect. Jori thought about her even more, especially when she glimpsed her throughout her shift.

Now, though she was here to see Erica and the new baby, she was disappointed that she wouldn't see Sawyer. She tried to shove that feeling aside as Paige opened the door.

"Good morning, Jori. Come on in."

She shifted the brightly wrapped present from under her arm into her hands and followed Paige to the living room. Erica sat on the couch and Tia, holding the baby, sat beside her. Tom and Brady occupied the love seat opposite them.

"Hey, Jori. Thanks for coming by," Erica said.

"How are you feeling?" Jori placed her gift on the coffee table in front of Erica and sat in a nearby armchair.

"Good. I'm taking advantage of all this help, because once I go home and Mom and Dad leave, I won't be sleeping much."

"Would you like to hold her?" Tia asked as she rose.

"She's beautiful, Erica," Jori said, carefully accepting the bundle wrapped in a soft pink blanket. "Hello, Taylor," she whispered to the sleeping baby.

Erica wondered if Jori was also thinking of the day she expressed doubts about her plans to keep the baby. Those doubts had dissolved the instant the doctor had placed Taylor on her chest. Distantly, she heard the front door open.

"Erica, are you here?" Sawyer called as she came down the hall.

Erica, Paige, and Jori shushed her in unison.

"Taylor's asleep," Paige said as she stood and offered Sawyer her chair. Sawyer waved her off. Instead, she perched on the arm of Jori's chair.

As she sat, Sawyer glanced at Jori. "Hi."

Erica watched Jori return the greeting with a shy smile. *Oh, no.*

"Hi there, gorgeous niece." Sawyer stroked Taylor's cheek with one finger. Her other hand rested on Jori's shoulder, and Jori didn't seem to mind.

Damn, I was hoping that wouldn't happen. Erica had been expecting the energy that burned between Sawyer and Jori to fizzle out. When Jori had told her she'd rejected Sawyer's advance, she'd expected that would be the end of it.

"Do you want to hold her?" Jori asked.

"You keep her. I don't want to wake her." When Paige asked Tom and Tia about their plans to drive back to Florida, Sawyer leaned closer to Jori and murmured, "I've missed you."

"We've been at work together every day," Jori whispered, and despite having rebuffed Sawyer's last advance, she felt a sizzle of excitement in response to Sawyer's words.

"Sure, but I haven't gotten you alone so I could—"

"Sawyer," Jori hissed, aware that any one of Sawyer's family members could overhear.

"I was just going to say I want to—"

"I mean it." Jori pinched the outside of Sawyer's thigh and

smiled as Sawyer tried to smother her yelp, but the baby in Jori's arms stirred anyway.

When she began to cry, Erica glared at Sawyer. "Nice going. I should make you change her."

"Oh, no. Let Grandpa have her." Tom took Taylor from Jori's arms. "Where are the diapers?"

"They're in the guest bedroom, Dad. But I can take care of it."

"I don't mind. I wasn't around to change your diapers, but I can make up for it with my grandchildren." He headed down the hallway toward the bedroom, murmuring softly to the still-fretting infant.

"I should get going. She really is gorgeous, Erica. And if you need anything, please call me." Jori rose.

"Thanks for stopping by."

Sawyer stood as well. "I'll walk you out." She followed Jori to her car and opened the driver's side door. "I really have missed you," she said when Jori paused beside her. "Maybe we could have lunch one day, or go out for a drink after work."

"Sawyer, I don't know how many ways I can say it. I'm not looking to get involved." She sighed. "And if you can't accept that, then maybe I shouldn't continue to work at Drake's."

"What? You wouldn't leave."

"I don't want to. But I will." Jori's expression was serious. "I can't keep telling you no."

"Why can't you give us a chance?"

"I don't need to. I know how it would end."

Sawyer couldn't argue that point; she had a pretty good idea how it would play out as well. But for the first time in a very long time, she feared she might not be the one to end it. She wanted Jori in ways she'd never wanted anyone, and it had her so conflicted that she didn't know whether to grab Jori and pull her close or run.

"Maybe the journey would be worth it," she said quietly, but Jori had already turned away.

❖

"What the hell was that?" Erica demanded as soon as Sawyer walked back into the living room. She hurried across the room and confronted Sawyer before she could escape.

"What?"

"You and Jori."

Never one to be left out, Brady jumped in. "What about them?"

"Didn't you see the way they looked at each other?"

"Obviously I didn't. So why don't you just tell me what you're talking about."

"Something is going on between them. Has anything happened that you didn't let me know about?"

"No," Sawyer said quickly. But Erica turned her accusing look on Brady.

Brady shrugged. "I guess they seemed pretty friendly the night we all went to the concert. But you know how Sawyer is. She's like that with everyone."

"Not like that," Erica practically snapped. Brady could be so aggravatingly unobservant sometimes. He had apparently missed whatever had transpired between Sawyer and Jori. She turned to Sawyer. "Damn it, I told you to stay away from Jori."

Tia laughed. "You tried to warn Sawyer off Jori?"

"What's so funny?"

"Well, that's like shoving them together." Tia's expression clearly indicated she thought that should have been obvious.

"Mom," Sawyer protested.

"No, it's not," Erica said. "I had a serious talk with her and asked her to leave Jori alone. There are a ton of other women around. Why does she have to go after the best pastry chef we've ever had?"

"You're worried about the restaurant?" Brady asked.

"Yes. And about Jori."

"Maybe Jori will ground her." When Erica gave him an incredulous look, he rushed on. "It could happen. Paige managed to tame me."

"But we're talking about Sawyer."

"Hey, I'm in the room," Sawyer interrupted.

Brady went on as if he hadn't heard her. "Okay, I wasn't as bad as she is. But does that mean there's no hope for her? She's our sister. Aren't we supposed to have any faith in her?"

"Brady, I'm not saying Sawyer is a bad person. Or even that her intentions aren't good. But Jori isn't someone I want her passing time with for a few weeks until she decides to move on."

"How do you know she doesn't really care about her?"

Sawyer sighed loudly.

"That's just it—she always thinks she cares for whoever she's involved with. But eventually she'll find flaws—either they're too tall, too short, too thin, too needy, or not needy enough. The list goes on, Brady, and you know I'm right."

"Hey!" Sawyer threw her hands up between them, and they both stopped and stared at her. "When you two are done listing my shortcomings, can I speak?"

"Unless you're going to tell me nothing's going on between you and Jori, I don't want to hear it."

"Well, we—"

"I don't want to hear it," Erica repeated, folding her arms over her chest.

"Mom, help me out here."

"Ha," Erica exclaimed before Tia could speak. "It'd be easy for her to take your side. She doesn't have to be here to clean up the mess you always make."

"Whoa, hold on. No one has ever asked you to clean up anything." Sawyer knew where Erica's irritation came from. Sawyer had been away at college the last time she'd allowed herself to really love someone, and she'd never shared that part of her life with her sister. Erica had witnessed only Sawyer's more recent quick escapes from relationships, and she still blamed Sawyer for the breakup that had cost her a close friend. Though Sawyer had insisted the relationship was never substantial enough for Erica's friend to sever their so-called friendship, Erica blamed Sawyer when her friend refused to answer her phone calls.

Tia finally interrupted. "Okay, girls. Enough."

"Think hard before you do this. Do you really want to hurt Jori?" Erica didn't wait for a response before she strode toward the kitchen.

When Sawyer turned away as well, Tia stopped her. "What's this all about? Are you dating Erica's pastry chef?"

"Jori, Mom. Her name is Jori. And she's not *Erica's* anything. She happens to work at Drake's, but I don't see what that has to do with—"

"Are you dating her, or not?"

Sawyer sighed and sat on the sofa. "No. We're not dating. But there's something—there's an attraction there. And I know she feels it, too."

"So, what's holding you back?"

"Erica's been on my case since the first day I met Jori. And I *don't* want to hurt her." Sawyer hesitated, not comfortable discussing Jori's background. "She had a tough life, and she deserves to be happy."

"And you're not the person to make her happy?"

"I don't know. No one else seems to think so."

When Tia silently studied her, Sawyer braced for the expected criticism. Tia, like Erica, always thought she knew what was best for her. But somehow Sawyer knew this time was different, Jori was different. And while she wasn't ready to admit she wanted anything more than to explore the sexual attraction between them, inside she knew she felt something she hadn't felt in years, maybe ever.

"Honey, what do you and Jori think? That's all that matters."

"I thought you'd tell me what I should do." Sawyer didn't try to hide her surprise at her mother's response.

"Would it do any good?"

"That never stopped you before."

Tia shrugged. "I just want you to be happy, Sawyer. That's all I've ever wanted. And if you've felt I went about it the wrong way sometimes, you need to understand that my intentions were good. But it seems like Jori has gotten under your skin. I could try to tell you what to do, but I think maybe this time you need to figure it out for yourself."

❖

Sawyer hurried across the apartment, grabbing her keys from the sofa table. Brady and the others were probably already downstairs waiting. She'd scheduled a meeting with the kitchen staff and servers to review the new menu, and she was already twenty minutes late. Knowing Erica would have been ready for the meeting early, she cringed.

So when, minutes later, she walked into a nearly empty dining room, she stopped short. Chuck and Jori sat at one of the tables and Brady leaned against the bar, ankles crossed.

"Where the hell is everyone? I posted a notice about this meeting next to the time clock, a week ago." Now Sawyer was irritated. She'd been stressed about being late, and most of her employees hadn't even been responsible enough to show.

"I let them leave," Brady said, not moving from his indolent pose.

"You—let them leave?"

Pushing away from the bar he strolled over to an open box on the table in front of Chuck, pulled out a folded menu, and handed it to her. "Yeah, since we obviously can't use these."

Sawyer snatched the menu out of his hand and opened it. Erica had briefed her on the specifics of the order. The weight of the paper felt right, the color scheme looked correct. "What am I looking for?"

"Well, my blue-cheese-crusted filet is stellar. But I don't know if it's good enough to charge three hundred and thirty-three dollars."

Chuck started to laugh, then covered it with a cough when Sawyer glared at him.

She scanned down and found the error. "Damn," she grumbled as she saw two more typos in the same column. "Well, I'll just call the printer and tell them they screwed it up. They're going to fix it before—"

"I checked the proof. It's exactly as you sent it in."

"And they didn't think to question a three-hundred-dollar steak?"

"They're printers, Sawyer. They don't proof the copy. They just make it up as it's sent in."

"Okay. I'll make the corrections and put in a new order. Thanks for handling that and I'm sorry I was late."

Sawyer glanced at Jori and found unwelcome sympathy in her expression. Without another word she headed for her office to call the printer. She had to straighten out the menu, and then she would have to call Erica and inform her of the mistake. She really didn't want to, but if Erica discovered she'd been left out of the loop, she'd be doubly mad.

Ten minutes later, Sawyer dropped the phone back in its cradle, struggling not to slam it down. The printer needed two more weeks to redo the order, and they weren't going to give her a break on the second batch of menus. Sawyer's insistence that the first set was unusable hadn't swayed the manager there. He maintained that the menu was printed exactly as ordered, and Sawyer couldn't argue.

It was her next conversation Sawyer dreaded, and even as she dialed the number she floundered for an excuse not to call Erica.

❖

"I know proofing menus isn't very exciting, but it's not that hard to get it right." Erica's response to hearing about the mix-up was as expected.

"Okay. I made it mistake. I'll get it fixed."

"Mistakes cost money, Sawyer. Or didn't they teach you that in business school?"

"God, Erica, can you get off my back for one damn second." Sawyer fought the urge to fling the phone across the room. Imagining it flying into pieces as it hit the wall gave her a moment's satisfaction, but that would just be another expense for Erica to bitch about.

"Well, you would think I could take a few weeks to have a baby without worrying about my sister running my restaurant into the ground."

"Yeah, you would think so, wouldn't you?" Sawyer agreed sarcastically. "Listen, I'll pay for the damn menus. I shouldn't have even told you about them."

"Don't you dare keep things from me. I want to know everything that's going on down there."

"Erica, you're going to have to learn to trust me. I know I'm not getting everything right, but I'm trying." Sawyer leaned forward, rested one elbow on the desk, and rubbed the back of her neck with her other hand.

"How am I supposed to trust you? As far as I can see, you only agreed to work at Drake's so you could get in Jori's pants, so—"

"That's not fair."

"Tell me it's not true." Erica raised her voice.

"It's not."

"Sawyer, I'm tired. Just deal with the menus, please."

Sawyer hung up, then circled the desk, needing to get out of the office. In fact, she was fighting the urge to leave the restaurant altogether. As she entered the kitchen she looked longingly at the back door and thought about how good it would feel to just walk out and get in her car.

"Sawyer, where are my apples? They should have been with this morning's produce, but I can't find them," Jori called, interrupting her escape plot.

Sawyer groaned, remembering how she'd dragged herself out of bed that morning when she heard the bell from the loading dock. She'd been asleep for barely four hours, and the last thing she wanted to do was go down and count food. She'd waited just long enough for the deliveryman to unload the truck, then quickly signed the receipt. She'd been meticulously checking the orders every day and hadn't found an error yet. But that morning, she had been upstairs crawling back into bed before the rumble of the delivery truck had faded.

"Sawyer?"

"Did you look in the pantry?" She crossed to Jori's counter.

"Twice."

"Well, I'm sure they're around here somewhere." So a bunch of apples were missing. Sawyer really didn't understand what the big deal was.

"I can't make my apple crisp without apples."

"Can't you just make something else?" Sawyer didn't even try to keep the irritation out of her voice. She was tired. She'd just had her fill of attitude from Erica, and she wasn't about to take more from Jori.

"I ordered them with this menu in mind. Now I'll have to scrape something together."

"Jori, if the apples aren't here, there's really nothing I can do about it, is there? You're the head pastry chef. Can't you just figure it out instead of needing me to hold your fucking hand?"

Jori didn't respond.

"Ladies, is there something I can help with?" Brady interjected from behind Sawyer. His tone held a warning that she was certain was directed at her, and it irritated her.

"Just make something else, please," Sawyer said, then turned away. She headed for the same office she'd fled earlier, now wondering if she could manage to hide in there for the rest of the day.

❖

"I don't need her to hold my hand," Jori muttered as she mashed bananas in a small bowl. She'd decided to make the bananas Foster upside-down cake she'd planned for tomorrow night. She would go to the farmers' market in the morning and get the apples for the crisp. "I don't need anyone."

She'd been proving she could handle things on her own since she was eight years old. It hadn't even taken a year in foster care for her to realize she would never have the loving, supporting parents that many of her peers took for granted. But these days she told herself she didn't care. She took a certain amount of pride in saying she'd provided for herself.

As she spread a mixture of melted butter, brown sugar, and cinnamon in a baking pan, she remembered the first and only time she'd returned to her childhood home, shortly after she began working at Drake's. She'd taken a taxi there and had asked the driver to turn around twice as she struggled to recall the directions to the house. The neighborhood had looked different than she remembered; most of the dilapidated homes were abandoned now. Two blocks over, a crop of government housing had been hailed as progress a decade ago. Jori recalled seeing the mayor conduct a ribbon-cutting ceremony on television and noticed it hadn't taken long before the residents here began to clear out.

She'd directed the driver to stop in front of a duplex that the owners had clearly given up on some time ago. Patches of weathered gray wood showed through chipped white paint, and jagged glass clung to the frames of several broken windows. She got out of the cab and paused on the sidewalk, weak with remembered fear even though over twenty years had passed since she'd last been in this yard. The grass and weeds were up to her knees, and she could barely see the paved walk as she approached the house.

The porch sagged dramatically at the far end, and the steps creaked as she climbed them. The door wasn't locked, and when she stepped inside, the sting of vivid memories assaulted her.

The house was empty, but as Jori wandered through it she saw it as it had been. She'd often come down to breakfast in the morning to find her mother where she'd passed out the night before, slumped over the yellowed and chipped Formica tabletop. And in the living room, her father had pushed the sofa against the wall so he could watch the fights on television without a glare from the nearby window. Jori had often crawled into the space between the sofa and the wall and pretended it was a portal where she could escape to a magical world free of the darkness and pain of this one. But when she opened her eyes she was still there and, looking back, that was when she'd learned that no one would rescue her and she'd have to rely on herself.

When her mind wandered too close to her past physical abuse, she instinctively jerked it away and forced her attention to the batter she poured over the cinnamon mixture and a layer of sliced bananas. She avoided those memories whenever possible, and she certainly wouldn't revisit them while standing in the kitchen at Drake's.

She retreated from those old monsters in much the same way she still backed away from situations that made her uncomfortable. She'd spent most of her life cloaked in self-imposed isolation, cultivating avoidance instead of relationships. But recently, the Drake family had become an exception to this practice.

Everyone, herself included, accused Sawyer of running away from intimacy, but Jori did practically the same thing. Sawyer was confident in a crowd with superficial social interaction but ran from a real, personal connection, whereas Jori was the complete opposite. When she thought about it that way, it seemed they might be the perfect complement for each other.

Sawyer seemed determined to ignore Jori's insistence that they not get involved. She could be short-tempered when she was tired or when she was pushed. And if they were in a relationship, she would probably try more than once to run away. But she was also open and friendly, and she made Jori laugh. She understood Jori's shyness and tried to ease it when she could. Jori recalled the night of the concert and the way Sawyer had tucked her against her side as if she'd wanted to shield her from the crowd pressing in around them.

While Jori was afraid of the outcome of pursuing anything more than a professional relationship with Sawyer, she couldn't deny the physical pull between them. She enjoyed their flirtatious banter, and just thinking about kissing Sawyer was enough to make her heart race and her body respond in amazing ways, if she gave her imagination free rein.

She glanced toward the hallway leading to the office and wondered if it was crazy to think a relationship with Sawyer could be worth risking her job. More than just her job, she'd be risking her comfortable emotional cushion. She hadn't truly let anyone close since she was eight years old. But no matter how much she tried to deny it, Sawyer was already too close. She could restore the distance between them quickly enough. A few weeks of acting cool and professional and Sawyer would probably lose interest.

But what if she didn't? What if she forgot about the fear and certainty that it wouldn't last and for once in her life simply let things happen? Worst case, she got her heart broken. Oddly enough, the thing she'd spent years trying to avoid didn't seem so bad anymore, because even heartache meant she felt something. And she hadn't realized how much she needed that. Isolation protected her from hurt, but it also kept her from the elation she'd felt in Sawyer's arms.

When she'd asked about the apples, Sawyer had snapped at her. But Sawyer hadn't directed her anger solely at her. She'd seen her frustration begin during the exchange with Brady over the menus. Again, she looked down the hall, wanting her, whatever her mood. By the time she put the cake in the oven, she had decided to reverse her usual instinct to withdraw from conflict.

She found Sawyer behind her desk, her glasses lying on its surface and her hands covering her face. At her determined knock, Sawyer glanced up.

"Come on in. I won't bite."

"Is something wrong?" Jori doubted that Sawyer *wouldn't* bite if provoked.

"That's a nice way of asking why I was being a bitch."

"Well?"

Sawyer rubbed her hand over the back of her neck. After the way she'd acted, she'd expected Jori to put an icy distance between them. "I need to get away from this place."

"Then let's go." Jori walked around the desk and laid her hands on Sawyer's shoulders.

"Where?"

"I'm not working Monday. Can you take the day off?"

Sawyer thought for a moment, then nodded. "Sure, I can leave Wendy in charge. What did you have in mind?"

"You decide. You're the one who needs some R and R. I'm all yours until Tuesday afternoon."

"All mine, huh?" Sawyer immediately pictured the two of them in bed for twenty-four hours. This sudden shift in the direction of their relationship confused her. She knew she'd been pushing the boundary Jori insisted on keeping between them, and maybe that was unfair. But was Jori changing the rules now? The hands kneading the muscles of her shoulders sure hinted that she was.

"Just remember, the point is for you to blow off some steam and relax."

"Oh, I can definitely see us blowing off steam." Spinning around, Sawyer grabbed Jori's waist and pulled her between her spread knees.

Jori had a pretty good idea what was going through Sawyer's mind, and though Sawyer sounded like she was teasing, Jori knew she was testing her willingness. They had been flirting from virtually the moment they met, and suddenly it felt as if they'd been leading each other to this moment and Sawyer was leaving the next step up to her.

She bent and kissed Sawyer, her decision sealed in the soft caress of lips, the thrill of arousal along her spine. Sawyer touched her cheek, and Jori wrapped her fingers around Sawyer's wrist, encircling it, feeling Sawyer's sprinting pulse.

She pulled back when Sawyer tried to deepen the kiss, conscious that they could be interrupted at any moment. "Monday. Let me know when and where."

Sawyer's face lit up, as if an idea had suddenly occurred to her. "Have you ever been whitewater rafting?"

"Are you serious?"

"Is that a no?"

"Well, I don't have a strong desire to be dumped in a river anytime soon."

Sawyer shook her head slowly. "No sense of adventure. I thought you said you were all mine."

"I did." Jori struggled not to stutter. Sawyer's eyes darkened as she drawled the words, *all mine.* Never before had Jori wanted so much to belong to someone, but she knew that wasn't what Sawyer had meant.

"So what's it going to be?" When Jori didn't argue, Sawyer said, "I'll pick you up at nine Monday morning."

"Okay." Jori covered Sawyer's hands, which still bracketed her hips, and pulled them away. "But right now, I need to get to back to work."

She turned toward the door and when Sawyer quietly said her name, she paused and looked back.

"Pack an overnight bag," Sawyer said, and Jori flushed with anticipation.

Chapter Fourteen

N ervous?"

"A little." Jori hefted the five-foot paddle in her hands as if testing its balance.

"It'll be fun," Sawyer assured her.

After their trip leader called them together, Sawyer grabbed two helmets from the nearby bin and led Jori closer to the assembly point. She'd been rafting before, but never with this company.

As the leader, a wiry man with thick gray hair and a deeply lined face, explained the basics of rafting safety, Sawyer studied the other three guides, two college-aged men and one woman, who would pilot boats filled with a share of the twenty people gathered around. The two men wore brightly colored swim trunks and were bare-chested and tanned golden. They leaned comfortably against the porch railing and watched as the crowd was divided into four groups, assigned to a guide, and instructed to board the old school bus parked nearby. The dark-haired woman, introduced as Lacey, would guide Sawyer and Jori, as well as four teenage boys.

The ride to the launch site took only a few minutes. They all disembarked and waited while the guides unloaded the inflatable rafts from the makeshift platform atop the bus.

"You're going to love this." Sawyer donned a yellow life vest.

Jori set the plastic helmet on top of her usual navy bandana and fastened the chin strap. "If I fall out, I expect you to pull me back in," she said as she shrugged on her vest.

Sawyer pulled Jori's vest closed and tightened the straps. "Too tight?"

"No. It's fine."

"Okay, my crew over here," Lacey called from near one of the blue rafts with Ocoee Whitewaters emblazoned on the side. She pulled her dark hair back and secured it with an elastic band from around her wrist before she put on her own vest and helmet. "Are y'all ready to have some fun?" As she looked at each of them in turn, she smiled and lines crinkled at the edge of her bright blue eyes.

When they'd all introduced themselves and staked out their spots in the raft, she issued instructions. "I'm going to steer from the back of the raft. You two guys in the front will set the pace. Everyone else, when you paddle, follow the person in front of you. There are a few basic commands. Obviously, when I say 'forward' you paddle front to back." She demonstrated with the paddle in her hand. "When I say 'back,' you go back to front. When I say 'drift,' don't paddle at all. We're also going to do some spins, and I'll call out 'right, forward, left, back.' I'll go over that again when we get ready to do it. Now, let's get this boat down there."

They all grabbed the strap strung through the rings in the side of the raft and carried it down the concrete ramp to the shore. The boys had clamored for the seats closest to the front, so Jori and Sawyer sat in the back, directly in front of Lacey.

Within minutes they were in the boat and drifting toward the first set of rapids. They plunged through the whitewater, clumsily trying to follow the paddling instructions Lacey called out. When their boat crested a large rock just visible beneath the water and dropped into the swirling wash, Sawyer blinked against the cool spray misting her face.

The water calmed for a stretch, and Lacey continued to shout commands interspersed with information about the river and type of rapids they could expect to encounter. The churning water was broken up with more even stretches, and at one spot they could get out of the boat and swim downriver before they reached the next bit of rough water.

She explained that the Tennessee Valley Authority controlled the dams on the river so even in the height of summer the water level stayed fairly consistent. A large wooden chute on one steep bank closely paralleled the twists and turns of the river, and during scheduled times the river nearly dried up while the water was diverted through the chute in order to generate power.

The boys were far too interested in teasing each other to pay much attention to the women. Sawyer and Lacey carried on an easy conversation, Sawyer questioning Lacey about her history as a guide and the changes in the river over the years. Feeling a bit left out, Jori sat silently and studied the treed slopes of the gorge on either side of them. The sky was azure and cloudless; nothing impeded the brilliant sun. Despite the recent run of temperatures over one hundred degrees, the breeze along the river was enough to make the heat bearable.

By the third set of rapids, they found their rhythm and were beginning to paddle in unison, each timing their stroke with the person in front of them. As they entered calmer water, Lacey told them they could get out and swim if they wanted to. One by one they slipped over the edge of the raft.

Jori slid into the cool water, then lay back and let her life vest keep her afloat. Though there were no rapids here, the current was still strong enough to carry them downstream. She closed her eyes.

A few feet away, Sawyer watched Jori. The rafting had been a great idea, but, more than that, being with Jori, away from Nashville, had recharged something in her that she hadn't even realized was drained. Their time together had both relaxed and aroused her. The pleasant three-hour drive down had been filled with music and casual conversation. When they reached the rafting outpost, Jori had stripped off her T-shirt to reveal a white bikini top that contrasted beautifully with her olive skin, and Sawyer had struggled to keep from leering. As Jori had boarded the bus in front of her, Sawyer's eyes had slipped down, of their own accord, to trace the waistband of her navy board shorts where they rode low on her hips.

Now she watched Jori floating a few feet away. Drawn to her but not wanting to disturb her repose, Sawyer swam slowly closer. But as she got within touching distance, Jori opened one eye and peeked at her. She reached out and captured Sawyer's hand, then drew her near.

"Are you enjoying yourself?" Jori asked.

Sawyer rolled onto her back and smiled. She glanced over to find Jori's eyes once again closed. "I am. Very much."

"Thinking about Drake's?" Jori's fingers curled around Sawyer's, the warmth of her skin penetrating the cool water gloving their joined hands. They floated side by side, their sandal-clad feet lined up in front of them.

"No." Sawyer smiled. Jori looked so cute with wet curls clinging to the edge of her helmet, and Sawyer was anticipating a relaxing dinner with her when they finished rafting. But when she thought about where the rest of the evening might lead, her stomach tightened like her skin beneath the hot summer sun.

"Good. I'd like to do this again."

"Me, too. In fact, I'm already planning the next trip. We could invite Matt and Davis."

"If we got a group together we could fill a boat by ourselves," Jori suggested.

"That would be fun."

Jori smiled, thinking it would be fun but it probably wouldn't top this day. She'd wanted Sawyer to have this time of relaxation but, she now realized, she'd needed this frivolous afternoon nearly as much. The time she spent away from work was often solitary, and even in her glass-blowing classes she usually kept to herself. But today, Sawyer's enjoyment of their outing enhanced Jori's. They drifted for several more minutes before Lacey called them all to the nearest bank. After they were settled back in the raft, she directed them to the center of the river.

"All right, folks. Are we chickens or heroes?" Lacey yelled.

"Heroes!" a couple of the boys called out, needing no further explanation.

Lacey laughed. "When we go through this next section, we can take the chicken route. Or," she paused, her blue eyes sparkling with mischief, "we can go the hero route and it's likely most of us will end up in the water. But everyone has to agree."

"Heroes," came the cry again from the front of the boat.

"Ladies?"

Sawyer glanced at Jori, clearly leaving it up to her. And Jori felt as if her answer was about more than just the raft route.

"I'm game." She knew if she'd said she wanted the tamer route, Sawyer would have backed her up. But when she looked at Sawyer, everything in her screamed to take a chance.

❖

Sawyer nudged the door open and led Jori inside. The small cabin was surprisingly spacious, especially the great room with its high ceilings and honey-colored exposed logs. Flat river stones had been sculpted into an impressive fireplace in one corner, and Jori could imagine how cozy the room would feel with a fire burning there.

Sawyer nodded toward a door to the right. "You can take that bedroom. I'll take the loft."

Jori stopped, not understanding what she'd heard. She'd assumed Sawyer would expect to share her bed. Apparently she hadn't needed to be so nervous and anticipatory all day.

Sawyer paused halfway across the room as Jori still stood by the entrance. "Is something wrong?"

She looked at the bedroom Sawyer had indicated and then at the loft. "Um, no. I thought—" She felt ridiculous.

"Jori, I'm not a dog." Sawyer slipped the strap of her bag from her shoulder and dropped it near the stairs. Skirting the rustic leather sofa in the middle of the room, she crossed to her, took her hands, and held them loosely. "You agreed to this trip so I could relax. Given that generosity, do you really think I planned it just to get in your pants?"

"I guess not." Jori was surprised by a surge of disappointment.

Sawyer grinned. "Of course not. That would be an added bonus." Jori flushed and Sawyer continued, "I didn't want you to worry about my expectations. You need a break as much as I do. Let's just have a good time."

Jori had never been the type to "just have a good time" without worrying about the implications. But she forced a smile. "Sure."

"Good. Now, let's clean up and find someplace to have dinner."

When Sawyer retrieved her bag and climbed toward the loft, Jori watched through the slatted railing, and Sawyer turned and deliberately grasped the bottom of her T-shirt.

"Jori, I'm starving and was looking forward to dinner. But if you're going to watch me undress, we may not make it out of this cabin." She pulled the shirt up, revealing a swath of skin.

"Oh, sorry." Startled, Jori rushed into her bedroom and closed the door.

She dropped her overnight bag on the bed and paced, distracting herself with the details of the room. The bed looked far too large for one person, with its handmade quilt that complemented the frame fashioned from natural pine boughs. She jerked her mind away from the image of herself and Sawyer crawling across that quilt. Sawyer had put the ball firmly in her court, and now she needed to decide what her next move would be.

In the attached bathroom, she discovered a whirlpool tub and glassed-in shower stall. Her mind overlaid a picture of Sawyer reclining in the gently churning water with one of Sawyer taking her, fast and hard, against the transparent wall. She pressed her thighs together to still the ache between them. At this rate she'd never make it through dinner.

She quickly showered and dressed in a pair of khakis and a dark green blouse. Exhausted from their day of activity in the sun, she suddenly found she was starving as well and hurriedly rubbed a dollop of gel into her wet hair, finger-combed it, and left it to air-dry.

When she entered the living room ten minutes later, Sawyer waited for her, wearing a white button-down tucked into dark jeans. She sat at one end of the deeply cushioned sofa, an arm stretched along the back of it and her legs crossed so a brown leather boot rested on her other knee. Sawyer's eyes roamed over her, drinking her in. When their gazes clashed, she thought Sawyer's relaxed posture was at odds with the intensity of that look.

Sawyer's casualness was possibly a ploy to draw her in and, she admitted, if that was case, it was working. Sawyer's apparent comfort with letting things progress or not intrigued her, made her uncharacteristically want to push the intimacy between them simply to see where it would lead. Jori allowed her smile to reflect her anticipation when she thought about what the evening might hold.

❖

"How's your pasta?" Sawyer asked before she took another bite of stuffed eggplant.

"It's good." Jori smiled over the rim of a glass of house burgundy.

They'd been surprised to find an authentic Italian restaurant tucked against the mountainside. Even after Lacey had given it her endorsement as the place to get a good meal, Sawyer had been skeptical when they'd pulled into the parking lot of the tiny building with wood-shingle siding. The red, white, and green awning over the entrance was the only hint they were in the right place.

But the restaurant had been packed when they walked in, wall-to-wall booths and tables crowded with a mix of locals and tourists. The hostess had seated them on the back patio, where the glow from strings of bare bulbs overhead lit a dining area that was otherwise intimately shaded by a canopy of trees.

"Did you enjoy rafting?"

"Yes. It was great. I never would have tried that on my own."

"And you only got dumped in the river once," Sawyer said seriously. She'd been apprehensive as she'd watched Jori disappear in the swirling water. But when she had surfaced and one of the boys had grabbed her life vest and hauled her into the boat, Sawyer had felt her galloping heart slow.

Jori laughed. "Yeah, no thanks to Lacey. I think she was showing off for you."

"She was not."

"She purposely steered us toward the roughest part of every set of rapids."

Sawyer dismissed the notion with a wave. "She probably knew those boys wanted an exciting ride."

"I don't think she even realized anyone else was in the boat."

Sawyer studied Jori. At first she thought Jori had been joking, but now there seemed to be a bit of seriousness behind her teasing. Her hint of jealousy, however misguided, thrilled Sawyer in a way no set of rapids could.

"Well, *I* noticed there was someone else in the boat," Sawyer said as she remembered how Jori had looked with her wet hair falling across her forehead and a broad smile on her face.

Jori caught her breath at the intimacy in Sawyer's tone. The candle flickering in the red glass votive jar on the table between them cast a dancing shadow over the planes of Sawyer's face, alternately hiding, then revealing the open appraisal in Sawyer's eyes.

"Sawyer, I—"

"Would you like dessert? Tiramisu?"

"No, thank you. I've eaten too much already." She pushed her empty plate away and accepted Sawyer's rapid subject change because she hadn't been certain what she was going to say anyway. But once again Sawyer had drawn her in, only to back off when the moment got heavy. "But please don't let that stop you from indulging."

"No, I'm sure it doesn't compare with your creations." Decisively, Sawyer swept her napkin from her lap and deposited it on the table in front of her.

"Flattery, huh? That will probably work."

"It's true. I still remember the chocolate cake you were making the first day we met."

"Princess cake," Jori supplied.

"You garnished it with strawberries and melted chocolate."

Jori laughed at the look of longing on her face. "Brady wasn't exaggerating about you and sweets."

"Not a bit."

When the waitress brought the check, Sawyer handed over her debit card, waving off Jori's offer to pay.

"At least let me leave the tip." While Sawyer signed the receipt, Jori laid several folded bills on the table.

They made the short drive back to their cabin in companionable silence. Jori was pleasantly tired and expected to be sore tomorrow, if she could even sleep. It was a good thing the loft was on the opposite side of the cabin, because

Sawyer's proximity inside the car had her body humming. She would definitely need some distance and perhaps a self-induced release. She didn't have that particular need often and had never considered herself an overly sexual person. But with Sawyer's tangy citrus scent teasing her and Sawyer's arm resting alongside hers on the center console, she couldn't think clearly.

Caught up in her thoughts, she didn't notice they'd stopped in front of the cabin until Sawyer lightly touched her arm.

"You okay?" Jori's distant expression concerned Sawyer. She'd been quiet during the ride back.

"Fine. I guess the day is just catching up with me."

Jori got out of the car and Sawyer sighed in relief. Once during dinner she hadn't been able to help herself and her composure had slipped. For a second she had felt as if Jori could sense the desire that stirred inside her. She wondered if Jori had been contemplating that moment as well, if she also felt like they were moving toward an inevitable encounter. *Or maybe I'm the only one who feels like I'll combust if I don't touch her.*

"Sawyer?"

Sawyer started and looked at her.

"You have the key."

She realized she'd been standing on the cabin porch lost in thought while Jori waited for her to unlock the door.

"Sorry," she mumbled as she opened the door.

Once they'd stepped inside, Sawyer reached around Jori to secure the deadbolt.

"Thank you for a wonderful day. I really needed this," Sawyer said.

She closed her fingers around the lock and stared at Jori's mouth. Jori moistened her lower lip and Sawyer realized she was only seconds from kissing her. She ached with the desire to close the space between them and could already taste her, need nearly overcoming logic. *Pull it back, Sawyer. Don't lose it now.* Only the voice in her head kept her from taking Jori right there, against the front door of the cabin. She would stick by her decision to let her make the move.

"I'm glad you enjoyed yourself. I did, too." Jori's voice held a slight rasp, as if she could see the battle raging within Sawyer.

"Good night." Sawyer kissed her cheek, carefully keeping the gesture light.

Hoping Jori didn't hear the tremor in her voice, she forced numb fingers to flip the lock into place. Then she backed away, though her body fought her at every inch. She fled before she could change her mind, seeking the safety of the loft.

Chapter Fifteen

Jori lay awake listening to the silence in the cabin. She missed the noise of the city, things she hadn't noticed until they were absent, like the sound of distant sirens. Instead crickets chirped and leaves rustled outside the window. Then an indistinct creak came from inside. A moment later the wooden stairs popped. Sawyer was coming down from the loft. Jori's heart fluttered in anticipation until she realized Sawyer wasn't headed toward her room. A glass clinked, then the faucet ran. She pictured Sawyer standing at the sink.

Just once Jori wanted to act without knowing where she was headed, to ignore the curl of anxiety in her stomach. She didn't want to think about Sawyer's apparent inability to do long-term, and in the time it took her to ease from bed and creep to the open door, she managed to convince herself that for tonight, it didn't matter.

Sawyer had left the lights off, and Jori could just make out her silhouette in the moonlight pouring through the window over the sink. A white T-shirt hugged her broad shoulders, and her dark shorts just covered the tops of her thighs. The shadows and silver moonlight created the impression of a black-and-white photograph, and Jori didn't need to see Sawyer's face to know that the androgynous lines would be striking in such a medium.

As she stepped into the room, the hardwood creaked beneath her feet and she stopped.

"I'm sorry if I woke you." Sawyer set the glass in the sink but didn't turn around.

Jori shook her head, then realized Sawyer couldn't see her. "I was awake."

"Can't sleep?"

Smothering a burst of doubt, she moved closer and slipped her arms around Sawyer's waist. "It's very quiet here."

Sawyer laughed softly. She covered Jori's hands and pulled them more tightly around her, bringing Jori flush against her back. "That's supposed to be a good thing."

"I know." She rested her cheek against Sawyer's nape. "And I thought after all that exercise today, I would sleep deeply."

"So..." Sawyer hesitated. "What's keeping you up?"

Jori considered her next words carefully. Despite the intimacy of their time on the river and at dinner, Sawyer seemed content to keep things platonic. But though she knew it could be a mistake, at that moment, with Sawyer's body against hers, *platonic* was the last thing Jori wanted. Her breasts against Sawyer's back and Sawyer's backside nestled against her crotch made her want to press even closer. "I've been lying awake wondering why you were sleeping so far away."

"Jori, I told you—"

"I know what you said." She slipped her hands beneath Sawyer's T-shirt and stroked her stomach, feeling muscles jump in response. "But are you really this chivalrous? Or are you purposely trying to make me crazy?"

She found her answer in Sawyer's sharply indrawn breath and quickly squared shoulders.

"I'm not." Sawyer turned and retreated until her lower back hit the edge of the sink.

It wasn't clear which question Sawyer was responding to, but from the hazy look in her eyes when Jori moved close and traced inside the neck of her T-shirt, she could guess.

"You know…" Jori was enjoying Sawyer's reaction to her touch. "You accused me of being a tease. But you've been teasing me all day."

"No. I just didn't want to pressure you." Sawyer stuttered slightly. Jori had come on this trip half expecting smooth seduction. *That* she had been prepared to fend off, but this genuine, maybe a little nervous Sawyer was endearing and oddly empowering.

"Yes, you said you just wanted us to have a good time." Jori deliberately trailed her fingers along the edge of Sawyer's jaw. When Sawyer's hands tightened at her waist, she smiled amid a surge of bravery. "I'm having a very good time. How about you?"

She wanted to blame the three glasses of wine at dinner, which still had her head buzzing. But in truth, Sawyer's nearness was the natural high that gave her the nerve to push her hands into Sawyer's hair, pull her head down, and kiss her.

Sawyer responded immediately as if she'd been waiting. When Sawyer opened to her, Jori let go of any hint of caution and poured herself into Sawyer's mouth, stroking her tongue inside.

Sawyer's head rushed with the feel of Jori against her, of Jori beneath her hands—the curve of her waist and the flare of her hips as Sawyer pulled them snug against her. Oh, God, she'd been fantasizing about this closeness for the entire day, for weeks even, and now that it seemed Jori wanted it as much as she did, she craved nothing more than to embrace it.

Backing through the living room, Jori nearly fell over an end table, but Sawyer held her up as they scrambled into the bedroom. Sawyer tugged at the hem of Jori's T-shirt and, when she raised her arms, pulled it over her head and dropped it on the floor. Her own shirt followed.

"God, you feel good," she moaned, smoothing her hands up Jori's sides to cup her breasts.

When she rubbed her thumbs over Jori's tightening nipples, Jori groaned and pushed her against the edge of the bed. Taken off guard, Sawyer fell back and Jori moved over her, straddling her hips. Sawyer reached for her breasts again, but Jori caught her hands and pressed them to the mattress above her head.

"Let me touch you," Jori whispered against her ear and Sawyer shivered, then met eyes dark and filled with exhilarating arousal. "Will you?"

"Yes." She would have given anything to feel Jori's hands on her.

Jori did touch her—urgently, as if she couldn't help herself—firmly squeezing a tight nipple and bringing Sawyer to the sharp edge of pain and pleasure. She slid down and sucked one into her mouth.

"Harder," Sawyer ground out as she buried her hands in Jori's hair. "Ah, God. Yes." She thrust against Jori's belly, seeking friction against her throbbing sex.

Jori reached between them and shoved a hand inside Sawyer's shorts. "I've been thinking about this all day. And you're so wet," Jori moaned as her fingers slid inside.

"For you." Sawyer's neck arched and she closed her eyes with the effort of holding off her orgasm as Jori's thumb circled her clitoris. *Too soon. Just a little longer.*

"For me," Jori whispered as she pulled away long enough to remove Sawyer's shorts.

She spread Sawyer's thighs and without hesitation pressed her mouth to Sawyer's flesh. The sweet feel of Jori's tongue circling her brought Sawyer close to the edge, too close. "Jori, wait, please. Slow down."

"Next time," Jori said and sucked her.

"Jori. Yes, oh, God." Sawyer's hips jerked. "Baby, please. There. Almost there," she managed seconds before she surrendered to the pleasure that thrashed beneath her skin, burned in her muscles, and coursed through her as if the silky strands of Jori's hair that wound around her fingers were live wires.

When finally Sawyer lay, spent, her body still vibrating, Jori trailed kisses up her hip and over her abdomen and chest until she reached her neck. Sawyer shivered and wrapped her arms around

Jori. She ran her fingers over Jori's back, tracing the angles of her shoulder blades and down her spine. She felt Jori smile against her skin and slowly roll her hips against her thigh.

Sawyer smoothed her hands over Jori's ass and pulled her even nearer, thrusting her leg higher.

"I need you," Jori said on a ragged breath. She grabbed Sawyer's wrist and guided Sawyer's hand between her thighs.

"Slow now?" Sawyer asked with a grin as she stroked inside. Her own body protested the statement with a renewed throb, but she ignored it in favor of the feel of Jori surrounding her fingers, of the back of her own hand grinding into her thigh.

"Not yet." Jori closed her teeth lightly on Sawyer's lower lip. "Too late for slow. I was more than halfway there from touching you."

"Okay," Sawyer whispered, curling her fingertips and thrusting deeper. "You can have your way this time, but later— I'm going to taste you."

"Oh, God."

Jori pumped her hips faster, her rhythm becoming erratic. Sawyer wrapped her other hand around Jori's neck and pulled her down to kiss her—hard, until with one final thrust, Jori collapsed against her shoulder.

Sawyer kissed her again, this time softly caressing her bruised lips. When she drew away she studied Jori's heavily lidded eyes.

"You—I—you caught me off guard. I mean, you're usually so shy."

"Not with you." She tucked her head against Sawyer's breast and closed her eyes.

❖

The warm sun slashing across the bed slowly coaxed Sawyer from sleep. She stretched, her muscles pulling pleasantly, and her head began to clear. The other side of the bed was empty, and she wondered how long she could avoid confronting what she and Jori had done the night before. She didn't want to risk disturbing the layer of satisfaction that lingered still.

"Oh, you're awake." Jori came in carrying a ceramic mug. "I would have brought you some coffee if I'd known you were up."

"I'll get some in a bit."

"I was going to jump in the shower." Jori sat on the bed and the edges of her terry-cloth robe fell to either side of her knees.

Sawyer squinted at the alarm clock. "I guess I'll go up to the loft and get ready. We should leave in a couple of hours if we're going to be back in time for work." She wanted to pull Jori back into bed and avoid the real world a bit longer.

Stalling, she angled her upper body enough to slide her hand under the hem of Jori's robe.

"Erica is going to be so mad," Jori said.

Sawyer froze, her fingers barely touching the top of a smooth thigh. She rose on one elbow and gazed at Jori for a moment before lowering her head to kiss Jori's knee.

"That's what you're thinking about right now? My sister?" Sawyer hooked one arm around Jori's leg and tugged her into bed. "Let's see if we can change that."

Jori barely had time to register the movement before she was flat on her back beneath Sawyer with her robe open to reveal her cotton briefs and tank top.

"Hmm. I was hoping to find you naked under there," Sawyer purred.

Jori laughed when Sawyer's hand found its way under her shirt. "That doesn't seem to be deterring you."

"Not much does when I want something."

"And, ah…" Jori nearly lost her train of thought when Sawyer's tongue brushed her earlobe. "Now that you've gotten what you wanted, do you still want it?"

Sawyer stopped and drew back, extricating the hand that she

had just closed over Jori's breast. "Are you really trying to pick a fight with me right now?"

"No. Yes. Well, I don't know." When Sawyer moved to lie alongside her, Jori shoved a hand through her hair in frustration. "Did we make a mistake?"

"Do you think it was a mistake?"

"I asked you first." Jori hated how needy she felt. That wasn't her. She'd been on her own, alone, for essentially her whole life, and she was fine with the status quo. She didn't need to rely on someone else, especially not someone notorious for running at the first sign of trouble or boredom. And Jori couldn't get Erica's warning about Sawyer out of her head. "I don't think you took me seriously the last time I said this, but I can't be involved with someone I work for."

Sawyer flicked aside the edge of Jori's robe with her fingertips, lazily pushed up Jori's top, and laid her palm on Jori's stomach. "Well, I will admit, it *is* much easier to take you seriously in this position," she said sarcastically.

Jori flushed, suddenly aware of how ridiculous her objections to their being together must sound considering the night they'd just had. The intensity of that first time hadn't yet faded when Sawyer had awakened her later to make good on her promise, stroking her to a maddeningly slow orgasm with her tongue.

Despite the teasing, Sawyer's eyes were serious when she next spoke. "Okay. Tell me about it."

"I was involved with someone at the last restaurant where I worked. Actually, she was the manager and our breakup was pretty nasty. She made things very difficult for me, and when I still didn't quit, she let me go."

"Was it serious?"

Jori considered the question and opted for a straightforward answer. "In the beginning I might have thought we had a future. But, no. As it turned out, losing the job hurt more than losing the girl."

"Jori, I'm not going to fire you."

Jori covered Sawyer's hand to stop its progress along her hip. She wouldn't be able to continue to carry on her side of the conversation if Sawyer kept touching her. "It may sound silly to you, but working with Erica and Brady is more important to me than any job I've ever had. I've never felt more like I belonged somewhere."

Sawyer sighed, rolled onto her back, and folded her arms behind her head. *We're quite the pair, aren't we? She's worried about her job, and I'm afraid I won't be able to be what she needs.*

"I do understand. But things are different for me. Erica doesn't try to control *you*."

"She worries about you." Jori turned on her side and propped herself up on her elbow.

"She worries I'm screwing up my life. She's never believed in my decisions."

"Do you?"

"What?"

"Do you believe in your decisions? Enough to stand up for them?"

"I'll make a deal with you," Sawyer said, aware that she wasn't answering the questions. "No matter what happens between you and me, if things get uncomfortable for you at work, *I* will leave Drake's."

"I can't ask you to leave your family's business."

"You're not. I'm offering."

"They're your family."

"And they always will be, whether I work there or not." When Jori turned away and started to sit up, Sawyer grabbed her arm. "Wait a minute. I know you think I can't take anything seriously. And maybe that's true most of the time. I don't want to make things difficult for you at work, but I enjoyed last night, a lot. And I'd like to do it again. Right now, in fact."

She kissed Jori's palm, and when she got no resistance she

lightly bit, then sucked the end of one finger. Jori moaned and took Sawyer's mouth insistently. Jori's uncharacteristic aggression made her heart beat erratically.

"Jori," Sawyer said when Jori's mouth moved to her neck.

"Hmm?"

"I promise you'll always have a place at Drake's."

"Okay."

Jori seemed to easily accept the promise Sawyer hoped she could keep.

CHAPTER SIXTEEN

Sawyer sat on a stool facing the dining room with her back resting against the edge of the bar. Brady perched next to her, his arm stretched behind her. The rest of the staff was gathered around the tables nearest them.

Jori was sitting next to Chuck, leaned back in a chair with her arms folded over her chest. Sawyer barely contained a wink and a wide smile as Jori's eyes met hers. It had been just over a week since they returned from the rafting trip, and, if possible, her desire for Jori increased daily. She enjoyed knowing that shy, reserved Jori so easily shed her inhibitions when they were alone.

Jori insisted they keep their relationship separate from work and had instituted a strict no-touching rule while at the restaurant. Sawyer did her best to respect it now that she knew Jori had been burned with a workplace romance. Usually they spent an entire shift flirting in the form of mumbled comments and eye contact, until she thought she might have to drag Jori into her office and lock the door. She had managed to convince her that the boundaries of Drake's did not include the upstairs apartment, so several times they had rushed up the back stairs in each other's arms after shift, and sometimes they actually made it as far as the bedroom.

Realizing she was staring at Jori, Sawyer forced her eyes to the notebook resting on her knee. "I need to make a few changes to next weekend's schedule." She flipped through several pages. "Vesticom Enterprises wants to have a management brunch here on Friday. So I'm going to need some of you earlier than usual." A couple of the servers volunteered right away and Sawyer made a note. Some of the college students always wanted as many hours as they could get, especially during the summer. "Okay. I'll have a schedule up tomorrow morning. They want to see a menu by Wednesday, so Jori and Brady, please stick around for a few minutes. Everyone else is free to go."

When the others had left, Sawyer moved to the table where Brady and Jori sat. She scanned the ideas she'd jotted during her meeting with the Vesticom representative.

"Guys, I really want this to go well. We got good word of mouth from the mayor's benefit, and I'd like to see us get more corporate attention. That's why I agreed to open early for this brunch even though they don't have enough people to reserve the entire dining room."

"Are we even making enough to cover the servers' salaries?"

Sawyer had sensed Brady's skepticism from the moment she'd introduced the topic. "Barely," she reluctantly admitted.

"Does Erica know about this?"

"Erica's not here." It probably wasn't fair to leave Erica out of this decision, but in the face of Erica's continuing doubt about her abilities, Sawyer was beginning to feel like she had something to prove. And for perhaps the first time, she actually wanted to prove it. She'd never cared much about excelling at any of her jobs. But she knew this brunch was a good move for Drake's and was proud of her part in pulling it together. "Think big picture, Brady. Sometimes we've got to take risks if we want the payoff. Vesticom is big business."

"Sawyer, we're not caterers. We've got a solid reputation as a family restaurant."

"So we shouldn't aspire to more?"

Brady shrugged. "We are what we are. Do you plan on sticking around to back up all these aspirations after Erica returns?"

Sawyer opted for a safe answer. "Right now I'm not planning anything beyond this brunch. If we can increase our demand for private functions, we become more exclusive."

"I knew a day would come when I'd regret letting my big sister run this place," Brady mumbled, but Sawyer sensed the good-natured teasing behind his words.

"You may as well. You let your wife run your house. What's the difference?"

"Okay, smart ass." He stood and headed for the kitchen. "I'll have a menu for you by this afternoon."

Jori hadn't moved. Now, her arms still crossed, she tilted her head. "Are you going to tell Erica?"

Sawyer pulled out the chair next to Jori and sat. "Eventually."

"On Saturday? When you can declare it a success in the same breath?"

"Well, that might take some of the sting out." Sawyer vacillated between feeling accountable to Erica and defiant. She'd been left in charge. Didn't that mean she should be able to manage the place without constantly checking with her? Even as she asked the question, she knew what Erica's answer would be. But she couldn't do anything about the brunch if she didn't find out about it until after the fact.

❖

Friday morning, the Drake's kitchen was active earlier than usual. The kitchen was fully staffed and Sawyer had scheduled enough servers to cover the tables. The aroma of baking pastries competed with the smoky smell of frying bacon. Jori carefully folded fresh blueberries into muffin batter.

"I need two cheese omelets and four ginger scones." Jori

barely glanced up as the order was called out by an incoming server.

"Five minutes," Chuck said as he expertly flipped the contents of one of the omelet pans in front of him.

"I need ten minutes on the scones," Jori shot back.

"How about eight," he suggested with a wink.

"I'll race you." Jori smiled and looked at Brady. "And you can't help him."

Minutes later, she and Chuck slid their plates onto the service counter at the same time. Sawyer hurried through the kitchen door just as the waitress spun toward it with her tray, narrowly missing a collision.

"Whoa." Sawyer danced around the other woman and turned to Brady. "The CEO wants to compliment the chef."

Brady nodded and untied his apron. "Schmoozing is my least favorite part of this job."

"I thought complaints were your least favorite."

"They are. But this is up there, too."

"Be nice," Sawyer warned.

"Yes, ma'am," he called over his shoulder just before he disappeared through the door.

Sawyer grinned and crossed to Jori. "How's it going in here?"

"We're keeping up." Jori forced herself to turn away, washing her hands in an effort to keep them occupied when what she really wanted was to grab Sawyer and kiss that sexy smile off her face. She'd been fighting those urges every time she got within a few feet of Sawyer.

"Sawyer, will you grab that tray of muffins out of the oven?" Jori asked as she turned off the water and dried her hands on the towel tucked into the apron at her waist.

Sawyer nodded, slid on an oven mitt, and stooped to pull the muffins out. Jori glanced at Chuck and suddenly wished she and Sawyer were alone. She would cross to Sawyer and bend her over the counter and—

"Jori?" Sawyer's tone penetrated her fantasy.

She jerked her eyes from Sawyer's backside. Sawyer was looking over her shoulder, and Jori smothered a gasp at the stark longing in her expression. Her gaze said she knew exactly what Jori was thinking about.

"Where do you want these?" Sawyer lifted the muffin tray but it slipped and reflexively she grabbed it with her unprotected hand. "Shit," she hissed loudly enough to turn heads. She dropped the tray on the counter and stuck her burned fingers in her mouth.

"Come here."

Jori pulled her over to the sink and held her hand under the cool stream while Sawyer continued to curse under her breath.

"I thought you were tougher than this," Jori teased, trying to ignore the sick feeling in her stomach at Sawyer's obvious pain.

"It really hurts. And it's your fault anyway."

"My fault?" When Sawyer tried to pull her hand back, Jori held on firmly. "Just a minute longer."

"Yeah. If you hadn't been looking at me like you wanted to sling me up on the counter and have your way with me, I wouldn't have been so distracted."

Jori flushed, knowing Sawyer wasn't far off.

"Well, maybe I'll have to think of a way to make it up to you." She stepped in front of Sawyer, turning her back to the other occupants of the kitchen to hide her purposely flirtatious expression.

"That sounds promising."

Mindful of Sawyer's injury, Jori carefully patted a towel against her hand. "Any suggestions?"

Sawyer slowly raised one eyebrow. "Maybe. You could *actually* sling me up on the counter and—"

"As interesting as that sounds," Jori gently examined her injured hand, "I think that might make Chuck uncomfortable."

Sawyer frowned. "Hmm, I guess I'll have to wait. But you

know I do have a key to this place so, after hours if you wanted to—"

Jori laughed. "You're obsessed."

"I'm just saying. We could even do it on Chuck's counter."

"Sawyer!"

"What? He'll never know."

"Okay, I think *you* need to get back to work." She steered Sawyer in the direction of the door, but before she pushed her away she leaned close and whispered, "And *I* will consider it and get back to you."

❖

"Long day, huh?" Brady asked as he took off his chef jacket, leaving only a navy T-shirt tucked into the loose cotton pants. He picked up his wallet and keys from the counter.

Jori nodded. "But the brunch went well, don't you think?"

"When I talked to the CEO he raved about Sawyer and talked about bringing his people back again. Can I walk you out?"

"I think I'll check in on Sawyer before I go." She and Sawyer hadn't made any plans, but they seemed to gravitate toward each other at closing time. When Jori glanced at Brady she found a knowing smile and looked away quickly.

"She's been in the office for over an hour," he said and held the kitchen door open for her. "She should be about ready to wrap up." Again, the smug grin.

As they stepped into the hallway, Sawyer emerged from the office. Jori warmed as Sawyer's lips pulled into a sexy grin.

"Hey there. You ready to go upstairs and—" She bit off the rest of her words when she noticed Brady.

"Hey, Sawyer," Brady greeted her with a touch of teasing in his voice. "I'll see you ladies tomorrow."

He headed for the back door, leaving them standing in the hallway. Jori searched Sawyer's face, but found her expression unreadable. She was nervous about how Sawyer would react to her family knowing what was going on between them. *Wonderful, Jori. You already know she can't commit. So why are you worrying about her family?* She'd been reminding herself that no matter how much it seemed Sawyer was taking things in stride, their relationship would inevitably end. Apparently Sawyer was built that way, and she hadn't indicated to Jori that this was any different. So she'd forbidden herself to have any expectations.

"I guess it's safe to assume Brady knows," Sawyer said quietly, as if to herself.

"I think so."

"And if Brady knows that means Paige knows."

"Maybe he didn't tell—"

"If he didn't, he will. He and Paige don't have any secrets. Besides, he knows Paige will love this."

"Why?"

Sawyer shrugged. *Because she wants me to be with someone. She wants me to be happy. And you make me so happy.* But she couldn't say that, so instead she sighed and said, "I guess I'll have to tell Erica. Brady won't keep it from her for long." She rested a hand between Jori's shoulder blades. "Are you heading home? Or do you—want to come upstairs?"

Jori carefully took Sawyer's left hand in hers and tenderly kissed the still-red skin. "I still need to make this up to you, so I better come up." Mindful of the injury, Jori led her toward the stairs.

Sawyer followed willingly, and closely, allowing her free hand to roam down Jori's hip and over her shapely ass. She was already imagining what she would do to Jori when, halfway up the stairs, Jori pushed her against the wall and devoured her mouth. Sawyer's legs tingled and if Jori's body hadn't pinned hers, she doubted her knees would have held her upright. These moments of aggression, so at odds with Jori's normally shy demeanor, still pleasantly surprised her.

"Jori. Upstairs." Jori's thigh was between hers, pressed firmly into her crotch.

"Here." Jori braced her foot against a higher step, gaining leverage, and pushed her leg up.

"Oh, Jesus." Sawyer wanted to let Jori take her right there on the stairs. They were alone in the building, and with Jori's thigh thrusting against her distended clitoris, it wouldn't take long. "Only a few more steps. I want you in bed."

"Then hurry."

They stumbled together up the remaining steps. Sawyer struggled with the lock, but, with Jori between her and the door, she couldn't see what she was doing, and Jori's mouth on her neck was making it hard to concentrate.

"Hurry," Jori said, her words a low vibration against Sawyer's skin.

She fumbled with the key once more before it slid into place and she swung the door open. Jori's arms tightened around Sawyer and her mouth found Sawyer's ear.

"Jori, I have to get my keys," she protested when Jori pushed her through the foyer toward the living room. Her keys dangled from the knob of the still-open door.

"What are you worried about, there's no one else in—" As Jori spun them into the room, she stopped so suddenly they both almost toppled over. Struggling to keep them upright, Sawyer glanced up and found Erica reclining on the sofa.

Erica stood slowly.

"You're early," Sawyer said. She hadn't been expecting Erica to move back until late the next day.

"I missed being in my own place. I would have come downstairs, but Taylor was sleeping and I didn't want to risk waking her." Her tone was controlled, but Sawyer could tell she was angry. "It looks like I came back just in time."

Jori released Sawyer and quickly moved away. Her face was flushed and her eyes downcast.

"How are you feeling?" Sawyer stepped slightly in front of Jori, shielding her from the irritation in Erica's eyes. She hoped

Erica would accept the subject change, if only in deference to Jori's presence.

"Fine. How was the brunch?"

"You knew?"

"I lived with Brady. You didn't think I would notice when he left for work seven hours early?"

"I was going to tell you tomorrow." Sawyer shifted uncomfortably, wishing she could figure out how to get Jori out of the room before Erica's anger boiled over.

Apparently, though, Erica was too mad to care who else was there. "Damn it, Sawyer. I *asked* you not to do this."

"Actually, if I recall, you *told* me not to. Look, you don't need to worry about it. If things don't work out, I'll leave Drake's."

"You're damn right you will."

"I know—what?"

"What?" Jori echoed as she stepped around Sawyer. She'd recognized Sawyer's attempt to protect her. But she didn't need anyone to take a bullet for her.

Erica's attention didn't waver from Sawyer. "I'm not losing my pastry chef because you couldn't keep it in your pants."

"That's not fair. You know I'm not like that."

"Do I? How many women have you dated in, say, the last two years?"

"What difference does that make?" The fire behind Sawyer's argument was fading.

"How long can you keep convincing yourself that it's their fault it hasn't worked out? At some point you need to entertain the idea that maybe it's you."

"Oh, that's nice, Erica." Sawyer's expression went cold. "But what's between Jori and me really isn't your business."

"Fine. But if you want it to stay that way, keep it out of my restaurant." Without waiting for a response, Erica stalked toward the kitchen.

Sawyer walked to the window and stared out. After several silent moments, she drew a deep breath and turned back toward Jori.

"I'm sorry about that."

"It's okay."

"No. It's not. But it's squashed for now."

Jori crossed to her and touched her shoulder. "I'm going home. Would you like to come with me?" It was obvious she wouldn't be spending the night there, and she sensed that Sawyer wanted some distance from Erica. Having her constantly on the premises now, instead of safely at Brady and Paige's, would strain Sawyer enough.

"You know, this kind of killed the mood for me."

"Sawyer, we don't have to have sex. I'm just offering an alternative to staying here tonight. It's up to you whether you take it."

Her words seemed to reach Sawyer. She took Jori in her arms and pressed her face into Jori's hair for a second before she spoke. "That sounds good. Thank you."

Jori rubbed Sawyer's back. "I'd like to talk to Erica. If you want to grab some things while I do, then we can take off."

"This is between Erica and me. You don't have to—"

"This involves me." Jori stroked the side of Sawyer's jaw. "I appreciate you trying to protect me. But she's my boss. I'm in it, too."

"Okay."

When Sawyer headed for the bedroom, Jori took a breath and walked into the kitchen. Erica stood at the counter dunking a tea bag into a steaming mug.

Jori wasn't confrontational and normally would try to find a way to escape this situation. But allowing her personal life to interfere with her professional wasn't an option. She'd learned those lessons the hard way. "Erica, can we talk?"

She waited, but Erica didn't respond. Instead, she draped the bag against the back of the spoon and wrapped the string around it. As the silence stretched, she dropped the spoon onto a nearby saucer and carefully lifted the mug.

Deciding Erica wasn't going to speak, Jori made another attempt. "I didn't mean for—"

"I tried to warn you."

"I think you underestimate her." Jori had come into the kitchen hoping to preserve her relationship with her employer, but instead she found herself wanting to defend Sawyer.

"How long have you known my sister?"

"A couple of months."

"Well, I've known her my whole life. Maybe you're overestimating her. I just hate to see her keep making the same mistakes."

"And being with me is a mistake?"

"She won't commit." Erica skirted the question. "Is that really a healthy relationship for you?"

Jori couldn't answer. If it was true that Sawyer couldn't commit, she knew it wasn't healthy, but by now she'd convinced herself that it didn't matter. What they had right now was good, and she wouldn't relinquish the time they had even if it was guaranteed to end. But she knew she harbored a hope in a corner of her heart that it wouldn't end—that this time Sawyer wouldn't leave, that *she* would be the one Sawyer couldn't leave.

"Jori, we're going to have to agree to disagree on this one. As an employee, your personal life is not my business. But I don't think of you as just an employee. I can't say this enough—I don't want to see you get hurt. And I think you're a good fit at Drake's. So I hope she keeps her word when all this is over."

"You want her to leave?"

Erica laughed humorlessly. "It's not about what I want. It's about what's best for my business."

Shouldn't it be about what's best for your sister? For your family? The fact that Erica was her boss kept Jori from replying aloud. And when Sawyer came into the kitchen, Jori no longer needed to come up with a suitable response.

"Are you ready?" Sawyer didn't look at Erica, but Jori did, expecting her to say something. But Erica seemed to have found something interesting in the bottom of her cup of tea and now ignored both of them.

So, instead, Jori nodded and followed Sawyer through the apartment. Sawyer took her hand as they walked outside.

CHAPTER SEVENTEEN

M aybe this wasn't a great idea. I'm not going to be very good company. We should probably have called it a night," Sawyer said fifteen minutes later as Jori led her up the stairs to her apartment.

"We're here now. Just come in." She unlocked the door and pulled Sawyer inside. Sawyer had held her hand all the way from the restaurant and released it only long enough to get out of the car when they arrived, then reclaimed it. She seemed unaware that she clung to Jori, and something about the unintentional vulnerability touched her.

She gestured across the room. "Sit. I'll be right there. Do you want something to drink?"

"Water would be good."

She grabbed two bottles from the refrigerator and joined Sawyer on the futon, then settled close and stretched her arm along the back of the cushion. "Do you want to talk about it?"

Sawyer shrugged and stared at the bottle as she rolled it between her hands.

"Listen, Erica was out of line—"

"She wasn't wrong. I appreciate your loyalty, Jori, but I don't deserve it. I've earned my reputation."

"There must be a reason. I don't buy the short-attention-span line, so don't even bother."

"The truth is, I do decide pretty quickly whether things are going to work out with a woman. But it's more about what *they* want, than what I want."

"What do you mean?"

The plastic of the bottle crackled lightly under the pressure of Sawyer's hands. "When I was younger, I really tried to have a long-term relationship. I got my heart broken a few too many times before I figured out the score."

Jori took the bottle from Sawyer and set it on the coffee table. "Which is?"

"I'm just not the type that women fall in love with, never have been."

Jori hadn't expected this explanation. She recalled the nearly instant attraction she'd felt. She'd thought Sawyer's smile contagious and her friendliness comforting. And for Jori, that was saying something, since she was never comfortable around strangers. "You're not?"

"No. I'm not." Sawyer forced a self-effacing grin. "You know those people described as having a *great personality*? I'm one of those people."

"You *do* have a great personality. I envy how outgoing you are, and how witty."

"Sure, because you don't have to worry about being outgoing."

"What does that mean?"

"Look at you. You're gorgeous. People notice you without you even trying. I don't make the same first impression. I fall back on being friendly and funny."

"You shouldn't have to 'fall back' on anything. You're a great person."

Sawyer shrugged. She knew what people saw when they looked at her, having never had any illusions about her appearance. She'd sometimes been described as cute and once as handsome, but the words that slashed through her mind when she looked at Jori—*beautiful, stunning, breathtaking*—had never applied to her.

"I have a mirror, Jori." Suddenly her surety fell away, a façade. And she hated her words, hated pointing out her own shortcomings and the weakness they revealed. She often forced the confidence she knew women found attractive, even in uncomfortable situations, in order to draw attention from her flaws—boring features hidden behind a pair of glasses. How could she expect to attract anyone with these looks? If she needed a reminder that she got the brains and personality in the family, she only had to look at Erica and Brady. Everyone had always told her she was the image of her dad, and he was no prize. Nothing like her mother and her sister, that was certain.

Having wanted Jori from their first meeting, Sawyer prayed she couldn't see her abrupt lapse in self-assurance. Suddenly she very much wanted Jori to see things in her that made her special. "Anyway, I've gotten away from the point. When I was younger I did have a couple of serious relationships. But in the end, I was a diversion while they were waiting for their soul mate."

"So somewhere along the way you convinced yourself that all women were the same, and we all wanted the same thing?"

"Well—"

"Do you think all women are shallow?"

"No, I guess not." It sounded ridiculous when Jori said it that way. Could she, without realizing it, have applied the faults of a few to all women? Certainly she'd used that as a reason to keep emotional distance, especially with Jori. She'd been so intent on seeming confident and assured that she'd been a complete idiot.

"Then why is it so inconceivable that someone could want to be with you, to really know you, Sawyer? But you don't let anyone close enough to give them a chance. How do you know one of the women in your past may have been good for you, but you didn't give her a real opportunity?"

"Are you trying to convince me to get back with one of my exes?" Sawyer tried for humor but it fell flat.

"I want to know why you're selling yourself short. Why you run."

"You don't ask for much, do you?" Sawyer said sarcastically, aware she wasn't answering the question. "I get enough of this from Erica."

Sawyer stood and took two steps toward the door before Jori grabbed her arm. "Okay. Hold on." Jori made a mental note: *Too much, too quickly.* Not releasing Sawyer's arm, Jori led her to the bedroom. "I didn't mean to get you all worked up."

She unbuttoned Sawyer's shirt and eased it off her shoulders, then released the clasp between Sawyer's breasts.

"I told you I wasn't going to be good company."

"Your company is just fine." She continued removing Sawyer's clothes and placed them neatly on the chair nearby, then gave her an old T-shirt. "Put this on and get in bed," she said as she changed her own clothes.

"I don't mind if you want to tell me to go," Sawyer whispered.

She wants *to run.* Suddenly, Jori very much wanted to know if she could convince Sawyer to fight that instinct and stay. She lay down and drew Sawyer's head to her chest, then sifted her fingers through her hair. "I don't want you to go."

Sawyer knew her body was tense with the desire to flee. It would feel so good to hear the door slam on her way out. Jori had ventured too close to the insecurities she had spent years carefully blanketing, and, without meaning to, Sawyer had revealed more than she usually did. But Jori's touch, the gentle caress against her scalp, distracted her.

Jori's patience lessened the frustration she usually felt when she thought about her past relationships and how they'd affected her. For months after the gorgeous woman in college rejected her, she'd been embarrassed to go out in public. And when she'd finally gotten the strength to try again with another woman, also beautiful, she repeated the same pattern. Things always started out smoothly, but at some point her partner would end things. Though her lovers trotted out the usual reasons—*it's not you, it's me* and *I'm just not ready for a relationship right now*—something inside Sawyer withered with each new heartbreak, and she became increasingly convinced each breathtaking woman she was involved with was simply tired of looking at her drab appearance every day. And try as she might, she was stuck with it.

Eventually Sawyer decided that being the one to initiate the breakup would minimize the hurt. She determined quickly that the relationship didn't have long-term potential and ended it first. Generally, this had been a good practice—for her. The women she rejected didn't always receive it well, though Sawyer rationalized that her percentages were pretty good. Only once had a woman screamed at her that she needed professional help.

But lying next to Jori with her wonderful hands in her hair, she could almost forget every failed attempt. She nestled closer against Jori's side and closed her eyes.

❖

Sawyer turned off the shower and stepped out. "Thank you for last night," she called through the open bathroom door as she toweled dry.

"Anytime. Do you want some breakfast?"

"No, thanks. I'll have to run by Erica's and get the rest of my stuff. She and I need some space right now."

"You can stay here, if you want to."

Sawyer stepped out of the bathroom. "Ah—I don't think—"

"I'm sorry. Forget it."

"Jori." The flash of rejection Jori failed to hide hurt. "It's not personal."

Jori paused with an open carton of juice poised over a glass.

Sawyer couldn't read her expression, but when she spoke the iciness in her tone was clear. "Of course it's not."

"So I'm going to call the office at my old complex and see if they have a one-bedroom open." Sawyer picked up her jeans from the chair and stepped into them.

"That's a good idea."

After she finished dressing, Sawyer crossed to Jori and slid an arm around her waist. "I want to see you again."

"You'll see me later at Drake's."

"I mean," she cupped Jori's jaw and kissed her lightly, "I want to *see* you. Not just sex. We could have drinks, watch a movie, or whatever you want."

"Okay. Maybe this weekend." When Sawyer kissed her again, Jori held her close and lingered.

❖

Twenty minutes later, Sawyer knocked on Matt's door. When he opened it, wearing his favorite boxers and a familiar faded T-shirt, Sawyer realized they hadn't gone this long without seeing each other since they'd met. She missed the comfort of knowing she could wander into the next room and talk to him about whatever was on her mind.

"I was over at the office checking on vacant apartments so I thought I'd stop in and say hi."

"I'm glad you did. Come on in, I was just making breakfast. How's Erica doing? She and the baby move home?"

Sawyer followed him to the kitchen and leaned against the counter out of the way while he fried bacon and eggs. "Yeah, she came back yesterday afternoon. A bit unexpectedly."

Matt loaded up a plate, and she took it and got two forks out of the drawer. As they settled at the table, she gave him an edited version of Erica's discovery of her relationship with Jori.

When she described the moment she'd realized Erica was in

the room, he laughed. "Man, I wish I could have seen the look on your face."

"I knew Erica was going to let me have it, but I thought she might wait until Jori left."

"What did Jori do?"

"She was cool. We went back to her place and talked for a while, then went to sleep. This morning she offered to let me stay with her for a while."

"How did she take it when you told her no?"

"How do you know I didn't take her up on it?"

"Come on, Sawyer. Even if you hadn't already told me you were over here looking for a place, I would've known you turned her down."

Sawyer didn't respond, instead taking a forkful of eggs.

"I think you should give Jori a chance."

"Who says I'm not? I was with her last night. We've made plans to see each other again." Once more, Sawyer found herself on the defensive.

"But you're waiting for it to be over."

"What's wrong with being realistic?"

"Okay, I know I'm not going to win this argument. All I'm saying is that Jori seems good for you. She's sweet, patient, and has a quietness about her that complements you."

"Maybe you should talk to Erica, because she doesn't see a relationship between Jori and me as a good thing."

"She's got a slightly different perspective than I do. It could be uncomfortable at the restaurant if things don't work out."

Sawyer shook her head. "I promised Jori I'd leave Drake's. Besides, I'm not going to work there forever."

Matt stood and stacked their empty plates. "Well, I can't help you with that. But I can offer you an alternative regarding your living situation. Move back in here."

She picked up their glasses and followed him into the kitchen. "Thank you. But you and Davis—"

"Davis wants to look for a house. There's no sense in you leasing another apartment, when this one will be free when we find a place."

"A house?" Sawyer had never seen Matt move so quickly with anyone.

"He wants a puppy, a golden retriever. So a yard, preferably with a fence—"

"A puppy?"

"I know it seems like it's too soon. But I really don't doubt that I love him. So, yeah, he wants a puppy. And I want to give him everything."

"If you're sure you guys don't mind." When Sawyer had gone to stay at Erica's, she had taken only what she'd need for several weeks, leaving most of her things at the apartment she'd shared with Matt.

"We don't. Besides, I don't think it will be that long. Davis already has his eye on a house that he heard is going on the market soon."

"Wow, a house." Things really were changing quickly.

He shrugged. "It's time to grow up and decide what I want from life."

Sawyer wondered if those were his father's words. When he'd graduated pre-med and announced his intention to sell cars instead of going to medical school, his father had been livid. For months, every time the two were in the same room, his father had thrown badly veiled barbs about wasted money and a shyster's living. But Matt had known what he wanted and gone after it. Sawyer envied his surety then and now.

"And what you want is Davis, a house, and a dog?"

"Yes." He wrapped an arm around her neck and pulled her into a hug. She wondered if she'd ever seen him so happy.

"Okay. But I'm not bearing any children for the two of you, so don't even think about it."

CHAPTER EIGHTEEN

A re you sure you'll be okay?" Erica asked for the third time in the fifteen minutes since Sawyer had walked through Brady's front door. She paced the living room, softly singing to the cooing baby in her arms.

"Yes. I've taken care of an infant before." When she paused, Sawyer touched Taylor's hand and felt the tiny fingers curl against hers. "I used to watch the boys all the time when they were babies, remember?"

"I know."

Erica and Derrick Ames were going to dinner with Paige and Brady, but Erica was nervous about leaving Taylor for the first time. Paige had called Sawyer earlier that day to ask if she would mind watching all of the kids. Sawyer was sure she'd heard a smile in Paige's voice when she'd told her to invite Jori over as well.

Though Ames had visited several times since Taylor's birth, Sawyer suspected Erica was nervous because this was their first real date. And she wondered if Paige and Brady had been invited along to buffer some of the pressure.

Erica had certainly dressed to impress. She wore a rich brown pencil skirt that ended just above her knees and showed off her shapely legs. Her wheat-colored silk blouse was the same shade as the lightest strands that wove through her French braid.

The only thing that detracted from her appearance was the towel tucked against her left breast and over her shoulder, to protect her blouse.

"You look nice."

"Thanks." Erica blushed.

During the three weeks since their argument, Erica and she had been politely distant, neither of them bringing up the dispute. They didn't discuss her relationship with Jori, but limited their conversation to Drake's, and even that was sparse since Erica hadn't returned to work yet. Sawyer had already decided that she couldn't change Erica's mind, so she could hope for only a silent truce and maybe time would prove her wrong. *Surely I am capable of a long-term relationship with the right person. Is Jori that person?*

"I'm going to feed her before Derrick gets here."

As Erica disappeared down the hallway, she passed Paige entering the living room. Paige's deep purple dress accented her trim figure, and a teardrop-shaped diamond nestled in the plunging neckline.

Sawyer whistled. "Wow, fancy. Where are you guys going for dinner?"

"Brady's been promising me we'd go to Antonio's for months. Tonight he's going to deliver." She winked at Sawyer. "Then maybe later when we get home, I'll deliver, too."

"Oh, man, that's my brother you're talking about. I don't need to hear that."

Paige laughed. "I let the boys rent a movie earlier, so they'll probably want to watch it. I put a pan of mac and cheese in the oven for dinner. The timer will go off when it's ready."

"Okay."

"Is Jori coming over?"

Sawyer shrugged. "She might stop by."

Paige looked like she wanted to say more, but the doorbell

pealed and she left the room. Sawyer heard her say, "Hello, Lieutenant."

"Please, call me Derrick," he said as she led him into the living room. He nodded at Sawyer and she returned the gesture. He looked every bit the gentleman in his dark gray suit, white shirt, and burgundy paisley tie. She guessed his jacket had been tailored to fit his broad shoulders.

"Are we ready to go?" Brady came down the hallway yanking on the knot of his tie. He crossed to Paige, who straightened it for him.

"We are now." Paige patted his chest. "Why don't you guys go start the car, and we ladies will join you in a minute."

"Yes, dear. Come on, Derrick, we can go out through the garage."

As they disappeared through the kitchen, Sawyer laughed. "You have him so well trained."

Paige waved a hand. "Please, men are easy."

"Compared to women, I'd have to agree."

"Your problem is not the other women, though. You're the complicated one."

"I'm complicated?"

"Well, being in a relationship with you is." Paige smiled as if trying to take the sting out of her words.

"Have you been talking to Erica?"

"Contrary to what you might believe, this whole family isn't against you." She touched Sawyer's shoulder. "And I understand more than you think. Before I met your brother, I wasn't very trusting. But I came around and, someday, you'll trust yourself enough, too."

Sawyer allowed Paige to wrap her in a quick embrace, then pulled away as Erica reappeared from the bedroom.

"The guys are waiting in the car," Paige said, picking up her small black clutch.

Erica nodded, then told Sawyer, "Taylor fell asleep. She'll probably be out for a few hours."

"We'll be fine. Have a good time."

"The boys are playing in their room, but if they get too loud make them go in the family room so they don't wake her." Paige squeezed Sawyer's arm before she moved away.

After Sawyer closed the door behind them, she went to the boys' bedroom. Intent on the video game they played, neither of them appeared to notice her standing in the open doorway. She watched in amazement as their little fingers manipulated the controllers while their onscreen characters battled in a flurry of kicks and punches. Each boy gloated that he was going to win and tried to bait the other into making a mistake. Their interaction reminded Sawyer of herself and her siblings when she was younger. Erica especially had been fiercely competitive, and the only thing that had changed over the years was the areas in which they competed. They weren't playing silly games now. Instead, Erica compared their lives and found Sawyer's lacking.

When Quintin bested his older brother, he jumped up and down chanting, then danced around, drawing his words out into multiple syllables. After the fourth refrain of "I won and you lost 'cause you're a big loser," Sawyer stepped in.

"Okay, boys. Let's go get ready for dinner. Wash your hands and meet me in the kitchen." Quintin was still whispering his taunt as he followed Daniel through the door. Sawyer palmed his head and slowed his progress. "Use soap. I'll know if you don't."

❖

Sawyer had just finished washing the dishes when the doorbell rang. She grabbed a towel, wiping her hands as she headed for the door.

"I'll get it," Daniel called from the next room.

"Look and see who it is before you open the door," she reminded him.

She reached the living room in time to see him peek out the glass panel alongside the door. Quintin hovered curiously at her side as Daniel pulled it open and stepped back to let Jori enter.

"Hi," Sawyer said. When Jori grinned back at her, she was surprised by a flood of pleasure just from seeing the spark in her eyes.

"Hi." Jori held up a plastic grocery bag and smiled down at Daniel. "I brought you guys something."

While Quintin clung to Sawyer's leg, Daniel rushed over and peered in the bag.

"Ice cream," he exclaimed.

"For sundaes," Jori said as she headed for the kitchen. "Who wants one?"

"Me!" Daniel followed and, lured by the promise of ice cream, Quintin trailed them.

As Sawyer walked into the kitchen and saw Jori unpack a carton of French vanilla ice cream, mason jars of topping, and a can of whipped cream, she wondered if the boys would ever go to sleep after ingesting so much sugar.

"Small sundaes, please," she said as she got out four bowls and spoons. "They just had dinner and bedtime isn't far off."

Jori twisted the cap off one of the jars and winked at Sawyer. "I've got homemade chocolate and caramel sauces."

"From scratch?"

Nodding, Jori put the jars in the microwave. "I made them this afternoon."

"Good Lord, you really are a woman after my own heart." Sawyer pressed a palm to her chest and stalked Jori across the kitchen, thinking, *If we were alone...*

"Help me up." Quintin's plea stopped Sawyer's progress. He stood on tiptoes next to the stool pulled up to the edge of the island. Daniel had already climbed up and now leaned the entire upper half of his body across the counter to watch Jori assemble the sundaes.

"Do you want chocolate or caramel?" Jori asked Quintin as Sawyer helped him scoot up to the counter.

"Can I have both?" he asked shyly.

"You certainly can." She spooned some of both sauces onto a small mound of ice cream.

"Oh, Lord, they'll never sleep," Sawyer muttered.

But they did. Two hours later, after watching the movie, she was tucking them into bed. Daniel had fallen asleep just before the credits rolled, so she had carried him and deposited him on the top bunk. Quintin climbed into the one below, then Sawyer sat down on the edge of his bed. He turned on his side and tucked one hand under his pillow.

"'Night, Aunt Sawyer." He looked at Jori standing in the doorway and said, "Thanks for the sundaes."

"You're welcome," she whispered.

"Sleep well." Sawyer smoothed a hand over his strawberry curls and kissed his forehead.

She stood and crossed to join Jori. "He gets his manners from Paige."

"He's sweet. They both are."

As they stepped into the hallway, Sawyer eased the door closed behind them, then led Jori back to the living room. "Would you like something to drink?"

"No, thanks. I should get going."

Jori turned toward the front door, but Sawyer grabbed her hand and pulled her back. She framed her face in her hands and kissed her lightly. "Stay. They'll be here soon. Stay, then come home with me."

When Sawyer's mouth moved to her neck, Jori's head dropped back and she moaned softly. "What do you have in mind?"

Sawyer nipped at her chin. "Do you have any of that chocolate sauce left?"

"Hmm, I think I do. But in that case, you'd better come home with me."

"Why's that?"

"Because I don't want to share with Matt and Davis."

Sawyer smiled and pulled her to the couch, tucking her against her side as they sat down. She picked up the remote and began to search for something to distract her until her family returned. Jori's head rested on her shoulder, and Jori's hand felt warm on her thigh even through her jeans.

A soft cry from the baby monitor sitting on the coffee table drew Sawyer's attention.

"It sounds like the princess is awake." She rose. "I'll be right back."

On her way to Paige and Brady's bedroom, she looked in on the boys, then, satisfied they were sleeping peacefully, she went into the room next door. Taylor lay in the portable crib fussing and waving her fists.

"Oh, what's the matter with my girl?" she whispered as she carefully picked her up. When she laid Taylor against her shoulder she knew what was wrong. "Ah, changing time."

As she put a fresh diaper on Taylor, she talked quietly to her. "Hey, little one, since I've got you here, there's something I've been meaning to talk to you about. You've got your mama's eyes, her nose, and it looks like you're going to have her hair, thank God." Taylor's father had jet-black hair, which he'd kept shaved. "You'll be a beauty, Taylor, like your mother and your grandmother. Nothing like your plain old Aunt Sawyer. You won't have to be a court jester like me. You'll attract all the women, or men, that you want without even trying."

Taylor scrunched her tiny features, then they smoothed and she cooed softly as if responding to Sawyer's words.

"But you really don't need to inherit your mother's

stubbornness. Maybe you could follow Aunt Paige when it comes to that. She has the patience of a saint. She'd have to, to deal with this family."

When Sawyer finished bundling Taylor back up, she carried her into the living room and settled carefully on the couch, laying Taylor against her chest and shoulder closest to Jori.

"Hi, sweetheart." Jori smoothed Taylor's pale wisps of hair, then kissed her forehead.

As Sawyer watched Jori, the familiar shard of fear folded within her. The undisguised longing in Jori's eyes as she looked at the baby reminded Sawyer of all that Jori had never had in her life.

"You want kids?" She knew the answer before she asked.

She could see each moment of pain, loneliness, and envy burn across Jori's expression and end with wonder. Then Jori gazed at her wearing a careful mask of concealment that nearly broke her heart.

"Four or five." Sawyer didn't think she imagined the emotion that choked Jori's words.

"Four or five? That's a handful."

"I want a big family."

"You need to spend some more time with these three and see if you still feel the same." Sawyer forced a light tone while doubt churned inside her. Did she dare toy with these emotions? She couldn't risk a relationship unless she was absolutely sure. Jori deserved everything that no one had ever offered her. She deserved something, and someone, special. Panic spread through Sawyer's chest when she found herself wishing she could be that special someone.

"These three are angels. Your children, now they would be a handful."

"Are you saying I'm hard to handle?"

"A little." Jori grinned when Sawyer pretended to look offended. "But I do so like *handling* you."

Taylor had drifted back to sleep and Jori curled against Sawyer's side. She tucked one hand inside Sawyer's and touched Taylor's foot with the other. Sawyer laced her fingers through Jori's, as if by clinging to this moment she could stave off her fears.

CHAPTER NINETEEN

Neither of them had moved when, an hour later, the front door opened and Brady and Paige walked in.

"Hey, guys," Sawyer said as Brady sat in the chair nearby and Paige headed down the hall to look in on the boys. "How was dinner?"

"Good."

"Where's Erica?"

"Outside." He grinned. "Saying good-bye to Derrick."

Before Sawyer could comment further, the door opened and Erica came in with a flushed face and goofy smile.

"Brady," Paige called as she came back down the hall. "Could you pack the crib and put it in Erica's car for her?"

"Sure thing."

Careful not to wake Taylor, Erica lifted her from Sawyer's arms, then sat in the chair Brady had just vacated. "How was she?"

"Perfect," Sawyer answered. "I'll go help Brady with your things."

Left alone with Erica, Jori shifted on the sofa and wondered if she should say anything to her. They hadn't really spoken since that night in the apartment, but earlier Sawyer had told her that Erica seemed content to let the awkward topic of their relationship drop.

Finally, she settled on polite conversation. "Did you have a nice night?"

Erica glanced at her, then back at her daughter, smoothing a hand over Taylor's fuzzy head. "I did."

"So? Are you going to see him again?"

Erica smiled faintly. "Yes, I think so. He asked if he could take Taylor and me for a walk in the park this weekend."

"He seems like a good guy." Having run out of small talk, Jori blurted, "I'm sorry we argued."

Erica regarded her with a thoughtful expression. "Perhaps it wasn't my place, but I was only looking out for you. You've obviously decided not to take my advice."

"I know it might seem the smarter thing to do. On paper, we're not the best match, but..." Jori wondered how to explain the need Sawyer inspired. She knew all of the reasons they shouldn't be together, many of them relating to her own family history. "Haven't you ever met someone and felt as if you really have no choice about whether to be with them? Like everything in you clamors to be near them, regardless of what the outcome might be?"

"Even if the inevitable outcome is heartache?"

Jori considered the question. Would she trade the feeling of being in Sawyer's arms for the guarantee of an even keel emotionally? "Even then."

Erica shifted forward in the chair, rocking Taylor when she stirred. She gazed at her daughter with the unconditional love of a devoted parent, the kind Jori had never known. And she wondered if Erica had finally found something that meant more to her than Drake's.

❖

Sawyer stretched out next to Jori on the bed and raised up on her elbow, then dipped a spoon into a bowl on the nightstand. "I've wanted to do this since the first day we met."

"Really?" Jori smiled as Sawyer drew the spoon across her bare stomach, leaving a trail of melted chocolate. Sawyer bent and dragged her tongue along the line. "Mmm, it's so much better when it's homemade."

"Ah, no bottled syrup for my girl," Jori said with a groan as Sawyer licked her skin again.

"I'm just glad you didn't let the boys eat it all."

Taking Sawyer's face in her hands, Jori pulled her close for a kiss. Their stomachs rubbed together, smearing the chocolate between them. "You taste good."

"So do you," Sawyer murmured, biting Jori's jaw.

"But I haven't had any chocolate."

"Then it's all you, isn't it?"

Sawyer traced the spoon across Jori's throat, then followed it with her tongue, feeling Jori's pulse beat heavily against her mouth.

"Hey, no marks," Jori said when Sawyer sucked the syrup from the side of her neck. "I don't need to explain hickeys to the guys in the kitchen." She rolled Sawyer onto her back and trailed her hand across her stomach. "You're a mess."

Sawyer smiled and caught Jori's wrist. She licked her chocolate-covered fingers clean, watched Jori's eyelids flutter, and heard her soft gasp. "I can't get enough."

"I'd be flattered if I wasn't convinced you were talking about the chocolate."

Sawyer coated another of Jori's fingers, then dragged her tongue along it. "Well, then it's lucky for me that you go great with chocolate." Sawyer emphasized her words by covering one of Jori's nipples with sauce. "Mmm, chocolate-covered nipple. My favorite."

Jori's laughter turned into a moan as Sawyer drew the nipple into her mouth. "Oh, that's nice. Bite it."

Sawyer closed her teeth on the sweet-flavored flesh and felt a surge of heat low in her belly as Jori's back bowed off the bed. She never tired of the rush that giving Jori pleasure brought, of feeling as if she were being let in on a secret when she watched Jori's reservation fall away while her orgasm spiraled through her.

"Can you come like this?" she whispered against Jori's breast.

"I wouldn't have thought so." Jori's voice was husky. "But, ah—God, maybe." Sawyer sucked her nipple, hard, until the muscles of Jori's abdomen and thighs hardened and Jori dug her fingers into Sawyer's biceps. Then she eased back, licking it lightly.

"Do you want to?"

"Yes." Jori's coiled body, so close to release, protested the sudden lack of pressure.

"How bad?"

"Sawyer, please." Jori clung to Sawyer, every nerve ending seeming to scream for stimulation.

Sawyer slipped her fingers down Jori's stomach, and Jori shivered beneath them. "I could spend hours touching you."

She gripped Sawyer's wrist and guided her hand down. "Then touch me."

Sawyer sifted lightly through the downy hair and barely pressed into her folds and grazed her clitoris.

"God, please, Sawyer. More."

Sawyer kept her eyes on Jori's face and Jori cocked her head to study her, resisting the urge to tug the wrist she still held and force Sawyer's fingers deeper. She could tell by the trembling in Sawyer's arm that she was fighting a similar impulse. Sawyer was teasing them both, and Jori wondered if Sawyer enjoyed it as much as she did.

"Do you like it when I beg?"

Sawyer gasped and couldn't hide her surprise at Jori's boldly spoken words. "Yes."

Jori smiled and lifted her hips, nudging Sawyer's hand. She wrapped a hand around the back of Sawyer's neck, pulled her head down, and pressed her mouth against Sawyer's ear. She bit

Sawyer's earlobe and felt the answering twitch in the fingers that still rested against her throbbing center.

"Does it excite you to know how much I want you inside me?" she whispered hotly in Sawyer's ear.

"Jesus, yes," Sawyer gasped.

The hoarse excitement in Jori's voice ripped through Sawyer, frying the connection between her brain and body and leaving her completely at the mercy of her senses. She was aware only of the feel of Jori squeezing around her as her fingers, seemingly of their own accord, slid inside—of the taste of Jori's mouth when she took it again, roughly—and of the scent of chocolate and sex as Jori rode her fingers toward orgasm.

"You should have let me shower with you," Sawyer said, staring hotly at Jori across the bed.

Jori laughed. "Uh-uh. I know what would've happened."

"I would have behaved. If you'd asked me nicely."

"Somehow I doubt it." Jori pulled back the clean sheet she'd put on the bed while Sawyer had finished her shower.

Amusement sparkling in her eyes, Sawyer blatantly trailed her gaze down Jori's body then back to meet Jori's. "You're probably right. I don't know that I can resist you when you're wet and naked."

Jori slid between the sheets and covered herself, enjoying the look of disappointment that crossed Sawyer's lovely features. She turned onto her side and looked back over her shoulder at Sawyer. "Get in here."

Sawyer spooned her and touched Jori's waist. Jori took Sawyer's hand and tucked it between her breasts, pulling Sawyer's arm more tightly around her. Her muscles felt like liquid and, relaxed and truly sated, she basked in the cocoon of Sawyer's body.

"That was rather decadent." She recalled how Sawyer had

made love to her, somehow blending each climax into a rise to the next, until she had weakly pulled Sawyer's hand away, whispering, "Please, I can't take anymore."

Though she would have thought it impossible, she'd felt a renewed rush of moisture between her thighs when Sawyer had leaned over her and said, "I like it better when you beg me *not* to stop."

Jori had distracted Sawyer by flipping her onto her back and licking a smear of chocolate from her chest. When, later, they lay coated in chocolate and sweat, Jori had declared them both in need of a shower.

Now, Sawyer nuzzled Jori's neck. "Complaining?"

Jori angled her head, giving Sawyer better access. "Oh, absolutely not. How do you do that?"

"What?" Sawyer pushed damp ebony locks off Jori's forehead.

"Wreck me so thoroughly."

"Just talented, I guess."

"And modest." Jori chuckled.

Sawyer traced her lips along the curve of Jori's jaw and the side of her neck. "When I'm with you—touching you, I simply don't want to stop."

"Mmm, I like the way you touch me."

Sawyer's stomach tightened at the slight growl in Jori's voice. She squeezed her thighs together to contain the throbbing arousal that threatened to surge again. Almost of their own volition, her splayed fingers stroked the underside of Jori's right breast.

"Don't even think about it," Jori warned. "I need more recovery time."

Sawyer stilled her fingers. "This is not just about sex, Jori. I like being with you. You're—comfortable."

Jori laughed. "That's a first."

"What?"

"I'm *comfortable?* That's what you say about an old pair of slippers."

"No, it's not."

"Yes, it is."

"I don't own any slippers." Sawyer grinned. "And even if I did, it's not the same thing."

"Then maybe you should explain it to me."

"Comfortable is—I can walk around in the boxers I only sleep in when I'm alone. Hell, just tonight, despite how self-conscious I've always been about my appearance, I was walking through your apartment naked. Comfortable is not worrying that I have to impress you or make some kind of impression. And that's great because I'm so busy—"

"Being comfortable?"

"I was going to say enjoying being with you. With you, I can be me." *I've never been completely me before.*

Jori rolled over in Sawyer's arms and fit one of her legs between Sawyer's. "I'm glad," she murmured drowsily.

Sawyer lightly stroked her fingers over Jori's back. When Jori pressed her face into Sawyer's neck, her soft wildflower-scented hair tickled Sawyer's nose. Jori's breathing evened out and Sawyer pulled back slightly to look at her face. Her eyes were closed, her lashes resting gently against her cheek. Sawyer dropped her head back on the pillow and smiled contentedly.

"Good night," she whispered into the semidark room.

"Mmm. I love you." Jori's voice was heavy with sleep. Her arms tightened around Sawyer's waist and she nestled closer, already too deep in slumber to feel Sawyer stiffen.

The next morning, Sawyer eased out of bed and was gone before Jori woke up. All the way to her apartment, she rambled to herself aloud, trying to figure out how she was going to explain her flight to Jori. She tried out every line she could think of and even tested the truth while she stood beneath the stinging hot spray of the shower. But the heavy mist of steam filling the stall couldn't erase the image of Jori's face or the memory of her murmured protest when Sawyer had slipped out of bed.

By the time she drove to work, she was no closer to having a plan, and her stomach was knotted with dread as she opened the back door to Drake's. But, as it turned out, she was granted a reprieve, however short, because when she walked into the kitchen Erica was there, pacing the length of the room and gently bouncing a crying Taylor in her arms. Brady, Chuck, and Jori were all doing prep work at their stations.

"Are you sure you're ready to come back? It's only been a month," Brady asked as he set a saucepan on the stovetop and added a healthy slab of butter to melt.

"It's been five weeks. And yes, I'm ready." To Taylor, she murmured, "Come on, sweetie. What's the matter?"

"Sawyer's got things under control here, if you need more time."

Sawyer briefly made eye contact with Jori across the room and averted her glance when she felt her heart hitch. She crossed the kitchen and leaned against Jori's counter, her back to Jori and her arms crossed over her chest. The scent of vanilla drifted around her, and she could hear the rhythmic sound of Jori's whisk against the sides of a stainless- steel bowl.

"I just need the rest of this week to find a sitter. I'll start back Monday."

Brady stuck his pinkie in the reduction taking shape in his saucepan and tasted it, then added a pinch of salt. "I might be able to help you out. Paige has been talking about doing some baby-sitting to make extra cash since both boys are in school now. In fact, she's already got names of a couple of families who might be interested. If you want, I can see how she'd feel about keeping Taylor."

"That would be great, Brady, especially since she'd be with family, too. I've been fretting about leaving her with a stranger." Taylor had finally calmed and Erica laid her in the infant car seat perched on a countertop a safe distance from where Brady worked. "So, um, Sawyer, I was thinking you might want to stay on after I come back."

"You were?" After all the trouble they'd had during the months Sawyer had been at Drake's, she didn't expect Erica would want to continue working with her.

"Sure. I'm still short a waitress."

Jori's whisk stuttered to a stop at precisely the moment that Sawyer realized Erica was serious. Sure, she'd never taken an interest in the family business before, so maybe Erica didn't have any reason to think she might want to now. But it still stung that Erica could so easily relegate her to server after the work she'd done managing in her stead.

"Waitress."

"Yeah, you've still got your uniform, don't you?"

Sawyer could tell from Brady's expression that he realized Erica's error. She turned away from his sympathetic gaze. Her blood ran hot but she kept her expression stone cold. She shook her head slowly, remembering how she'd returned the uniform to the linen closet the day Erica had collapsed—the day she'd assumed the reins of Drake's. Temporarily, she reminded herself.

"Why wait until Monday, Erica? Why don't you just take over right now?" Sawyer drew the keys to Drake's from her pocket and tossed them on the counter in front of Erica. "I'm done."

She didn't even look at Jori as she headed for the back door, ignoring Erica's confused exclamation and Brady's plea to return and talk about it. Head down, she had the engine of the Solara cranked and her hand on the gear shift when she heard a knock on the car window. Without looking up, she pressed the button to roll down the glass.

"Sawyer, hold on a minute." Jori touched her shoulder.

Her pride only dented but not destroyed, Sawyer held up a hand to silence her. "She's on her own."

"Sawyer—"

"Not now," she snapped. Jori's fingers still rested on her

shoulder and their warmth seeped through her shirt, making her long to step out of the car and pull Jori into her arms. She wanted so much from Jori. More than she had from anyone in so long, maybe ever. And that thought alone had her searching the street for the quickest escape route.

"Please, talk to me. I know Erica upset you just now."

"I can't talk about that right now."

Jori suspected that Sawyer's behavior wasn't entirely about her anger with Erica. "Are we not okay? Because I thought things were going well with us, and last night was—well, incredible. Then this morning I woke up and you were gone."

"I need some space."

"Okay. I'll call you later, and—"

"Jori, I need to sort some things out."

Jori pulled her hand away and stared at Sawyer, confused. She'd watched Sawyer's enthusiasm for her work at Drake's grow with every day, so despite any pretense to the contrary, she knew Erica's apparent inability to see Sawyer's accomplishments had hurt her feelings. But that didn't explain Sawyer's absence that morning or the distance between them now. *She needs space.* Jori could almost manage to deny the trickle of fear at not knowing what "space" meant for them, but she couldn't ignore the slash of pain in her chest.

She stepped back and was barely clear of the car when Sawyer backed into the street and took off.

Sawyer maneuvered through downtown traffic more aggressively than she should, ignoring two honking horns and one angry motorist whom she was sure would have flipped her off if she'd glanced his way.

Instead, she drove back to her apartment on autopilot while replaying the conversations with both Erica and Jori. Her anger with Erica was easy to figure out. Erica always made it plain that she didn't expect too much from her, and then when she didn't put forth the effort to prove her wrong, Erica practically gloated.

What surprised Sawyer more was the hollow feeling in her

chest when she thought about Jori. She usually knew when a relationship was about to end. It began as an itch beneath her skin and blossomed into full-blown restlessness eased only when she finally broke it off. She had come to expect the rush of relief that followed the last time she saw a woman. But with Jori, she didn't feel any of the usual cues. She was happy when they were together, and when they weren't, Jori was always on her mind, in sweet anticipation of when she would see her again.

But that had changed the night before. Jori's murmured declaration of love had been so quiet, Sawyer almost hadn't heard it. As the words sank in, Sawyer's heart had kicked with fear as she realized how much she wanted—no, *needed*—that love.

Jori had snuggled against her and Sawyer had wished she never had to let her go. Somehow, while she was preoccupied with the pace of life, love had sneaked in on her. She'd barely slept, wanting to ingrain the feel of Jori into her arms, because she knew in the morning she would flee. Sawyer simply couldn't bear the knowledge that Jori now had the power to devastate her.

"Fucking coward," she muttered. "Guess I'm job hunting again." In the past, she'd enjoyed the process of looking for a new vocation. Usually, she was tired of what she'd been doing and anticipated the promise of starting over. But today felt different, and she refused to examine why.

CHAPTER TWENTY

Sawyer stood on Brady and Paige's front porch holding a gift bag decorated with a red cartoon sports car. She glanced once more at the driveway. She'd parked behind Erica's Land Rover so she had a pretty good idea what to expect when she got inside. She hadn't spoken to Erica in two weeks, having ignored several phone calls from her.

She knew she was being stubborn and she wasn't ready to give in yet, but she hadn't been able say no when Quintin had called and invited her to his birthday party. So she took a deep breath and pressed the doorbell. Seconds later feet thundered on the other side of the door, and when it swung open Quintin stood there flanked by his brother and six of their friends.

"Hey there, birthday boy." Sawyer ruffled his already mussed hair as she stepped inside.

"Aunt Sawyer, I'm five. I'm catching up to Daniel, he's only six."

Sawyer smiled at his logic. Once again she saw a reflection of her early relationship with Erica.

"No, you're not, dummy. I'm going to be seven in two months," Daniel asserted, making it clear he wouldn't let his brother pull even with him.

"Don't call your brother a dummy," Paige said as she came

from the kitchen. "You boys go play and let Aunt Sawyer come in the house, please."

Sawyer followed Paige into the living room, trying to appear as if she was glancing around casually. Derrick Ames sat at one end of the sofa and Brady in the chair nearby.

"She's in the kitchen." Paige paused as she passed Sawyer. "Why don't you go in there and help her with the cake."

"I don't think—"

"That wasn't a request."

Paige's tone was unexpectedly firm, and when Sawyer looked at her, her expression didn't invite argument.

"Yes, ma'am," Sawyer muttered.

Erica was opening a box of birthday candles when Sawyer entered the kitchen, and suddenly Sawyer remembered the day an older boy had asked fifteen-year-old Erica out. But the Drakes wouldn't let their daughters date until they were sixteen, so they didn't allow her to go.

"It's not fair," Erica had screamed at their mother. "Sawyer's old enough, but she's not pretty, so nobody even wants to date her. So why can't I go?"

All these years later, Sawyer recalled this comment and others like it. Now, it seemed ridiculous that she would let Erica's childish frustration color her view of herself. Those three little words, "she's not pretty," had stuck in a soft spot deep inside her and festered for years. And coupled with her confusion about her sexual orientation during that time, Erica's barbs had fed the doubts about her self-worth that grew each time she looked at herself in the mirror.

When she stripped away what she now knew was a normal sibling rivalry, she realized she was stronger than she'd thought. And she knew she should decide for herself what she wanted for her life, not let Erica's past resentment cripple her.

As Sawyer crossed the room, Erica looked up and paused before she counted out six candles. Sawyer picked one of them up and swirled it between her fingers, tracing the spiral grooves carved in the sides.

"You haven't returned any of my calls," Erica said quietly as she sank the candles into the thick white icing on the cake in front of her.

Sawyer shrugged. "I've been busy."

"I wanted to offer you a job."

"You shouldn't have any trouble finding another server."

"Oh, I've already hired another server." Erica paused again, and when she spoke apology laced her tone. "But I'm having trouble finding a trustworthy manager."

Sawyer knew her astonishment showed on her face. "I don't think me working for you is a good idea."

"You wouldn't be. We'd be working together." Erica held out her hand and Sawyer gave her the candle. "I've had some time to really take in the changes you made at Drake's while I was gone and I'm impressed. The new scheduling system is so much easier. And the CEO of Vesticom called. He wants to make the brunch meetings a quarterly event for his people, and he's reserved the private dining room for an annual employee-appreciation dinner."

"That's nice, but I still don't think us working together is good for either of us."

"It could be. Listen, I'm sorry. I didn't give you enough credit for your hard work, and I've meddled in your life. But you have to know why I've acted this way."

Sawyer did know. But she didn't think it would be easy to break such a long-standing pattern in their relationship.

"So here's my plan. You come back to Drake's, as co-manager, and handle the bulk of the management. I want to split my time between that and the kitchen—with Brady. I know it's not a foolproof solution. You and I will probably still butt heads. But we're family, Sawyer, and if the three of us work together, we could all benefit. We'd each have a lighter workload and could spend more time away from the restaurant. Since I went back to work, I feel like Paige is raising my daughter, and I'd love to have more time with her."

Sawyer considered Erica's proposal. It had merit, but one big drawback. She would have to face Jori, and she wasn't sure she was up to that yet. Since they last spoke, Sawyer had almost convinced herself they were both better off if they ended it—until she lay down at night and longed for the feel of Jori's soft skin against hers. But, she reminded herself, she'd just decided she would go after what she wanted in her life, and, truthfully, she wanted Jori.

As if reading her mind, Erica said, "And as your first official act as manager, I need you to help me keep my pastry chef."

"Keep your pastry chef?"

"She gave me her resignation letter yesterday."

"What? Why?"

"She wouldn't say, but I suspect it has to do with you. Damn it, Sawyer, this is why I asked you not to go after her. I knew you would screw up my staff."

Sawyer rolled her eyes at the familiar chord of accusation. "Okay. I can't change overnight." Erica acknowledged her slide back into their old dynamic. "Just fix it, please. I don't want her to leave. I'd like it if you two could at least find a way to work together."

Sawyer sighed. "I'll talk to her." *Tomorrow.*

"Get her to stay," Erica ordered, then her voice gentled. "You really love her, don't you?"

"Yeah. I guess I do."

"Then tell her."

It was certainly the last advice she thought she'd ever get from Erica.

"I know what I said about the two of you. But she's miserable, and you look like you haven't slept in days. Maybe I was wrong. If there's a chance you can make each other happy—well, you both deserve that."

"She makes me more than happy, Erica." Sawyer searched for the words and finally settled on the simplest explanation. "She fills me." That's when she knew she couldn't end things with Jori. For the first time in years, she would risk heartbreak for the chance at happiness.

❖

By the next night Sawyer still didn't know what to say to Jori. She'd rehearsed the conversation about a hundred times, trying out every scenario she could think of, from Jori embracing her right away to Jori forcibly throwing her out. Fearful that she would upset Jori, Sawyer decided to wait until after Drake's closed to talk to her. So when she arrived early, she stalled by going to the bar and ordering a beer, which she nursed for the next hour.

The bartender, a slim brunette, leaned against the bar and met her eyes. "Last call, sugar."

"I'm good." The bar area had emptied until Sawyer was the only one still perched on a stool.

"I heard you don't work here anymore."

"Nah, I just took a few days off. I'm back starting Monday." She rolled the bottom of her empty bottle in slow circles against the scarred mahogany.

"You going to hang around and walk me out?" The brunette winked suggestively.

Sawyer laughed, knowing she was teasing. "Now, I don't think your husband would like that very much."

"No. Probably not."

Sawyer glanced at her watch. "I'll catch you later." She stood and crossed the dining room.

As she walked into the kitchen Chuck, Brady, and Jori looked up. Sawyer saw surprise cross Jori's features, followed by a flash of emotion Sawyer couldn't identify, and then her expression went blank. Jori held a sharpening steel in one hand and a large chef's knife in the other. Chuck and Brady, perched on stools nearby, seemed to be hanging out, keeping her company.

"Hey, boss," Chuck called out. "You miss us?"

"Sure do, Chuck."

"So come on back."

Sawyer moved toward Jori until only a counter stood between them. "Guys, can you give us a minute?"

Chuck glanced uncertainly at Jori, but Brady stood without hesitation, slightly tugging Chuck's sleeve as he passed him. Sawyer smiled at Brady, appreciating the display of trust.

"Don't leave Drake's," Sawyer said when they were alone.

The steady rasp of the knife blade against the steel faltered, but Jori's eyes stayed on her task. "It's too late. I've got another job lined up. Friday is my last day."

"Where?"

Setting down the knife, Jori gave a defeated sigh. "Does it matter, Sawyer?"

It's not here. Sawyer blinked, realizing she'd heard the unspoken words as clearly as if Jori had said them.

"Erica doesn't want to lose you."

Now Jori did look up, her expression incredulous. "That's why you're here? Well, I'm so sorry, Sawyer, but I'm not interested in soothing your stupid conscience."

"Erica asked me to come back, to manage Drake's with her."

Jori remained silent.

"But if it means the difference in you staying or going, I won't do it. You belong here."

The quietly spoken words pierced Jori's heart, but the blood that spilled into her chest was cold and constricting. She wanted them to be true. She wanted to belong at Drake's, more than she'd ever wanted to be anywhere. But she couldn't be here, around Sawyer's family, without a constant reminder of her. And it was even harder to think about being here *with* Sawyer, knowing that she had turned out to be another person in her life who had walked away from her.

"Tell me, Sawyer. Why did you leave?"

"Erica pissed me off. Besides, she was coming back. I wasn't needed anymore."

"Cut the bullshit. You know what I mean." Jori drew a deep breath. "Why did you leave *me*?"

"I just needed to think."

"So I don't hear from you for two weeks?" Jori was mortified to feel tears welling up. "God, I hate how pathetic you've made me sound," she muttered.

"You don't sound pathetic."

"Come on, I'm practically begging you to tell me why you didn't call. I don't think I could sound more needy." Jori had always clung to her independence, which was one of the few positives she could attribute to her childhood. She'd never *needed* anyone. In the few relationships she'd had, she had honed her ability to exhibit just the right amount of reliance while still holding most of herself back.

"Shit." Sawyer shoved both hands into her hair and blew out her breath on a heavy sigh. "I got scared."

"Of what?"

"I don't even know if you remember, I mean you were nearly asleep and maybe you didn't realize what you were saying, but I freaked out."

Jori spun away in frustration and leaned against the sink. "If any of that was supposed to clear things up—"

"You said you loved me."

Jori turned back and stared. The emotion was real, but she didn't remember saying the words. And Sawyer had just given her an out to deny it, if she wanted one. But the flicker of fear and confusion in Sawyer's eyes made Jori want to make her face it, because seeing the weakness in Sawyer somehow made her feel better about her own. She could need Sawyer, even let Sawyer see that need, and not be so afraid that she would frighten her away.

"And you don't love me. You could have just said so—"

"No." Sawyer stepped around the counter and stopped when only inches separated them. "I mean, I was scared because I do."

"You do?"

"And I was—I *am* afraid of disappointing you. I know about your past, and I see how you've been hurt by it. And given my track record, I was afraid I would hurt you more. I want you to have everything, Jori. I know no one in your life has ever promised you forever."

Jori steeled herself against Sawyer's words, against Sawyer's understanding of her loneliness and inability to trust. "It doesn't matter—"

"So let *me* be the first." Sawyer reverently traced the line of her jaw with one finger. "I love you, Jori Diamantina. I would do anything to make you happy. I want to be the person you turn to, the person you can rely on."

"How am I supposed to depend on you?"

"I know I haven't given you much reason to believe I can stick around. But if you give me a chance I'd like to change that."

Jori shook her head. "I ask again, why should I believe you?"

"Because I can't imagine being without you." Jori's expression remained neutral, but Sawyer thought she detected the tiniest tightening around Jori's mouth.

"When trouble starts, you want to run. I'm more of the stay-and-talk-it-out type."

Sawyer searched for the words to explain. "What's wrong with needing a little bit of space to sort things out? Just because I don't want to sit around and analyze every detail until I can't breathe, let alone think."

Hurt flashed across Jori's face. "I don't like it when you leave."

Suddenly Sawyer realized how her absence must have made Jori feel. What, to her, had been time to clear her head had felt like abandonment to Jori.

"Okay." Slowly she nodded. Testing the waters, she took Jori's hand but was disappointed when Jori only let hers lie there passively. "I'll try to stay and talk, if you'll try to understand when I need some time to process things."

"As long as *some time* doesn't mean two weeks."

She stroked Jori's cheek and was encouraged when Jori leaned into her palm. "I'm sorry. I've never been that good at relationships, but I can do better. I've never wanted anyone so much." Sawyer paused before she added, "I've never needed anyone before."

"Really? You're not just using me for my desserts?" The hint of a smile deepened Jori's dimple.

In answer, Sawyer kissed her, and what began as a gentle persuasion flared into a heated fusion of mouths. Sawyer stroked her tongue along Jori's lips, eased back, then returned for another quick kiss. And when she smiled at Jori, she knew it was with the goofiest of grins. "Well, where else am I going to find a woman who'll give me free rein with the chocolate sauce?"

"Mmm, the first time I caught you watching me drizzle chocolate on a plate I knew you'd be easy." Jori tapped a finger against Sawyer's chin.

"You saw that, huh?"

"You were practically drooling." She slipped out of Sawyer's grasp and put away her knives. "Walk me to my car?"

"Yes." It seemed that Jori was keeping some distance between them, and Sawyer wanted to push. But she didn't, because she realized she'd been pushing Jori in one way or another since they met. It was time to let Jori be in control.

"Let me grab my bag. I'll be right back."

Jori returned from the locker room minutes later with a brown leather messenger bag slung over her shoulder. They walked out side by side, their shoulders brushing lightly as they stopped next to Jori's car. Jori stepped close and Sawyer wrapped her arms around her. When Jori rubbed the back of her fingers absently over Sawyer's bicep, Sawyer guessed she didn't even realize she was doing it, and though it was probably silly, Sawyer enjoyed the unconscious caress. She liked thinking that Jori might need to touch her.

"I'm parked around front." She kissed Jori, then eased back, prepared to put her in her car and send her home, even though she was currently conjuring up images of Jori naked beneath her.

As if reading her mind, Jori said against her lips, "Come home with me."

"I'll meet you there." She stepped back, opened Jori's door, and waited until she was settled before closing it. She stood there and watched Jori back out and drive up the street before she cut through the alley toward the front of the building and her car.

❖

Jori awoke to a buzzing noise in her head. Sawyer stirred against her back and the arm around her waist tightened, then relaxed again. She smiled to herself, thinking how glad she was that Sawyer had come to her damn senses. When she hadn't heard from Sawyer, Jori had been crushed, but her pride wouldn't let her call Sawyer.

Instead she'd tried to keep busy and ignore the aching fissure in her heart. She'd even flirted with her glass-blowing instructor, but soon realized that was a dead end. She couldn't look at another woman without comparing her to Sawyer. Even work didn't make her happy. She'd never particularly thought Sawyer looked like her siblings, but she began to see Sawyer in Erica's features and realized that when Brady smiled, his eyes sparkled in much the same way as Sawyer's. Surrounded by reminders of Sawyer, she had seen no other solution than to leave Drake's.

When Sawyer had walked into the kitchen the night before, Jori had almost flung herself across the room and into Sawyer's arms. Only her sense of self-preservation, cultivated over many years, kept her standing on the other side of the counter.

Jori heard the buzzing again and Sawyer shoved lightly against her. "Answer your phone," Sawyer murmured against the middle of her back.

One of the two cell phones sitting on the nightstand vibrated against its surface. Jori picked it up and passed it over her shoulder. "It's not mine."

"Oh." Sawyer rolled onto her back and Jori turned over to face her. Sawyer flipped the phone open. "Hello. Hi, Mom, what time is it?"

Jori glanced at the clock and saw that it was barely past eight. And since she had an idea just how little sleep Sawyer had gotten the night before, she wasn't surprised when she growled at her mother's response.

"We really need to talk about the time of your phone calls." She glanced at Jori. "My mother says hello."

"How did she know?" Jori whispered, feeling her face flush.

Sawyer covered the end of the phone. "Probably Brady. Yes, Mom, I'm listening to you—of course—you're right—"

Sawyer continued trying to get a word in with her mother, and Jori drew back the edge of the sheet covering Sawyer. When it slid over her bare breasts, Sawyer pulled it back into place, gave Jori a stern look, and whispered, "On the phone with my mother here."

Jori pressed her lips to Sawyer's other ear. "Better hang up. We don't want her to hear me make you moan." She slid her hand between Sawyer's legs and squeezed.

"Ah, Jesus." Sawyer flinched and grabbed Jori's wrist.

"Gotta go, Mom. I'll call you later." She barely waited to hear Tia's response before she closed the phone and tossed it over the edge of the bed. "I think my mother approves of you." She released Jori's wrist, rolled her onto her back, and slid on top of her, levering her upper body away to look at Jori.

"Enough talk about your mother." Jori wrapped her arms around Sawyer, her hands following the graceful lines of her back.

"My whole family approves," Sawyer said softly as she brushed a strand of hair off Jori's forehead. Sawyer's eyes were tender and deeply reflective. "You've helped me find my place among them again." The corner of Sawyer's mouth lifted. "I'd been a bit lost for a long while. But you calm things inside of me that I've never been able to put words to."

Sawyer slowly lowered her body to rest fully against Jori and turned her face to Jori's neck. She reached behind her, grasped Jori's hand, pulled it around, and held their joined hands between their bodies.

With her other hand, Jori cradled the back of Sawyer's head, then pressed her lips to Sawyer's forehead. "I love you," she whispered and felt Sawyer's murmured response against her own skin.

"You belong right here." Sawyer squeezed Jori's hand.

Jori smiled. *Yes. This is home.*

About the Author

Born and raised in upstate New York, Erin Dutton now lives and works in middle Tennessee. But she makes as many treks back north as she can squeeze into a year because her beloved nephews and nieces grow faster every time she is away. Recently, she has rediscovered inspiration in her surroundings and is constantly trying to find new ways to capture those images. In her free time she enjoys reading, movies, and playing golf.

Her previous novels include two romances, *Sequestered Hearts* and *Fully Involved*. She's currently working on a Matinee romance, *Designed for Love*, which will be published in November 2008. She is also a contributor to an erotica anthology, *Erotic Interludes 5: Road Games*, and an upcoming romance anthology, *Romantic Interludes 1: Discovery* from Bold Strokes Books.

Books Available From Bold Strokes Books

Falling Star by Gill McKnight. Solley Rayner hopes a few weeks with her family will help heal her shattered dreams, but she hasn't counted on meeting a woman who stirs her heart. (978-1-60282-023-4)

Lethal Affairs by Kim Baldwin and Xenia Alexiou. Elite operative Domino is no stranger to peril, but her investigation of journalist Hayley Ward will test more than her skills. (978-1-60282-022-7)

A Place to Rest by Erin Dutton. Sawyer Drake doesn't know what she wants from life until she meets Jori Diamantina—only trouble is, Jori doesn't seem to share her desire. (978-1-60282-021-0)

Warrior's Valor by Gun Brooke. Dwyn Izsontro and Emeron D'Artansis must put aside personal animosity, and unwelcomed attraction, to defeat an enemy of the Protector of the Realm. (978-1-60282-020-3)

Finding Home by Georgia Beers. Take two polar-opposite women with an attraction for one another they're trying desperately to ignore, throw in a far-too-observant dog, and then sit back and enjoy the romance. (978-1-60282-019-7)

Word of Honor by Radclyffe. All Secret Service Agent Cameron Roberts and First Daughter Blair Powell want is a small intimate wedding, but the paparazzi and a domestic terrorist have other plans. (978-1-60282-018-0)

Hotel Liaison by JLee Meyer. Two women searching through a secret past discover that their brief hotel liaison is only the beginning. Will they risk their careers—and their hearts—to follow through on their desires? (978-1-60282-017-3)

Love on Location by Lisa Girolami. Hollywood film producer Kate Nyland and artist Dawn Brock discover that love doesn't always follow the script. (978-1-60282-016-6)

Edge of Darkness by Jove Belle. Investigator Diana Collins charges at life with an irreverent comment and a right hook, but even those may not protect her heart from a charming villain. (978-1-60282-015-9)

Thirteen Hours by Meghan O'Brien. Workaholic Dana Watts's life takes a sudden turn when an unexpected interruption arrives in the form of the most beautiful breasts she has ever seen—stripper Laurel Stanley's. (978-1-60282-014-2)

In Deep Waters 2 by Radclyffe and Karin Kallmaker. All bets are off when two award winning-authors deal the cards of love and passion... and every hand is a winner. (978-1-60282-013-5)

Pink by Jennifer Harris. An irrepressible heroine frolics, frets, and navigates through the "what ifs" of her life: all the unexpected turns of fortune, fame, and karma. (978-1-60282-043-2)

Deal with the Devil by Ali Vali. New Orleans crime boss Cain Casey brings her fury down on the men who threatened her family, and blood and bullets fly. (978-1-60282-012-8)

Naked Heart by Jennifer Fulton. When a sexy ex-CIA agent sets out to seduce and entrap a powerful CEO, there's more to this plan than meets the eye...or the flogger. (978-1-60282-011-1)

Heart of the Matter by KI Thompson. TV newscaster Kate Foster is Professor Ellen Webster's dream girl, but Kate doesn't know Ellen exists...until an accident changes everything. (978-1-60282-010-4)

Heartland by Julie Cannon. When political strategist Rachel Stanton and dude ranch owner Shivley McCoy collide on an empty country road, fate intervenes. (978-1-60282-009-8)

Shadow of the Knife by Jane Fletcher. Militia Rookie Ellen Mittal has no idea just how complex and dangerous her life is about to become. A Celaeno series adventure romance. (978-1-60282-008-1)

To Protect and Serve by VK Powell. Lieutenant Alex Troy is caught in the paradox of her life—to hold steadfast to her professional oath or to protect the woman she loves. (978-1-60282-007-4)

Deeper by Ronica Black. Former homicide detective Erin McKenzie and her fiancée Elizabeth Adams couldn't be happier—until the not-so-distant past comes knocking at the door. (978-1-60282-006-7)

The Lonely Hearts Club by Radclyffe. Take three friends, add two ex-lovers and several new ones, and the result is a recipe for explosive rivalries and incendiary romance. (978-1-60282-005-0)

Venus Besieged by Andrews & Austin. Teague Richfield heads for Sedona and the sensual arms of psychic astrologer Callie Rivers for a much-needed romantic reunion. (978-1-60282-004-3)

Branded Ann by Merry Shannon. Pirate Branded Ann raids a merchant vessel to obtain a treasure map and gets more than she bargained for with the widow Violet. (978-1-60282-003-6)

American Goth by JD Glass. Trapped by an unsuspected inheritance and guided only by the guardian who holds the secret to her future, Samantha Cray fights to fulfill her destiny. (978-1-60282-002-9)

Learning Curve by Rachel Spangler. Ashton Clarke is perfectly content with her life until she meets the intriguing Professor Carrie Fletcher, who isn't looking for a relationship with anyone. (978-1-60282-001-2)

Place of Exile by Rose Beecham. Sheriff's detective Jude Devine struggles with ghosts of her past and an ex-lover who still haunts her dreams. (978-1-933110-98-1)

Fully Involved by Erin Dutton. A love that has smoldered for years ignites when two women and one little boy come together in the aftermath of tragedy. (978-1-933110-99-8)

Heart 2 Heart by Julie Cannon. Suffering from a devastating personal loss, Kyle Bain meets Lane Connor, and the chance for happiness suddenly seems possible. (978-1-60282-000-5)

Queens of Tristaine by Cate Culpepper. When a deadly plague stalks the Amazons of Tristaine, two warrior lovers must return to the place of their nightmares to find a cure. (978-1-933110-97-4)